Let's Pretend

Also by Laura Vaughan

The Favour

Let's Pretend

Laura Vaughan

CORVUS

Published in hardback in Great Britain in 2022 by Corvus,
an imprint of Atlantic Books Ltd.

10 9 8 7 6 5 4 3 2 1

A CIP catalogue record for this book is available from the British Library.

Hardback ISBN: 978 1 83895 205 1
Trade paperback ISBN: 978 1 83895 206 8
E-book ISBN: 978 1 83895 207 5

Design and typesetting benstudios.co.uk
Printed in Great Britain

Corvus
An imprint of Atlantic Books Ltd
Ormond House
26–27 Boswell Street
London
WC1N 3JZ

www.corvus-books.co.uk

MIX
Paper from
responsible sources
FSC® C013056

This book is for Hannah Bailey. *Nazdrave!*

I'll tell you the truth,
Don't think I'm lying:
I have to run backwards
To keep from flying.

– Old rhyme

PART ONE

CHAPTER ONE

'You know what I blame?' growled Nina. 'Me-sodding-Too. All the men are running scared. Even the shameless ones. I mean, it's all very well for the A-listers to come over all snooty about the casting couch. *They* can afford it.'

I was used to Nina mouthing off after failed auditions, so I just laughed and passed her the joint.

Nina and I first met at the age of ten, at a call-back for a yogurt commercial that neither of us got. Twenty-two years later and we're still bonding over our mutual rejections.

'Christ – if only I'd known my casting-couch power peaked at sixteen. In those days, they'd be happy with just a handsie, too.'

'Ew.'

'You're just jealous cos none of the dirty old men wanted *you*. They tagged you for an uptight little madam, and they were right.'

I blew her a kiss. It's never a good idea to rise to Nina's baits. Even as a kid, Nina was the edgy one, accessorising her own quirky niche with big nerd glasses and a shit-eating grin. I've never known how seriously I should take her tales of juvenile debauchery – then or now. But the Momager, for all her faults, kept me on a tight leash. Nina's mum is a drunk.

3

This is one of the many reasons the Momager's never approved of our friendship. 'Shop-soiled' was how she once described Nina, when she was still a teen. Nina didn't seem to bother with puberty, mind you, going straight from quirky-cute to *va-va-voom*. On her good days, she has a louche, jolie-laide sexiness that makes other girls seem insipid. I'm sometimes surprised it hasn't served her better.

The fact is, Nina Gill's spot on the 'Where Are They Now?' rankings is several places below mine. She gets by on the back of her residuals, supplemented by experimental theatre gigs and the occasional art-house movie, usually involving nudity.

'You and me should do a porno,' she said another time. 'We'd clean up. Little Miss Snowflake and the Disney Slut.' And later, 'We're two sides of the same fucked-up coin, baby.'

There are two things you should know about me. One is that I was briefly famous when I was four. The other is that I had a nose job when I was fifteen. These things are not, of course, unrelated.

To a great many people, Lily Thane is synonymous with Little Lucie, the winsome orphan who made a wish on a snowflake. ('All I want for Christmas is a daddy of my own!') Nobody expected *Snow Angels* to become a hit. It was a low-budget Brit romcom, with a cast of unknowns and an incongruous magical twist. But twenty-eight years later it's still on repeat every festive season, having somehow earned the status of a Holiday Classic. There I am, a tousle-haired, rosy-cheeked moppet, gazing upwards as the first cellulose snowflakes begin to fall. Forever frozen in my four-year-old glory.

I was only on screen for twenty minutes. The focus of the movie was the romance between nerdy Tim Randolf and sassy older sexpot Honey Evans. But even now, people will clock my name and ask me about it. ('So, what's Sir Tim *really* like?' 'Did they let you keep one of the snow mice?' 'Were you frightened of the icicle goblins?') The thing is, for a lot of people, that film looms larger in their childhood memories than it does in mine. I mean, c'mon, how much do *you* remember of what you were doing age four?

Off the back of *Snow Angels*, I had three more small film roles and a run of commercials and voice-over work. But the brutal truth is that a kid who is absolutely adorable at, say, four may not be the least bit adorable or even attractive once they've outgrown their dimples. Aged fifteen, I'd been pathetically relieved to acquire visible cheekbones. Alas, the loss of puppy fat came with a price: my nose was now distractingly prominent. Or so I thought.

When *Snow Angels* came out, reviewers liked to mention that the scene-stealing child actor who played Lucie came from a 'theatrical dynasty'. It's true that Pa and his two siblings are all performers of sorts, and my cousin Dido has a couple of Olivier awards in her loo, but none of them are what you'd call household names. In fact, we can only boast of one bone fide National Treasure: my grandfather, Sir Terence Thane, formerly Terry Stubbs, the butcher's son from Ealing who scaled the thespian heights along with Sirs Larry, Ralph and John. His nose was almost as famous as his Lear, and was long and arched, with flared wings. We've all inherited a version of it. On the right sort of profile – Dido's, for example – it is both handsome and distinctive. On others, it's simply all-conquering.

Either way, getting rid of the nose wasn't the liberation I'd hoped for. The new model was narrow and straight, with a demurely rounded tip. It made my face look neater, sweeter but also oddly unfinished. Work picked up, at least at first, but my late teens and twenties were filled with pilots for series that never got sold, forgettable British crime dramas and my most recent gig, the American legal dramedy *Briefs*.

Otherwise, my film credits are mostly along the lines of Pretty Girl on Plane, Prostitute at Party and Crying Bridesmaid.

If I had kept my nose, would it all have been different?

Would I still have agreed to beard for Adam Harker?

What then?

Ah, what then.

When the PR blitz began, it made for a cute anecdote: 'We were childhood sweethearts!' Like everything else, this was essentially bollocks.

I first met Adam when I was twelve and we were both enrolled at stage school. Students called it the Fame Factory, as if mock disdain could cover up the rancid whiff of our ambition. My first few years there were not happy ones, on account of the puppy fat and the nose. Meanwhile, the only name Adam had made for himself was that of a cocky little shit. He was small and squat and acne spattered, yet possessed of unshakeable confidence. 'Ten years from now,' he used to say, 'all these talent-show losers will be dining out on how they went to school with me.'

Adam was a year older than me, so we only got to know each other when we were cast as brother and sister in a play about an upper-crust family at war over their inheritance. They were small parts in a fairly awful show that folded after a month, but as the only juveniles on set we spent a certain amount of time backstage together. We used to play card games and take the piss out of the director, as well as the Barbies 'n' Kens (Adam's term) back at school. Adam liked hearing about the Thanes, too. 'A pedigree like that's the real deal,' he told me once, with a solemnity that surprised me.

'Sure, he'll be a great *character* actor,' the Ken dolls sneered when rumours of Adam's on-stage charisma began to spread. Then he got his growth spurt, his skin cleared up and, for a while, his rise seemed as effortless as it was inevitable.

At the age of nineteen, after rave reviews for his part in ITV's World War I drama *The Last Hurrah*, Adam headed to LA. From there he bagged a BAFTA for playing Brad Pitt's troubled son in art-house flick *Silent Hour*, which was followed by a few small but well-received parts before being cast in *Wylderness*, billed as the biggest dystopian fantasy franchise since *Hunger Games*. The box-office returns were disappointing, however, and when they didn't film the third of the trilogy, Adam's trajectory began to stall. There were rumours of difficult behaviour, an on-set bust-up that halted production on a film that was later shelved. His prediction that he'd be the Fame Factory graduate we all name-dropped had come true only up to a point. Most people knew who he was, but indistinctly.

'Adam Harker's a meth head,' said Nina authoritatively, the same afternoon as her #MeToo rant. 'He got a bit too much into character during that Deep South family saga. Hasn't been able to shake the habit since.'

'Says who?'

'The make-up girl on the *Evening Standard* shoot. So there.'

Nina always claims the most successful stars are nursing the darkest secrets. Drugs, violence, paedophile rings … She's got a lot of contacts in showbiz-adjacent roles, so she's better informed than most. But I also happen to know she makes stuff up and sends it to the blind gossip sites just for shits and giggles. I can see the appeal. I mean, *I* want to believe it. It's certainly easier on the ego to assume the famous and beautiful are also the miserable and the damned.

'I wish you'd dig up some dirt on the Thanes.'

'Pfff. No one gives a crap about your family.' Nina looked mischievous. 'Though I did hear Dido's shagging a spear-carrier.'

'No!' I was delighted. My cousin Dido is three years older than me and the heir apparent to Sir Terry's luvvie legacy. People still rave about her Lady Macbeth, and her Hedda is almost as fawned over as her Antigone. My one comfort is that she's too much of a snob to take her talents mainstream.

Actually, that's not true. I also take comfort in the fact that Dido's husband is a dick. Hence the spear-carrier, presumably.

'You can ask her about it tonight,' said Nina. 'He's fresh out of RADA and hung like a donkey. Allegedly. Mind you, those Shakespearean codpieces can be very misleading.'

'Dinner. *Shit.*' We'd spent the afternoon in Nina's flat, getting stoned and watching Fred Astaire movies. It's Nina's thing when she's had a setback. Those big monochrome dance numbers are trippy at the best of times, like an Escher print come to life, but weed slows them down. It's very soothing. Too soothing on this occasion; I now had less than an hour to straighten out and get to Dido's. It was her standard invitation: 'Just a kitchen supper, *super* relaxed, *super* fun crowd.'

For Dido, 'fun' means worthy yet snide. Habitat for Humanity meets *Mean Girls*.

Dido and Nick live in a large house in Highgate. Patchily painted in Gothic hues, it's chilly and cluttered, with stacks of Nick's unpublished novels and Dido's scripts piled up everywhere. There's quite a lot of dog hair, too, courtesy of Hotspur. Hotspur is an Afghan hound. Hotspur looks very much like Dido, but of course nobody has ever dared point this out.

As I said, it's not an inviting house. The location of these famous kitchen suppers is in the basement; the fittings are unvarnished wood, and the crockery looks like it's been thrown together by depressed Scandinavian pre-schoolers. But the thing about my cousin is that she can *really* cook. In interviews, she'll say things like 'feasting people is how I show love' and it's not entirely bollocks. Dining chez Dido means platters of fragrant meats melting from the bone, lacy lacquers of chocolate and slicks of spiced butter, swirls of boozy cream. The hostess herself will barely touch this largesse. She'll pick at a slice of fruit or paring of cheese, all the while eating us up with her eyes.

After retrieving a key from under the usual plant pot, I slunk in late, red-eyed and dishevelled, hoping to find the party in full tipsy swing. But the eleven people gathered around the kitchen table looked disconcertingly alert. Except for Nick, perhaps, who was doing the rounds with a carafe. The sloshing way he poured suggested he'd had a head start on the rest of us.

'Darling Lily,' said Dido, arms flung wide. 'We're all so thrilled you could make it.'

I wasn't sure if this was a dig. It can be hard to tell with Dido. I think she honestly believes she's doing me a favour with her condescending suppers and cast-off clothing and unsolicited advice.

'And how gorgeous you look!' Definitely a dig, then.

Dido's studied carelessness on the domestic front extends to her own appearance. She favours mannish tailoring, oversize shirts and ugly shoes. ('Who does she think she is?' sniffs the Momager. 'A lesbian?') But Dido can carry it off. She lopes about on her endless legs, curtained by swirls of her endless hair, that famous nose jutting forth like the prow of a very sexy ship. The kind with billowing sails and lots of guns.

'Isn't she adorable?' Dido declared to a narrow bearded man sitting at the more shadowy end of the table. 'Gideon, have you met my adorable cousin? Lily, this is Gideon. He's a music journalist and *the* most fascinating man.'

She ushered me into the seat next to him. Within seconds, a loaded plate of food was steaming in front of me. The gloom of the basement was barely alleviated by a scattering of hurricane lamps, so it was hard to tell exactly what I was eating. The pot had left me ravenous in any case. Blindly, I forked in various richly spiced and scented mouthfuls, as introductions to assorted artistes and do-gooders were made.

Dido had recently finished a run of *Mary Stuart* at the National, and the conversation I'd interrupted was moving from Schiller to Goethe. 'Not a fan of Weimar classicism?' Gideon asked in a stage-whisper.

'It doesn't come up much in my line of work.' I was too busy shovelling in food to pay attention. There was butter on my chin and I didn't even care.

'Aren't you an actress too?'

'Ah, but Lily's in actual "showbiz",' Dido trilled from the other end of the table.

'Right.' I took a long swig from my glass. 'Here to represent the bread-and-circuses division of Thane, Inc.'

'Oh, so *you're* the child-star,' said somebody else.

'I took a lot of growth hormones before coming out tonight.'

Nobody laughed.

'I remember you from *Briefs*,' said the woman across from me, so graciously it was clear she thought she was throwing me a lifeline. 'Weren't you the bitchy one? With kleptomania? The Honourable Hermione Whatnot.'

'Hancock. Yeah. It was a … fun role.'

'One of my guilty pleasures. Mostly, I watched it for the power-dressing.'

It turned out she was a lawyer. Human rights, inevitably. She started to tell me – archly, but in great detail – all the ways that TV shows get the legal profession wrong.

'What *I* find off-putting about those glossy American dramas,' said Gideon, cutting in, 'is how they make up their leading ladies to look like drag queens.'

'Oh, I know.' Human Rights made a moue of distaste. 'False eyelashes and ridiculous hair extensions and all that contouring goop.'

'People get self-conscious with high-definition,' I said, sounding defensive in spite of myself.

'Why should they? Seems to me everyone on the telly these days is a perfect ten. Or eight, minimum. Take a girl like you.' Jovially, Gideon speared an asparagus from my plate.

11

'You don't need three inches of slap to look fuckable.'

I turned my chair towards Nick, who was on my other side and had contributed even less to the general conversation than I had. He's quite good looking, in a sneery sort of way, but tonight he looked more than usually morose. Maybe Nina was right and Dido *was* carrying on with some oversized codpiece. I supposed I should feel sorry for him. 'So tell me about the new book ...'

Nick had an agent for a while, but they parted ways over the direction of his latest effort, which was written in the voice of a drug dealer from the Bronx who believes he's the reincarnation of the Earl of Rochester. Writers and actors share the impulse to be as overweening as they're insecure; the difference is that actors, even failed ones, have a pathological need to win over their audience. Nick has never felt the need to ingratiate himself with anyone. Thanks to family money, he's under no pressure to produce a bestseller. Or any kind of seller, in fact.

'Ever thought about self-publishing?' I asked at the end of his monologue on the relationship between gansta-rap and seventeenth-century erotic poetry.

'*Vanity* publishing?'

'Well, not exactly. I mean if, like you say, traditional publishing's so corrupt ... and, you know, the model's broken, why not look elsewhere? You'd get total creative control. And that could be good. Right?'

'Honestly, Lily.' He looked at me coldly. 'Asking a novelist if they've thought about self-publishing is like asking an actress if they've considered porn.'

'It's hardly –'

Gideon leaned in. 'Maybe you should expand your range. A webcam girl who quotes Schiller ... Think about it.'

'Excuse me. I've just remembered there's somewhere I have to be.' I got up from my chair, which scraped dramatically against the floor, knocking into Hotspur in the process. Amidst the anguished yelping and flurry of dog hair, there was no hope of a swift exit. Dido insisted on escorting me to the door.

'Are you sure you have to dash? I know how good you are at putting a brave face on things but Uncle Lionel *did* mention you're at rather a loose end ...'

'Right. Luckily for me, your guests had some tips for getting into porn.'

'You funny creature! But you *will* let me know if there's anything I can do to help?' She was thrusting a Tupperware filled with leftovers at me, followed by an enormous woolly muffler thing. It was possibly one of Hotspur's blankets. 'Anything at all. Promise me.'

'How about an introduction to one of your casting-director chums?'

Dido actually blanched. 'I, ah, thought you didn't do theatre ...'

'I'm kidding! But thanks anyway. It was a lovely evening. Except for Gideon. He's a perv.'

She raised her brows. 'I'm sorry, darling. I thought you were too stoned to notice.'

CHAPTER TWO

I dumped the Tupperware and the muffler by the side of the first bin I passed. Maybe some deserving Dickensian orphan would find them. Then I wandered around aimlessly for a bit until I eventually found myself in a pub.

It was the kind of place I'd only ever gone into by accident. It was cavernous and dimly lit, with an ancient Axminster carpet and wooden fittings that looked like they'd been varnished with gravy. It wasn't busy, even though it was near ten on a Saturday night, with just a handful of old duffers propping up the bar. In one corner, a trio of Japanese tourists were glumly picking over the remains of what looked like truly terrible fish and chips. I headed straight to the toilets.

They were mercifully unoccupied, though I still made sure to flush to cover any noise as I vomited. All Dido's exquisite feasting. All those buttery, creamy, bloody-meaty mouthfuls gurgling off to the sewer. I felt much calmer, as well as cleaner, afterwards. It's not a big deal. I've never used laxatives and I'm basically too lazy for excessive exercise. But I like my thigh gap and this is a shortcut to keeping it. Standing by the basin, I felt the reassuring jut of my pelvic bones.

I'm a pretty girl, I know that. The big blue eyes. Those radiantly white teeth. The honeyed locks. That adorable nose.

I'm still young enough to get trashed and go out with unwashed hair and no lipstick and get away with it.

You don't need three inches of slap to look fuckable.

It was a mistake to look in the mirror, all the same. My cheeks looked blotchy in the harsh fluorescent light, and there was a tiny broken vein in the left crease of my nose. I made a mental note to go to the dermatologist and get it zapped before the Momager noticed. Were my pores getting bigger? And what about the crinkles starting at the edges of my eyes? Vomiting up food is like vomiting up the rot inside, the sludge and stink we all carry around with us. But you can't purge this kind of decay.

I went back to the bar. I was feeling light-headed and my throat hurt. The old geezers had moved to a table so there was just one other person sitting there, a young guy in a beaten-up leather jacket and a baseball cap, nursing his drink with a leave-me-alone hunch I could relate to. I ordered a double rum and Coke. Diet, obviously.

'Do I know you?'

I didn't even turn around. 'You absolutely do not.'

'Ah, but I think I absolutely do.' His voice was slurred, but not aggressively so. 'Didn't we go to school together?'

'Really? That's your line?'

'Try this one, then: "How he loves you. How he loathes you. How he devours us all!"'

This time I actually looked at him. '*Adam?*'

'"The worm-eaten apple of Daddy's eye."'

He was quoting his lines from that crap play we did when we were kids. I was amazed he'd remembered it. I was even more amazed Adam Harker had remembered me. I glanced around the pub, but nobody had given us a second glance.

'You know, you were pretty good in that thing.'

Condescending prick. 'Wish I could say the same.'

He laughed. 'It's Lily, right? Lily Thane. What've you been up to since?'

The question was as unwelcome as it was inevitable. Adam's Hollywood ambitions might have come unstuck, but he was still several leagues of success above me. Just last year, he'd been the villain in a prestige HBO thriller about political corruption. And he had a film coming out this autumn – a war movie. I didn't know much about it, but the director, Kashif 'Kash' Malik, was said to be a hot new talent.

I swallowed some more of my drink. Sticky fake Coke, with the nail-polish whiff of cheap rum. Childish yet bitter, just like me. 'Oh, you know. Playing klepto lawyers and drunk bridesmaids. Toothpaste ads. *Poirot*. Disappointing my mother.'

'Well, as long as we're disappointing our parents we must be doing something right.'

The smile that followed was conspiratorial. Intimate. I was now regretting the unwashed hair and lack of make-up. My throat still burned from the vomit. Furtively, I reached into my bag for gum.

To be fair, Adam didn't look in great shape either. He was unshaven in a patchy way that suggested it wasn't designer stubble, and there were dark rings around his eyes. Their smoulder was bloodshot. I remembered what Nina had said about him being a secret meth head. Tonight, I judged, he was merely drunk.

'So what brings a girl like you to a dive like this?'

I drained my drink and signalled for another one. Then I told him about Dido, and pervy Gideon, and Hotspur's muffler. I remembered he'd always liked hearing about the Thanes back in the Fame Factory days. And he seemed to be listening, albeit in a slightly unfocused way.

'And what's your excuse?' I finished.

'Hm?'

'A nice boy like you in a place like this. Et cetera.'

'Among the civilians, you mean?' Adam belched. 'Wonky faces. Fugly clothes. Crap hair. You ever have that moment? When you step out of your bubble and realise how unbelievably *dingy* most people are?' He raised his glass in a toast. 'So here's to the beautiful people and those who screw 'em. Over and under and every which way between.'

It was obviously a blackly private joke. Neither Adam's reference to beauty nor the sourness with which he said it had anything to do with me. All the same, I wondered – feverishly – where he put me on the scale. In any London bar, I'm pushing ten. But at an LA casting? An eight. Maybe only a seven-point-five. And that average will slip with every year.

The gorgeousness of female movie stars is generally uncomplicated. It's why I'd got rid of the nose. (Ha. A vain hope, that one, in every sense.) But the big male stars, the most admired and iconic ones, often boast some knot or crookedness or quirk. Maybe that's what we need to take them seriously. Adam the ugly boy had grown into a startlingly beautiful man, and this was partly because of – not in spite of – the pitted skin on his right cheek. He had the bone structure for heroic but there was always something else behind it – something jagged, wolfish. Blue-black hair and bruised blue eyes. Seeing the trace of his acne scars up close, I felt a drunken tenderness towards both our former selves.

'I'm thinking of getting out,' I said abruptly. 'Of the bubble and everything else.'

'Whaddya mean?'

'I've been in the business since I was four. All the castings and callbacks … all that smizing on demand. I guess I can't remember the last time any of it felt like a choice.'

'Why should acting feel like a choice? If you've got talent, it should be an imperative.'

'Ugh. You sound like my cousin.' I was nettled: I'd been expecting sympathy.

'I don't believe you, anyway. You still want this more than anything else. You're like me, I've always known that. Desperate.'

I didn't know what to make of this, so I laughed. 'Are you seriously telling me you've never had any doubts about your talent or where it's taken you?'

'Nope.'

'Well. Nice to see success hasn't gone to your head.'

'OK. Fine. Maybe there was this *one* time …' He paused. 'After the studio killed off *Wylderness 3*, there was a review of the first one that got stuck in my head.' This time the wait was so long I almost thought he wasn't going to continue. '"Adam Harker struts and scowls so prettily it hardly seems to matter he's dead behind the eyes."'

'Miaow.'

'It was the *Guardian* critic.'

'Bitter old hack.'

But Adam was still frowning. 'The reviews that get under the skin aren't the unfair ones. It's the ones that show you what you're afraid of.'

Our conversation had abruptly sobered up. Last orders were called; we said our goodbyes soon afterwards. If there had ever been a moment when Adam was going to invite me back to his, I'd missed it. It was probably just as well, I told myself. He was the same cocky shit he'd always been, just drunker. And I wasn't wearing good underwear. And he'd taken my number in any case.

He didn't call. I'm sure I wouldn't have heard from him again if it wasn't for our second chance encounter. Yet that night in the pub was a turning point all the same. Not even a year later, as I stared at Adam's lifeless body in the swimming pool, his ring on my finger, I found I couldn't pin down the moment when there was no going back.

I *was* guilty, though. And desperate. It's best you know this from the start.

CHAPTER THREE

The day after our meet-cute, when I still thought Adam might call, I sat down to watch the first *Wylderness* movie. Adam had dated his A-list co-star, Casilda Fernandez, for over a year, and seeing her in action was as depressing as I'd feared. She was all Bambi eyes and golden curves, fetchingly showcased in a post-apocalyptic outfit of ripped leather. Although they'd kept the acne scars, the camera heightened Adam's features so they had an almost fearsome symmetry, artfully infused with both light and dark. I didn't think he looked dead behind the eyes. But he didn't look quite human either.

For the first shirt-less scene, our hero was rescuing someone from a poisoned lake. Adam's lean muscled torso filled the screen. The film was only 12A but the camera lingered, knowingly, on the abdominal glisten of fake sweat. That was the point at which I stopped the film. I was starting to feel like a voyeur. Sex makes me a bit queasy anyway. All that frenetic rubbing and sucking, the squelches and smells ... as an act, it's demeaning; as a performance, it's exhausting. Of course it's always going to be better on screen.

I didn't sleep well that night. It was partly because of the film and partly because I was thinking about that quote from the

Guardian critic and how all these years later Adam could hardly bear to repeat it. You have to be a bit of a masochist in a profession that requires you to knock on the door of rejection time after time. Sometimes the burn of humiliation is almost a thrill. Like the tang of stomach acid on the back of my throat. But we've all had the dismissals and takedowns that do more than sting. Those are the moments of annihilation. The thunder clap and the ringing of static that follows, drowning everything else out … That night, I woke up clawing at the sheets, my breath rank and heart racing. What had Adam meant when he fixed me with that adamantine blue stare and said, *You're like me, I've always known that. Desperate.* I couldn't even remember how he said it, whether he had been light-hearted or loathing.

A week passed with no contact from Adam. I tormented myself by chasing him down the internet rabbit hole: reviews, interviews, fan-sites, gossip blogs, *Wylderness* slash fiction … His new film would be out in October. Adam played a traumatised US veteran of an unspecified Middle Eastern war, whose breakdown was dramatised with hallucinogenic scenes inspired by Shakespeare's play *Pericles, Prince of Tyre*. For an art-house movie, it was picking up a lot of buzz.

Filming on *Tyre* had finished in January. More recently, Adam had been appearing on Broadway in *Long Day's Journey into Night*. He needn't worry about those reviews, at least. 'As big brother Jamie, Adam Harker has a formidably magnetic presence,' swooned the *New York Times*. 'Catch him while you can.'

Fat chance.

It had now been exactly five months since I'd been booked for anything. I prostrated myself on the sofa, listlessly scrolling through the *Backstage* ads. *Must be comfortable with nudity … Proud of her sexuality; happy to wear push-up bra … Petite/thin, wears revealing party attire … Drop-dead gorgeous and knows it … Drop-dead gorgeous but doesn't know it …* And my personal favourite: *Looks intellectual but is still smoking hot.*

Ninety-five per cent of these ads were for actresses under the age of thirty. Did I really want this life 'more than anything else'? *Still?*

Despite everything that happened, I truly believe Adam had what it took to become one of those undeniable, immortal things: a movie star. It was different for me; I've always known I don't possess that kind of heat and light. That's one of the things I'm grateful to the Momager for. She knew from the start that I was never going to be an Ingrid Bergman. Instead, I was to be the girl with unclouded eyes and a guileless smile, who will sell you anything from a belief in true love to kale-soup cleanses. The girl who brightens chat shows and romcoms and shampoo ads because she looks like a better version of your best friend or first sweetheart. A face that when it fills your screen feels like a homecoming.

Trouble is, there are literally thousands of girls who could fit this bill. We act, we model, we sing and we dance. We're as interchangeable as we're appealing. And for a while, I was less interchangeable than the rest because of *Snow Angels*. I was already gift-wrapped as a happy memory.

It still wasn't enough. I don't know, even now, if Little Lucie held me back rather than pushed me forward. Either way, a pathetic part of me still believes I can outgrow her. That all I need is one last lucky break, and I'll be able to prove all the clichés wrong and that everything was worth it. I will find a role or give a performance that's such a perfect fit it will redefine me forever. And once that's done I'll be free to give up and move on. Little Lucie will be left behind for good. Dead and ice-bound, where she belongs.

Or so I kept telling myself.

'Oh, darling,' the Momager exclaimed as soon as she saw the nest of fast-food wrappers I'd made for myself on the sofa. She put her hands to her face. 'Is it time for me to *really worry*?'

Not for the first time, I regretted giving my mother a key to my flat. In minutes, the festering contents of my fridge were binned in favour of celery, tofu and brown rice milk. (I don't think the Momager knows about my eating habits or that she'd necessarily disapprove. She told me that when she was at ballet school, the girls used to eat cotton wool soaked in orange juice to suppress their appetites.) Curtains were flung back and cushions plumped. She even lit a scented candle. As a final touch, she fluffed out my hair and dabbed some gloss on my lips. I sat up straighter, despite myself. 'There,' she said. '*Much* better. And I have a nice surprise for you. Talia's in town – did you know? I ran into her outside Selfridge's, of all places. She's dying to catch up. And she's got an invitation for you. Some party or launch event on Saturday night. I said you'd be thrilled.'

'Talia is very far from thrilling. And I don't want to go out. I'm on a break from all that.'

'Nonsense. You've wallowed long enough, and it's starting to show. Talia knows *everyone*. It's time to start putting yourself out there again. Who knows who you'll meet or what might turn up?'

'Pimping me out to C-list It girls isn't going to reignite my career.'

'Please don't be confrontational, Lily.' My mother took on a martyred air. Nina calls it her Dying Swan. 'It's very unkind. You know I'm only trying to make you happy.'

She and Pa met when they were both in *The Tempest* at the Old Vic (appropriate, really, seeing as their six-month marriage was as stormy as it was short-lived). Pa was Alonso; the Momager was one of the dancers hired to be Prospero's sprites. Despite her training, she was never a classical ballerina and mostly picked up gigs in West End musicals or ballroom-dancing shows. But she has always looked the part of a prima: dainty and upright, with snap-able wrists and a crown of white-blonde hair. Her steeliness is swathed in chiffon.

My agent handles the majority of my career requirements; these days, the Momager is reduced to curating my social-media accounts. Even so, there are occasions when I like to get her perspective on things. Her instincts are usually right. And she never needed to be pushy, or at least not during her stage-mother days. Her trick was to give the impression that she'd arrived at the position by accident, swept up by the irresistible tidal wave of her daughter's talent. She would hint at the burden of her responsibilities with a brave and selfless smile; her negotiations were conducted with an air of trusting hopefulness that others – most of all me – found very hard to disappoint.

———

So I went to the party with Talia, and also Nina, who finds Talia hard to take but never says no to a free ride. Talia's the only child

24

of Flora Templeton, the English aristo-model, and US retail tycoon Joey Banks, and as such gets invited to everything. Although she's five or six years younger than me it feels like we've been crossing paths forever; we're more than acquaintances but not quite friends. Talia prefers the term 'influencer' to 'socialite', designs jewellery or swimwear, possibly both, and is always ever-so-keen for me to attend her various charity fundraisers and launch parties and first nights.

Tonight was the private view of a fashionista-turned-artist's début. Her financier boyfriend had hired the gallery: a converted warehouse in Shoreditch, replete with steel pillars and exposed ceiling joists. Assorted glamazons flitted about, their sparkle made even more effervescent by the raw industrial space.

'Lily, Nina, over here!' Talia called out as soon as we got in. She click-clacked across the concrete floor, arms outstretched. 'Oh,' she said, 'but you're *stunning*. The two of you! Look at that dress! Look at your *hair*! God. I hate you both. Argh!' Beside me, I heard Nina suppress a groan.

Talia has her mother's Disney-princess eyes and nose and mouth, but these features are all bunched up a little too closely together and look slightly incongruous on her face, which is broad and square like her father's. Efforts to further emulate her mother include a boob job, ear-pinning and a chin-reduction (according to Nina, at any rate, who may not be the most reliable source). Still, I know the signs of someone who isn't at ease in their own skin. They're there in Talia's jittery, gym-whittled frame and the gnawed flesh around her synthetic nails.

'Isn't the show great? I'd love to have a talent like this. All that *purpose*. It's inspiring.'

Talia has the naivety of those born into extreme wealth. 'Absolutely,' I said, though the art on the distressed brick walls looked pretty underwhelming to me. It was mostly neon scribbles of bad poetry, superimposed over grainy photos taken backstage at fashion shows.

'You heard about my latest project? I'm excited, I really am. It's this ethical skincare company and they want me to be a spokesperson, so – hang on.' Talia had caught sight of another friend. 'Christian! You *beast*, why didn't you let me know you were coming? This place is *so you* –' She turned back to us. 'Two minutes! Don't talk about me once I'm gone. Promise? Ha, I'm kidding. Kidding! OK, I'll be back –'

Nina slumped extravagantly against the wall. 'Thank Christ. I've already heard all I can take about sustainable mud-packs for your fanny.'

'You two met up?' I was surprised; I didn't think Nina and Talia hung out without me.

'I was at a loose end. I guess Talia does for me what I do for you.'

'And what's that?'

'You know: makes my own life look slightly less pitiful by comparison.'

At least she said it with a grin. I wanted Nina to be in a good mood; I wanted both of us to have a good time. I'd made an effort, in a backless silk dress the colour of midnight. Nina was rocking her nouvelle vague sexpot thing. I collected two negronis from a passing waiter and clinked glasses with determined cheer.

'Bottoms up.' Nina downed hers in one. 'Ack.' Then, 'Stone the crows. Isn't that Adam Harker?'

26

She sounded interested rather than impressed. It wasn't like he was even the biggest name in the room, since it was the kind of party where most people were at least vaguely recognisable, or desirable, or both. Life in the bubble, as Adam had put it.

And there he was, in the flesh.

I looked away quickly. It would be awkward running into him again, and not just because he hadn't called. We might not have seen each other naked but I felt our last encounter had been unexpectedly exposing, all the same. Luckily the gallery was becoming as crowded as it was cavernous; Adam would be too busy schmoozing models to notice the likes of Nina and me. One more drink and I was headed out of there.

'Hello again.'

'Oh. Hi.'

I'd been on my way to find Talia, to tell her that Nina and I were moving on. And there he was, abruptly in my path.

Everything was different. My hair was blow-dried and my lingerie was designer. Adam looked more like his on-screen avatar. Taller, rangier, lazily assured.

He smiled down at me. 'So you're a connoisseur of art as well as old men's boozers.'

'Actually, I'm here for the models.'

He laughed. 'I was going to give you a call, wasn't I?'

'I don't know. Were you?'

'Right now it looks like I definitely should've done.'

'Lily! Thought I'd lost you. Oh!' Talia stopped. 'I'm sorry. Am I interrupting?' She laughed skittishly, fingers pressed to her mouth, and peeping out at us from under her My Little Pony mane.

'Adam,' said Adam, putting out his hand.

'Yeah, hi, we actually met before, briefly? At Lula Burstein's summer party? I'm Talia …?'

'Of course,' he said, with an easy warmth that was so practised I felt sure he hadn't a clue who she was. 'Great to see you again. It's turning out to be quite a reunion.'

She beamed. 'So how do you two know each other?'

'Lily and I were stage-school brats together, back in the day.'

I became aware that a man with a camera was hovering expectantly in front of us – the event's official photographer. 'Gotta pay the piper, right?' Adam murmured in my ear, before slinging his arm around my shoulder and pulling me in. The camera flashed several times. When the photographer moved on, Adam didn't immediately release me. Instead, I felt his fingers on my bare back, tracing something on my skin. Our eyes met, mine still dazzled by the camera's flash. But the next moment he saw someone he knew and was called away.

'What. Was. That?' demanded Nina, suddenly by my side.

'The chemistry between the two of you is *insane*,' said Talia.

'Please. He's just working the room.'

Nina narrowed her eyes. 'Weren't you spotty teenagers the last time you met?'

'Actually, we bumped into each other the other week.' Miss Insouciance.

'Bumping uglies, was it?'

'Hardly. It was just a drink in some awful pub. We're not – ow.'

Talia had nudged me sharply in the ribs. '*Act cool*,' she hissed. '*He's coming back over.*'

This time, Adam stayed. When a section of the party moved on to a neighbouring bar, we moved with it, and from there to somebody's house. The rooms were long and dark, painted in the same inky colours that Dido favoured, but lit by sparse gleams of crystal and gilt. In the shadows, the guests had their own glister – the flashes of mirth in their teeth and eyes, the gloss of money everywhere else. They were all strangers, except for Adam; I'd lost Talia and Nina somewhere along the way. It didn't matter. His hand was still on my back. The tips of his fingers were cool; my skin shivered.

At some point a tray was brought out, neatly arranged with razor blades and mirrors and white baggies. 'You don't have to,' said Adam when he saw me hesitate. So of course I dipped down to one of the slimmer lines, avoiding my own reflected eyes. There was no hesitation on Adam's part, and I remembered Nina's drug gossip again. But, 'Whew,' he said, pinching his nose, so smiling and surprised it looked like innocence, and as my own sinuses sparked and fizzed, we leaned in for our first kiss. I tasted smoke and chemicals, a trace of sweetness from his cocktail, and then he moved his mouth away from mine, across my cheek, where he bit me, hard, just above the jaw.

I recoiled, swearing, and the other people in the room momentarily paused. 'You *animal*,' said someone admiringly, and for whatever reason, I started to laugh, a little too loudly. To soothe me, or to shut me up, Adam kissed me again. 'You're delicious,' he murmured. 'Unbearably so.'

I went to find a bathroom and splash some water on my face. The bite mark was striking in a good way. I looked beautiful. Exhilarated. The stimulants buzzed through me even as I stood still. When I came back, Adam wasn't in the main room. It took

29

me a while to find him; he was smoking in the alcove under the stairs.

'You want to get out of here?'

He considered me. 'Not with you. Not like this.'

I was too wired to feel wounded. I wanted to laugh again. 'Fuck you, then. Or not.'

'Don't misunderstand me – I want to see you again. But clearly. Soberly.' He put his head to one side. 'How do you hold up in the cold light of day, I wonder?'

'Better than you, I'll bet.'

'You're probably right. You've still got a touch of the ingénue, just about. Little Lily …'

'There's never been anything the least bit ingénue about you.'

'Maybe not.' Adam reached out and put a finger on my cheek, where he'd bitten it. 'Jesus. I can't think what came over me.'

'Ah. This is where you tell me what a terrible person you are and how I should stay away for my own good.'

'What if it's true?'

'Even if it is, you should come up with a better cliché.'

Watch out, I'm bad news is how a person positions themselves as irresistible while admitting they're irredeemable. But I can't deny it: I was warned there would be trouble ahead. Maybe I should have returned the favour.

'I'll call you,' said Adam, and I nodded, and by then it was too late for either of us.

CHAPTER FOUR

'Oh, darling! You clever girl!' The Momager came whirling into my bedroom, all of a flutter. 'Would you be *terribly* annoyed if I said I "told you so"?'

I scrubbed the sleep gunk from my eyes and squinted at my phone. OK, so it was ten o'clock on a Wednesday morning, but it was still definitely time to change the locks. 'You told me so about what?'

'About the power of networking and putting yourself out there! Really, you look adorable.'

She was thrusting one of London's freebie newspapers under my nose. It was open at the 'On the Tiles' social diary section. A whole page was devoted to the fashionista's art show opening. One of the picture captions read: 'Adam out of the Romance "Wylderness"?' And there we were both were, looking pretty cosy, I had to admit. *Spotted: Adam Harker and former child-star Lily Thane, getting up close and personal in a corner.*

I rolled over and pulled the duvet back above my head. 'Yeah, well, don't go buying your wedding hat.'

It was already bad enough that Talia and Nina messaged me every day to ask if he'd called. (He hadn't.)

'Sweetie, don't put yourself down. Adam looks *very* enamoured in this photo. I'd go as far as saying you made a bit of a conquest. I remember him from your school days, of course. Such a funny-looking little chap! Amazing the transformational powers of puberty –' She leaned in to pull off the duvet, then did a double take. 'Whatever happened to your cheek?'

The bite mark was faded, but there was still a purplish mottled mark.

'I … got some pigmentation lasered off.'

'Poor you. I always find aloe vera helps with the bruising. Anyway, it's lovely to see that Adam's doing so well. He's had a few lean years, by all accounts, but it's starting to look as if he's turned a corner. Because his new film could be quite a big deal, couldn't it? Artsy war movies always do well at award season. And –'

'Is there a point to this? Or are you just reciting his IMDb page?'

Then my phone rang.

'Bet that's him now!' my mother warbled. I shooed her away. 'Hello?'

'It's Adam.'

'Adam. Hi.' My hand went to the bite mark. I went hot all over. 'How are you?' I said formally.

'Very well, thank you for asking.' Adam sounded amused.

My mother had actually put her fist in her mouth and was chewing her knuckles in agitation. Somehow, she managed to look dainty while doing it. I sprang out of bed, frogmarched her out of the bedroom and closed the door.

'So,' he said. 'Ready for the cold light of day?'

———

Coffee and a stroll in the park. Easy-breezy.

(Drop-dead gorgeous but doesn't know it.)

(Looks intellectual but is still smoking hot.)

I channelled the Momager for my final primp.

'I don't mean to pressure you, darling,' I said breathily to my reflection in the bathroom mirror, 'because you know how proud I am of you, but I cannot stress enough what a wonderful, wonderful opportunity this.'

I dabbed on some lip-stain, turned up the collar on my biker jacket and pulled the neck of my T-shirt down low. Tweak, tug, tweak. 'Adam can open a lot of doors for you, sweetie. Put in the right amount of effort, and who knows where things might lead?'

Then I hunched my shoulders, infusing my voice with a teenage whine. 'What if we're, like, fundamentally incompatible?'

I looked at the mirror sternly. 'I'm only saying don't rule anything out.' Cue the dazzling smile. 'Eyes on the prize, darling. That's all I ask. Eyes on the prize.'

'There she is.'

I had forgotten how tall Adam was. He had to stoop to kiss my cheek. He smelled of liquorice and wood smoke.

'Sorry. I was – the time – stuff got away from me.' I took a moment to catch my breath. Hopefully my cheeks were prettily aglow. 'I was talking to my mother.'

'About me?'

'You know, there *are* other topics of conversation.'

'Not half as interesting, surely.' His smile slanted. Under the shadow of the trees, his face was dappled gold. 'Walk with me.'

So off we went. In silence, we contemplated the blue sky and summer-bleached grass, the glittering leaves. Bonfire smoke drifted lazily across the path.

'You know,' Adam said after a little while, 'I remember meeting your mum backstage during that play we did. She was rather charming.'

'Well, there's an iron fist in that velvet glove.'

'That's no bad thing in a manager.'

'But a little wearing in a parent.'

'No doubt. Still, all things considered, you seem pretty stable for a former child-star. Unless there's a sex tape or shoplifting conviction I don't know about.'

'You're speculating that I'm not quite as wholesome as I look?' Maybe Adam was only interested in slutty coke-heads. No – if that was the case, we'd have hooked up at the party. Instead, he'd made a point of meeting up in the fresh air, two green-juice smoothies in hand. 'Fact is, I'm plain vanilla with a side of square.' Coquettish smile. 'At least within working hours.'

No reaction. 'Is your mother still your manager?'

Oh God. 'Sort of. Not really. I mean, that's her job title. Self-appointed job title. Mostly, she just replies to comments on my Instagram.'

I braced myself for the inevitable piss-take. (Who did I think I was? A Kardashian?) But Adam simply nodded, as if he was storing the information away for future reference.

We ditched the smoothies for coffee from a stand and sat down on a bench to sip them. A couple of people glanced at us as they passed by, then looked again. I didn't flatter myself that they were looking at me. Adam's jet-black hair was covered by a beanie; he wore a nondescript navy jacket, beaten-up jeans, scuffed work boots. But even away from the flattering camera angles and filtered light, the make-up artists and the photoshopped shoots, people like him carry a lustre of their own.

'What about your dad?' he asked.

Ah, Lionel Thane. The golden youth with the weak jawline and slightly too close-set eyes. In a different age, with a marginally better chin, he might have been a matinee idol; instead, he's had to eke out the classical stage roles by playing upper-crust cads, cowards and the occasional Nazi. Poor old Pa.

'Vague. Distracted. Fond.'

'The Thane name must open some doors.'

If only. As acting dynasties go, I'd say we're pretty second rate. Three of us are currently actors of, as we know, varying success. Then there's Dido's parents: the avant-garde theatre director (Uncle Felix) and feminist playwright (Aunt Naomi). Plus Pa's opera-singing wife Adele, Aunt Sylvie, the alcoholic ex-Bond girl, and her son Blake (briefly an Australian soap star, now a yoga instructor in Bali). But, 'We're not exactly the Redgraves,' was all I said.

'Your grandad's Lear is still the best I've ever seen. I must've watched the RSC recording a dozen times. A tough act to follow ... Your dad – he's supportive of your career?'

'I think he's come to accept we can't all be Shakespeareans.'

'And thank God for that. *Briefs* was a good gig. One of the top-three ratings earners for the network, right? And I saw some of that crime drama you did last year. *The Dreamer.* It's just been added to Netflix.'

Oh ho – so I wasn't the only one to indulge in some light cyber-stalking. I perked up immediately. The drama in question was a Scandi-noir-style thriller set in the south London suburbs, and I'd played the daughter of one of the chief suspects. The reviews were admiring, but we'd been scheduled opposite a cosy period drama about land girls, and so the viewing figures had been less than stellar.

Adam's next words raised my spirits further. 'You were really good,' he said, snark-free. 'I believed in you. A natural sociopath.'

'That's me.'

Eyes on the prize, darling. Eyes on the prize. I casually twirled a strand of hair and tilted my face at the angle I use for head shots.

However, Adam failed to respond. Somehow we were in a flirtation-free zone. I tried asking my own questions, though none of them got me very far. Adam's PR liked to highlight that he was from an 'ordinary' background (father a scaffolder, mum a school administrator), unlike the public-school types who hang out in Dido's kitchen. But when talking about his family, Adam sounded as if he was referencing mere acquaintances. He was similarly reticent about his new film, trotting out a few bland soundbites about what a 'privilege' it had been to work on.

I'd auditioned for the wrong part, I realised. He wanted some druggy party girl after all. The dewy-eyed meet-cute of that newspaper photo belonged to somebody else's life.

Adam's next words confirmed it. He got his phone, typed something out, then looked up with an efficient smile. 'I'm sorry, I have to head off now. There's a meeting I can't get out of.'

'Sure.' *Don't call us, we'll call you.*

'But this has been great. Perfect, in fact. Let's meet up again soon.'

Huh?

We'd reached the park gates. Several knots of people were milling about in the sun; there was a holiday atmosphere. Adam suddenly pulled me close, brushing the hair from my eyes and looking at me intently.

'I mean it, Lily. I think this could be something special. Unexpected, but special. You'll see.'

I was sceptical. A self-protecting instinct, I guess. The next evening we went to a bar, but Adam was preoccupied and on edge. A fan came over asking for a selfie, and although he obliged, he was fairly terse about it.

'Did you understand what you were getting into with that snowflake film?'

The question came out of nowhere and it took me a moment to respond, partly because I was distracted by the way Adam, leaning back in his chair, had rucked up his T-shirt, exposing a thin strip of stomach. And, yes, washboard abs.

'Well, I come from a family of performers. As you know. I grew up assuming that's what people did. Sure, my mother pushed me, but it was also something I enjoyed – wanted – from the start.'

Most people assume that the Momager is the way she is because she never headlined for the Royal Ballet and so made me a surrogate for her frustrated ambition. 'But the truth – and I can only ever admit this to you, darling – is that I never really wanted to be a ballerina. I wanted to do my dancing in *heels*. Sparkly ones! I wanted bright lights and sequins and big-band music. Ginger Rogers, not Anna Pavlova. The Thanes could never understand that kind of dream, let alone respect it. Your father's family have many fine qualities but, one has to admit, they do rather like to suck the joy out of things …'

And there *was* joy in our shared enterprise, at least in the beginning. As a kid, my mother and I were two gal pals together, out to conquer The Business We Call Show. I'm sure the Momager enjoyed cocking a snook at the Thanes as she shepherded me through assorted child beauty pageants, junk-food commercials and TV melodramas where I'd lisp 'I'll wuv you fowever!' next to an ailing parent's bedside. The way she sees it, however, is that she saved me from the kind of disapprovingly intellectual hothouse Dido was raised in. 'Meaning isn't only found in serious things, sweetie. There can be truth and beauty in light entertainment, and it will touch *far* more people's lives than your cousin moping about in Ibsen.'

'Basically, I liked feeling special,' I told Adam.

'Nice. Any actor who says they don't want to be famous is lying. Inside all of them, inside every performance ever given, there's this small sweaty child, stamping his feet and shouting till his voice is hoarse: "Look at me! Look at me! Look at me!"'

I laughed. 'But that's never quite enough, is it? Because then it goes: "Love me! Love me! Love me!"'

Adam was silent for a while. 'My mum's Irish, so when I was a kid, we'd spend the summer holidays with my aunt and uncle and cousins in County Kildare. They didn't live in romantic picture-postcard Ireland. It was a crap little house in a crap little town. There was nothing to do, and it always seemed to rain, and me and my sister and the cousins would bicker, endlessly.'

He sat forward again and took a swig of beer. 'I slept on a blow-up mattress in the loft. I'd lie there thinking about how I'd performed that day. How many times I'd made people laugh. Or frown. Or just, you know, listen to me. And when I closed my eyes … the rain on the skylight, it sounded like applause.'

It wasn't much of an anecdote. But even now, after everything, I remember the bleakness of his face as he said it.

The next moment the darkness was gone, so swiftly I almost thought I'd imagined it, as Adam leaned into me and lowered his voice to its most velvety tones. 'So … where do you think we are, right now?'

'I think you're playing games,' I said lightly.

He touched the nape of my neck. Despite myself, my skin shivered. 'You seem like a girl who enjoys the thrill of the chase.'

'Mm. And you're starting to seem like a third-rate pick-up artist.'

That made him draw back. 'So why are you still here?'

I had to laugh. I kept it flirtatious, though. 'Desperation. You said we have that in common, if you remember.'

He nodded, quite serious again. 'I did.'

I thought back to our parting in the park, and the way he had brushed my hair out of my eyes. There had been something so intimate about the act. Like the way he'd looked at Casilda Fernandez on screen – and in real life too, presumably – that intoxicating mix of hunger and tenderness. I wondered what it must feel like to be looked at with such intensity. But Adam Harker was an actor. A good one. He could look at anyone that way if he chose.

––––––

'He's a self-loathing narcissist, obviously,' said Nina on the phone. 'But so are ninety-five per cent of actors. This can't have come as a surprise.'

I stuffed another three butterscotch cookies into my mouth. They came from the emergency pack (family size) I'd stashed under the kitchen sink and tasted like sugared cardboard, but the rhythmic munching was calming to my jangled nerves. Through a mouthful of crumbs, I said, 'So who *should* I be dating? My accountant? Some Tinder random? One of Dido's groupies?'

'Beats me. I mean, I'd totally bang him.' Nina cackled. 'Even though he's probably a selfish arse in bed too. Men like that never make any effort.'

Adam emailed me about an hour after dropping me home after our second date. (His goodnight kiss had barely even been PG – appreciative, gentle. *Polite.*) He had to travel over the next week, he said, and would probably be out of contact, but he wanted to meet up soon. As I purged the butterscotch cookies, and the tub of chocolate ice-cream and pastry cheese-puffs that followed, I told myself I was flushing away all schoolgirl hopes of Adam Harker too. But it turned out I'd misjudged him. The night before he was due back he messaged to see if I was free to meet him the next day at his manager's office.

My agent belongs to a small if respectable firm, whose slightly chaotic office is just off Oxford Street. My manager is technically my mother. Adam was represented by one of the big Hollywood agencies. His manager, Victor Green, was one of the founding partners of Penfold Green. Its HQ was a modern town-house in Soho and had the understated luxury of a smart hotel. As soon as I was buzzed in I began to regret my raspberry-coloured knit dress and tan boots. The outfit didn't look as sophisticated as I'd thought when leaving the flat.

I was expecting Adam to meet me in the lobby. Instead, I was greeted at reception by a chic Asian woman who introduced herself as Grace Tang, Adam's publicist. Her handshake was firm, her manner brisk. 'Thanks for coming, Lily. Before I bring you to Adam, would you mind taking a minute for some paperwork?'

Confused, and trying not to let it show, I followed her into a spacious office. A grizzled man with tired eyes was sitting behind the desk.

'Victor Green,' he said. His teeth were excessively white. 'It's good to meet you. Adam speaks very highly.'

He didn't say anything else for the duration of the encounter. I was uncomfortably aware, however, of being under his scrutiny throughout.

Grace passed over the paperwork, along with a pen. 'I'm sure it's not the first of these you've come across, and it's all completely standard. But if you have any questions, please do ask.'

Holy shit. It was an NDA. I had, in fact, signed one of these before, for the crime drama. In that case it was just a promise not to give away the final twist. This was different. As I skim-read the jargon, I realised I was essentially agreeing to keep all my interactions with Adam private. If I shared 'confidential information' about him with friends, family, publishers, social networks or media outlets, I would face legal action. I'd also have to pay an upfront fine of £100,000 in addition to any costs incurred from breaking the agreement.

WTAF?

This was the sort of contract celebrities impose on their household staff or guests at an especially private party. Some stars also ask their sexual partners to sign them, as a protection against kiss 'n' tells. Just the idea of it made me feel cheap.

Walk away, dammit. Walk.

Trouble was, I was burning with curiosity.

Victor Green continued to watch me speculatively from behind the desk.

My palms were sweaty as I picked up the pen. I waited a long moment. Then I signed. It didn't look as if I was going to see Adam again if I didn't.

'That's great. Thank you,' said Grace blandly. 'Adam's just through here.'

He was sitting on a leather sofa set against a plate-glass wall. The view behind him was filled with rooftop slopes and angles and pearl-grey sky. In front of him was a black glass coffee table with a single espresso cup in the middle. He was wearing an expensive-looking blue shirt, open at the neck. The mid-century sofa, the skyline, his lounging pose turned the scene into the kind of advertorial you'd see in high-end lifestyle magazines. Maybe he was about to sell me a pen or a watch. A coffee capsule.

Adam smiled as I came through the door, but didn't get up. Self-consciously, I perched on one of the uncomfortable designer chairs.

'Hi.'

'Hi.'

'Would you like anything to drink – coffee? Water?'

Presumably there was a bell to summon minions, concealed in the wall. 'I'm fine, thanks.'

'So you signed the NDA.'

'Yup.'

'Sorry about that. Victor insisted. He likes to be thorough about these things.'

'I see.'

'No, you don't. You're pissed … it rather suits you.'

'I'm wondering what I've let myself in for, that's all. Are you going to pull a Weinstein?'

'Would you want me to?'

I hardened my stare. 'That's not funny.'

'No. My apologies. You're right. So let me set your mind at rest – I'm not going to "pull a Weinstein". Because, one, I'm not a rapist pig. And, two, I don't sleep with women.'

It took me a moment. 'Oh,' I said witlessly.

'Explains a few things, does it?'

Actually, it felt like I'd missed a step on the stairs. I cleared my throat. 'Some. Maybe.' *Pull yourself together.*

'There you have it: my deep dark secret.' Adam's lounging was almost aggressively relaxed. 'Again, I'm sorry about the NDA. I know you're no snitch. But my team are a touch paranoid on the subject. We've got big plans, and I'm sure I don't have to spell out how me being exposed as a raging homo could derail them.'

I cleared my throat again. 'Even now? I mean, there are some pretty mainstream names who are –' I realised how patronising this sounded and came to a halt. 'Sorry. I'll shut up.'

'That's OK. I take your point in that, yes, there are queer actors enjoying successful careers. But here's the thing: *Hollywood*

43

still hasn't got a major star who is out. By that, I mean an A-lister who's out in the peak of their career – not twenty years past it. Studio bosses remain very leery of gay actors playing straight leads. And if an aspiring star came out to them … do you really think the men in suits would still bet millions of dollars on their box office, that they'd have the same power to pick the best projects, the most in-demand co-stars? That they'd be allowed to have the odd flop or misstep and get away with it?'

His delivery of this speech surprised me. I wouldn't have expected it to sound so obviously rehearsed. 'Well …'

'I've already been the Next Big Thing, remember. For all of five minutes, over ten years ago. I didn't make it then, but now … maybe this could be the start of my second chance. *Tyre* – the new film – the buzz is good. Promising. If things go to plan, it could turn a corner for me. Open up those golden doors … Trouble is, everything's so fucking *fragile*. Even if I do everything right, I still need to be lucky. Or else it could all fizzle out. Again.

'I can't make my own luck. But I can control a lot of other things. Image, brand, marketability. My sexual orientation is a part of this. And the fact is, it will always be a weakness until the point I become too big to fail.'

'I can, uh, see that.'

'Then lighten up! I don't have a problem with who I am. Believe me, I'm *very* comfortable with my sexuality.' Now his smile had a private sleekness. 'I'm also comfortable keeping my personal life under wraps. Which is where you come in.' Adam leaned forward. 'Little Lucie. Lovely Lily. How'd you like to star in my fauxmance?'

44

CHAPTER FIVE

This was the deal Adam Harker presented me. In return for playing the part of a dutiful girlfriend, which would include photo ops, interviews and public appearances as required, my own career would be 'materially advanced' above and beyond any promotional benefits of being seen on his arm. The contract would initially be for six months, with the option to extend it further if all parties were satisfied with proceedings.

Adam's war film would première in September, at the Telluride film festival in Colorado. A six-month contract would cover a big chunk of the festival and award-season circuit. Adam wasn't just asking me to be his fake girlfriend: I was being invited to be his red-carpet plus one.

And yet my mind was elsewhere – the kisses. The fondles. The bite.

'You strung me along. You *played* me.'

'We've got natural chemistry. Anyone can see it. So can you blame me if I got a little caught up in the act? It was a seductive fantasy.'

Liar. I still wanted to believe him.

I began to pace the room, imagining the checklist. *Single, photogenic wannabe required. Industry experience preferred. No fame-whores or homophobes.*

Adam looked amused. 'C'mon. This is how all relationships start: first an audition, then a performance. Don't tell me you'd already fallen for me.'

'I'm not *that* much of a masochist.'

'Look, I'm sorry I wasn't entirely – pardon the pun – straight with you. But I was hardly going to do the Big Reveal to someone I barely knew. When we bumped into each other again, I didn't have a strategy in mind. I just remembered you as being a nice kid, and you seemed to have grown up to be a cool person, so one thing led to another and ...' He shrugged. 'In the interest of full disclosure, I think you should know that Grace has been against this. Or you, specifically. Vic took a bit of convincing too. They like the Thane name, it's true. Adds kudos. Class. But they think I should be aiming for a more obviously advantageous relationship, with an established star.'

Fair point. I was an ex-child-star whose career was on the slide and was still managed by her mother. Not exactly a catch. 'Another Casilda Fernandez, you mean.'

Adam shook his head. 'The studio set that one up. A straightforward promotional arrangement to titillate the *Wylderness* fans. Cassy's nice enough but thick as mince. We never had anything to say to each other outside of work.

'Ideally, I'd be linked with one of the girls from *Tyre*. But one's married and the other's just started dating Kash so ...' He shrugged. 'I told Victor that if I'm going to have to spend a certain amount of time pretending to romance somebody, I'd like it to be someone I actually enjoy hanging out with. Someone I can be open with, who hasn't come straight off the PR assembly line. Someone with a bit of an edge.

'You don't have to decide now, Lily. Go away and have a think. If it's not for you, it's no big deal. My team has plenty of candidates on the books. But we can be of use to each other. I think we could also have a lot of fun.'

'Is this what you meant by "unexpected but special"?'

His grin was wolfish; his eyes were little-boy blue. 'You won't regret it. Trust me.'

I think Adam believed those things he told me. I think it was largely true that he chose me on impulse, based on the serendipity of our meeting and a sense of connection that felt genuine at the time. Truth, of course, is a many-layered thing. The week he'd said he was away travelling and out of contact, his team would have been doing their due diligence on me; however anodyne I appeared in their report, Adam was sharp enough to discern I was more hot mess than ingénue. Because for all his talk of control and calculation, Adam was drawn to risk. Maybe my messiness made him feel even more superior; maybe he just fancied the idea of a partner in crime. Either way, he'd sensed something raw and ragged in me, right from the start, and that's what attracted him.

I was a good candidate in another way. The Momager. Adam said he and his team would prefer to deal with her directly and keep my agent out of the loop. The fewer people involved in our arrangement the better, he said. He'd have done due diligence on her as well. Despite her apparent flakiness, the Momager was discreet and a shrewd negotiator. But when all's said and done, she was essentially a talented stage mother, not a founding partner at Penfold Green.

My collaboration with Adam was never going to be an equal one. I knew that the fine print of our contract was always going to be to his advantage. The truth is, in the beginning I was too greedy, too needy, to care.

I didn't admit this to myself, of course. Not at first. I even pretended to my mother that I was wavering. We held the summit in her living room.

The Momager's pose reminded me of Adam's. She was on the chaise-longue, wearing the pink pussy-bow blouse that's part of her power-dressing ensemble. There was even an espresso cup on the table in front of her. She was doing a much worse job of pretending to be nonchalant, however.

'I can't believe this is even up for discussion. This is absolutely a win-win situation for us. What have you got to lose?'

I looked pious. 'Only my integrity.'

'Nonsense! This is a perfectly straightforward PR arrangement. *Lots* of big names embark on them for all *sorts* of reasons. It's a Hollywood tradition – the "bearding" aspect in particular. No, don't roll your eyes at me, sweetie. I know what I'm talking about. A "lavender marriage" they called it, back in the day. Like Rock Hudson and the secretary. Just think, you and Adam could have one too!'

'You cannot be serious.'

'I am entirely serious, Lily.' She put down the espresso cup and fixed me with her most no-nonsense stare. 'Not about marriage, necessarily – though, let's face it, nobody's getting any younger here. But an opportunity like Adam Harker won't come around again.'

'Are you saying I can't make it on my own?'

'Darling, we have to face facts. When you weren't promoted to a series regular on *Briefs* … well, that was a body blow. Now that you've hit your thirties, you're at a very delicate time in your career. Dating Adam Harker isn't just a potential game-changer – it's a lifeline.'

'Only if his new film turns out to be a sleeper hit. And to be honest, it sounds pretty niche.'

'So? Even if it bombs, you'll still have had red-carpet exposure. Press opportunities. Your name in all the right circles. And there's nothing so easy as pretending to be in love! Of course, I'll want to see some real incentives before we sign up. We need to find out exactly what Adam's team are prepared to commit to. You should definitely get a clothing allowance, for instance.' She gave a happy sigh. 'It's fascinating, really … Adam seems almost *aggressively* masculine on screen. But perhaps it's different in real life? You must have had a hint, surely. Is that why you were so coy about that photo in the gossip column?'

Jesus. 'Let's try to leave out the offensive stereotypes, shall we?'

She ignored me. 'The funny thing is, this has actually worked out much better for us than if you were dating Adam for real. There won't be any uncertainty. Everyone will know exactly where they stand.'

When I didn't answer, she came over to where I was sitting and knelt beside me. 'I'm sorry if I'm getting ahead of myself, sweetie. I'm just so excited for you, that's all. After all your troubles and disappointments, I really feel you deserve this. Don't lose sight of why we got into this business in the first place. It wasn't ever supposed to just be about work, or making a name for yourself. It was about adventure. Glamour. *Fun*. Because we used to have fun, didn't we, the two of us? In the old days?'

'I miss those days.'

She put her cheek against mine. 'I miss them too.'

We found out what was on offer by the end of the week.

The NDA section of the contract included financial penalties if the no-disparagement clause was breached. There was also a weight management and appearance clause, offset by use of a stylist, provision of clothes for red-carpet events and a proportion of personal grooming expenses. The cost of my dates with Adam, travel and hotel accommodation would be covered, but instead of a subsistence allowance or fixed fee, Adam's team was to secure me an audition for the pilot of *Hollow Moon*. Adapted from an international bestseller, and pitched as *Game of Thrones* set in space, it had been lavished with a huge budget and a lot of hype.

Much fuss was made as to what a big deal this was. Strings pulled, favours called in, et cetera. The truth was, it was in everyone's interest for me to have my own gig. Adam Harker, being groomed for his second shot at stardom, shouldn't be dating a has-been.

I now saw that Adam's reticence about *Tyre* was superstition. He didn't want to jinx it. When he talked about the movie he was struggling to suppress the treacherous swell of hope. It was a low-budget indie and only the second film to be made by its director. Yet people were already saying Kash Malik could become that rarest of Hollywood beasts: a maker of art-house films that turned into box-office gold.

'When I first read the script I wasn't sure if it was genius or utter bollocks. The dream sequences – trips – whatever you want to call them – they're pretty out there. But it came together. The vision.' Adam gave a brittle laugh. 'At least, I fucking hope so.'

He told me this during one of our first official dates. Photos of Adam and me 'canoodling', as the Momager called it, sprang up like mushrooms on all the major gossip sites. We were stars of our very own Richard Curtis movie, the most scenic parts of London providing a sugar-sprinkled backdrop for our PDAs.

'No offence, but who gives a crap?' asked Nina, as she and Talia squinted at a photo on *Popbitch* of the two of us larking about at Bermondsey market. 'Adam's not been hot since *Wylderness*, and even then he was only pushing B-list. Either it's a really slow week in the gossip office or his PR's calling in a lot of favours. Do you have a tame pap following you around or what?'

Not much gets past Nina.

'Adam's got a new publicist. She's a bit over-keen, apparently. Trying to stir up interest ahead of the new movie.'

'Why isn't he dating someone who's actually famous then?'

I hadn't told anyone about my upcoming audition for *Hollow Moon*. 'Aren't my perky tits and magnetic personality enough?'

'Magnetic, sure … like those plastic alphabets kids stick on a fridge.'

'You *guys*.' Talia's never understood our schtick. She looked between us anxiously, like the child of quarrelling parents. 'Lily doesn't need to be an uber-celeb for Adam to be into her. Look how smitten he was at that party. Just think – if I hadn't invited

51

you, then you two probably wouldn't have connected again, and this whole romance might never have happened. It's *synchronicity*. No coincidences are meaningless, I really believe that.'

'It does make for a heartwarming story,' Nina agreed. 'I mean, the guy was so smacked-up he literally tried to chew Lily's face off.'

'Is that true?' Talia asked, goggling.

'Barely.'

'Oh. Well, I think you're such a photogenic couple. And I love your new hair.'

I'd had a bit of a makeover, it was true. No more going out with unwashed locks and last night's eyeliner. 'You should quit wearing black,' Adam had told me. 'It makes you look tired. And tired is halfway to old.' He looked at me thoughtfully. 'I think you should upgrade your highlights, too. Something warmer, maybe with a bit of red in it.'

We were having a drink at my place. I was going through my wardrobe to pick an outfit, while Adam lounged on the bed and scrolled through his phone. Just like any ordinary couple getting ready to go out on a Saturday night.

I tossed the black halter-neck I'd picked out to one side. 'Is this the bit where the gay BFF does the makeover montage?'

'I'm not your BFF. As far as this romcom's concerned, *you're* the blink-and-you'll-miss-it sidekick with the sassy asides.' He snickered. 'In casting terms, you might as well be the token black girl.'

At least I had a real casting coming up. *Hollow Moon* was my first brush with sci-fi, though the aliens and spaceships were supposedly background dressing for an epic tale of dynastic power struggles and the clash of civilisations. All the major parts had been cast, even though the feature-length pilot wasn't due to start shooting until after Christmas. But then the actor cast as Lys Azuriel had been forced to pull out, due to another project overrunning. It was her role that had been dangled in front of me.

Ironically enough, I'd unsuccessfully auditioned for the show a month or so before – for the walk-on part of an android maid (AKA sex-bot). The role I was up for this time was an actual lead. I read the character breakdown in one greedy gulp: '*We first meet Lys as a naïve, somewhat spoiled young priestess who is only beginning to explore her powers as a star-seeker and seer. But after being captured by sky-pirates, she learns to use her natural wit and resilience to not only survive, but thrive, in the cut-throat world of Ark'aan politics ...*'

'*Hollow Moon*'s the golden ticket. Prestige TV with a movie budget, a built-in fandom via the books. I can't see it not being ordered to series.' This was from my agent, Judy. She knew about the relationship, if not the contract, with Adam, and if she was shrewd enough to suspect that wheels had been greased on my behalf, she didn't say. We were both pretending I hadn't already auditioned for it, too. 'They're only seeing a couple of other people at this stage. Lys is a great fit; I'd say she's there for the taking.'

The day before my audition I had a visitor.

It was Adam's manager, Victor Green. He still looked tired, and grizzled in a prematurely aged way, but his teeth looked freshly whitened. Sharpened, too. He gave the impression that he was passing through the area and had spontaneously decided to drop by. Coffee was offered and accepted; *Hollow Moon*'s potential was favourably appraised. Gracious things were said about the Momager.

'How's everything going with Adam?' he finally asked.

'Fine. Great, I mean. He's an easy person to get along with.'

'I'll admit I had my reservations, but so far your arrangement looks to be working out well.'

'I'm sorry the, uh, circumstances – I'm sorry there has to be an arrangement at all.'

'Are you?' he asked drily. 'Well. Adam's the only person who can decide in what direction his life goals take him and how he wants to present himself to the world. My job is helping him to achieve that as smoothly and comfortably as possible. I don't pull the strings.'

Don't you? I longed to ask, but didn't quite dare.

'I am, naturally, protective,' Victor continued. 'A successful managerial relationship has to work on a personal level as well as a professional one – you and your delightful mother are proof of that. That's why I consider Adam's emotional health to be as integral to his success as his billing at the multiplex.' He took a sip of coffee. 'Mm, delicious … Tell me, how much powder is Adam putting up his nose these days?'

'I – we –' I was caught out. 'He doesn't get high with me, if that's what you're asking.'

'No?'

'No.' This was largely true. Since the night of the private view, our evenings had involved nothing stronger than booze and a bit of weed.

'That's as I thought,' Victor said amiably. 'There's nothing wrong with the "work hard, play hard" dynamic per se. But it's something I like to keep an eye on. Not just Adam – this goes for all of my clients.'

'Right.'

'That's one of the reasons I'm pleased you're on board, Lily. I haven't always been so positive about the people in Adam's life.' Another appreciative sip of coffee. 'For instance, there was a young man … Rafael, I think the name was. He had a connection to Adam's agent in LA and he and Adam were close for a while. Has Adam ever mentioned him to you?'

I shook my head.

'It wasn't the healthiest relationship. Rafael liked to party, and he got Adam into some unfortunate habits. He wasn't discreet, either. I didn't interfere, but I have to admit to being very relieved when the affair burnt itself out, even though it left Adam in a bad way. It was around this time that he began to attract a somewhat unfortunate reputation. Up-and-comers can't afford to be difficult, as I'm sure you know.'

I did. I do.

'He's over it now, obviously. Lessons learned. These days he seems relaxed, upbeat. Amenable. I'd like that to continue. You understand?'

'Um, sure.'

'You're clearly a sensible girl. It'll be an exciting time ahead – parties, festivals, premières. A lot of fun. A lot of opportunities. A lot of *pressure*. Especially for Adam. So if you see any signs that things are going … off-kilter, shall we say, I would appreciate the heads-up.'

I shifted uncomfortably in my seat. 'Are you asking me to spy on him?'

'I'm asking you to keep an eye on Adam for his own well-being.' Victor rose to his feet. 'It's the responsible thing to do, Lily. I'm sure I don't need to tell you that this is very much in your interests, as well as the rest of the team's.'

I was meant to be intimidated by this conversation. But if it was my job to report to Victor on Adam, then maybe Adam didn't hold all the cards. I had some leverage too.

My first audition for *Hollow Moon* had been like all the others. Waiting in a corridor with a line of other young women who looked vaguely the same as me. An hour later, being shown into a dark box. The stale air, the table cluttered with coffee cups and half-eaten sandwiches. The men slumped behind their monitors like bored teenagers. The desperation oozing from my pores. *Look at me. Love me. Please.*

This occasion was different. There was no wait, no other candidates on parade, and the casting director herself met me at the lift. 'Lovely to see you again, Lily.' She claimed to remember me from my audition for the sex-bot part. 'Now, of course, it seems absurd that you didn't try out for Lys in the first place.'

That was because I wasn't one of the favoured few who'd been invited to. I smiled politely.

'Seeing you in *The Dreamer* was a revelation, to be honest. It really showcased your range.'

You were really good, Adam had said. *I believed in you.*

A natural sociopath.

We went through to the audition room. I was nervous, of course, but in the good way, when adrenaline hums in the blood and everything around you seems extra sharp and clear. Afterwards, the director exchanged looks with the producer and murmured, 'Very nice.'

The director was small and eager, with bitten-down nails. As he talked, his oversize glasses kept slipping down his nose. '*Hollow Moon* may be set in space, but it's flesh-and-blood human drama that drives the story. The lust for domination, for sex and power … There won't be anything gratuitous, obviously, but we need the passions we show on screen to be authentically gritty. Real. Will you be comfortable with that?'

'Of course,' I said, as if I'd expected nothing less. *Authentically real* … Definitely code for tits out. And/or explicit sex scenes. My agent hadn't mentioned anything. Was this because she didn't know or hadn't wanted to put me off?

I realised I'd momentarily zoned out from what the director was saying. Something about how they'd hoped to get the actor playing the sky-pirate captain, Jarkus, to read with me, but that he was away filming in Australia. 'So for this next scene,' he continued, 'I want you to seduce us. Show us Lys's sensual side.'

Oh, fantastic.

There are few things less sensual than attempting to be sexy on demand in front of a group of strangers in a nondescript room in a nondescript office in the middle of the day. The new pages were already being passed over to me; I'd have a few minutes to read them through and gather my thoughts, then we'd be off.

The red light of the camera blinked. The casting director gave an encouraging smile. 'Whenever you're ready.'

I closed my eyes for a moment, picturing the scene. Lys is planning to escape the sky-pirates. At a crucial moment, Jarkus appears. Has he come to seduce her, and is he going to use force or charm? Either way, Lys needs to catch him off guard, disarm him. Both are concealing their real feelings; it's not immediately clear who is in thrall to who. I looked out at the room with Lys's eyes, as she tries to hold the gaze of the pirate-king. Amused, superior, rakish … Of course it was Adam's face that appeared to me.

I took a deep breath.

Watch out, I said. *I have a weapon.*

CHAPTER SIX

Filming on *Hollow Moon* wasn't going to start, coincidentally or not, until January, close to when my six-month contract with Adam was up for review. The timing made me jittery. Even though I'd 'won' the part, every actor knows you can't count on a job being booked until the show or film or commercial is actually broadcast with you in it. I'd need to continue my winning streak with Adam, too.

But in the early days, as with any real relationship, Adam and I were honeymooning. Adam was on his best behaviour; I was eager to please. Not too eager, of course. Adam didn't like neediness. He liked me feisty. Feisty ... but knowing my place.

It was a tricky balance. We weren't lovers but we were still something more than friends. I hadn't reached this level of emotional intimacy with any of the other men I'd dated (mind you, I'd never committed to dating anyone for as long as six months before). But with Adam, this kind of honesty felt easy. Perhaps all I'd ever needed was practice. Or else sex was more of a distraction than I'd realised.

I think Adam was also enjoying the novelty. Out on our public dates, or private debriefs, we talked with an openness that I sensed was new for him, too. We tried out the same questions any new couple asks. Are you a morning person? Who's the most awkward member of your family? What's been your worst unrequited crush? And do you believe in The One?

No, I said. Maybe, said Adam. Yes.

I could barely contain my surprise. Adam the closeted gay man was one thing, Adam the closet romantic quite another.

'The trouble is, my kind of Mr Right is very much Mr Wrong. See, this is why I'd always need a fauxmance, even in some parallel universe where I could be an A-list homo. I'd still have to have a twink version of you for public consumption. You know: some glad-eyed fairy to keep house and bake cookies, while I'd be banging Mr Bad News on the side.'

I thought of Victor's warnings about the toxic ex. 'And what would be so bad about him?' I asked lightly. 'Sex, drugs, rock 'n' roll?'

But Adam answered me seriously. 'No. I know what's bad for me, and it's none of those things. Because they don't make me weak – not when used properly.'

'Weak ... as in vulnerable?'

'I'm at my worst when I'm at my weakest. Isn't that true of everyone?' His frown lifted. 'That's why you're perfect for me, Lily. You don't ask me for anything I can't give. You might even make me want to be a better person.'

'How's that?'

'The act! You're so good at it. The way you look up at me when we're on parade? Cheeks flushed, lips slightly parted, eyes starry ... There's a moment when I almost believe it. When I can almost believe in me and you: two good and happy people in love.'

I rested my head on his shoulder. 'Then let's pretend it's true.'

You're perfect for me.

Actually, I was a disaster for him. That's often the way of great love, isn't it? At least in the stories.

(OK, so calling our relationship a 'great love' is pushing it. But love *was* there. Sometimes. I'm sure of it.)

It's my only consolation.

The night before the news of my casting in *Hollow Moon* was announced, I took Nina out for drinks. I was actually desperate for an evening in – over the past couple of weeks, Adam and I had razzle-dazzled at the Groucho, Shoreditch House, some hipster dive in Brixton, the opening of a designer store and the première of a play. How did Talia do it? I wondered, as I layered on the under-eye concealer. *(Tired is halfway to old.)*

Nina was silent after I broke the news. Then, 'Why are you telling me this as if it's a death in the family?'

'What? No –'

'Or like I'm one of those women who can't get knocked up and then their best friend gets pregnant with twins.'

'I didn't mean –'

'So you can't believe that I'd actually be happy for you. Have you any idea how crap that makes me feel?' She knocked back her drink. 'You're my best friend, Lily. Pretty much my only friend, if I'm honest. You're my squad. So you should take it as a given that when you get a win, I'm fucking *proud*.'

'I only … I … I'm sorry. You're completely right. I just didn't want you to think I was getting full of myself. I know how random this all is.'

'Random. Uh-huh. Isn't one of your Spacebilge producers also backing Adam's new film?'

How the hell did she know this stuff? 'What happened to just being happy for me?'

'I can be happy *and* cynical. C'mon, babe, we both know how this business works. Either you screw them or they screw you. Of course you've gotta play the game.' She chinked her glass against mine. 'Here's to the successful turning of tricks.'

I was feeling rattled when I got home, and so I called Adam, even though it was late. He must know about navigating friendships in a profession where everything's a competition and everyone's a rival of sorts. But his attempt at comfort wasn't what I wanted to hear.

'You don't need Nina now. You've got me.'

'She's my best friend.'

'She's an also-ran. She's always been losing to you, hasn't she? Now she's losing some more. I can't see the two of you lasting past our contract.'

I got a bit teary at this point.

'Ugh. Ignore me.' Adam sounded embarrassed. 'I'm jealous, most likely. I've had two mass-dumpings by mates: first, the people who ditched me once I started to outshine them, then all the people who ditched me the moment my career went off-track. The sad truth is that you're my entire entourage.'

'That's what Nina said to me.'

'Must be nice to be so in demand. Hey,' he said, lightening the mood, 'while we're on the subject of frenemies, here's a question we haven't tried yet: who's your nemesis?'

'How do you mean?'

'Your uber-rival. The girl who's just like you, but always on your best day. The girl who gets two out of the three parts you go head-to-head for. You, with no bad side.'

I closed my eyes and I was eight years old again. Ten. Fourteen. Lining up in a corridor among a row of other little blondes. The covert appraisals in search of a pimple, fat ankles, bad hair. The obligatory smiles, cheap as the scent of vanilla body mist ... The faces came and went. The fashions changed; the years passed. But yes, there was always one. That one particular girl who was always fairer, thinner, perkier. More shine to her smile. More of a swing to her hips. Me, with no bad side. *Her*.

I could smell the vanilla. I could taste the bile. But I didn't want to get into specifics. 'There've been too many to count. That's the problem with being generic.'

'Is it? The story goes that if you meet your doppelganger, it's a warning of death. No wonder actors are neurotic.'

'So who's yours?'

Adam laughed. 'Ah, but *I'm* the nemesis. The one guy everyone else loses out to. Just wait and see.'

The weekend before the première of *Tyre* was Pa's birthday party. To my surprise, and slight consternation, Adam took it as a given that he would attend.

'What's the big deal? I've already met your mother.'

'That was excruciating enough.' (The Momager had flirted shamelessly throughout. When I tried to remonstrate, she laughed her most tinkling laugh and said, in earshot of Adam, 'Don't be silly, sweetie. Everyone knows it's all pretend!')

'So who are you ashamed of – me or your family?'

'They can be a bit much, that's all.'

'The Thane dynasty in their pomp. I can hardly wait.'

Pa's seventy-first was in fact fairly low-key: a buffet lunch at the Sussex vicarage he shares with his second wife, the soprano Adele Grange. It would be the usual crowd – Adele's musical friends, a handful of raddled elderly actors, assorted local grandees. And the Thanes, of course; most of whom are too self-involved to be very observant. I still had an obscure dread of being caught out.

'The trouble with me and your father, darling,' the Momager once told me, 'is that poor Lionel realised quite early on that nobody was ever going to ask him for his Lear. And then he made the mistake of assuming I was the same, just because nobody wanted my Swan Princess. The Thanes have always respected highbrow failure more than lowbrow success. No wonder your Aunt Sylvie drinks.'

There's a portrait of Sir Terence as Lear in Pa's entry hall, facing a painting of my grandmother, the musician Hermione Cox, at her cello. They were both dead before I was born. This is usually something I regret, but today I felt it was probably for the best. Their painted gaze was quite judge-y enough.

I found Aunt Sylvie, her Bond-girl cheekbones haughty as ever but make-up halfway down her face, glugging gin on the stairs. Dido's parents, Uncle Felix and Aunt Naomi, smoked austerely on the terrace as Milo and Sebastian, my six- and eight-year-old half-brothers, circulated with the canapés and matching scowls of concentration. Dido, regal in a grey silk kaftan, was holding court in the drawing room, Hotspur frisking at her heels. Nick brooded in a corner. Pa, meanwhile, was hamming it up no end as the gracious paterfamilias.

'The new young man,' he said to Adam in his archest manner. 'Do you know, you're the first of Lily's swains I've been introduced to?'

'To be fair, she tried her best to keep me away – she's convinced I'm going to embarrass her horribly. I'm a Thane groupie, I'm afraid.' Unctuous smile. 'You and your *Archester* colleagues have performed a Sunday-night coup. How does it feel to have the nation hanging on your every word?'

Pa was playing the (ig)noble earl on Julian Fellowes's latest corset fest.

'Mm, it does seem to have struck a chord, doesn't it? Of course, it's pretty broad-brush stuff ...'

'That's why it's a real masterclass to see what you do with the script. All the subtleties are your own.'

'I think I just threw up in my mouth a little.'

'What was that, Lily?'

'Nothing, Pa. I was just saying that Adam and I should get a drink –'

'*Adam*,' Dido declaimed, swooping in. 'We meet at last.'

I braced myself. But in the event, my cousin was as much of a pushover as my father. I was almost disappointed – I'd expected more of her.

'I was there for the opening of *Phaedra*, of course,' Adam told her. 'One of the highlights of the year. I even slunk backstage to tell you so ... but wasn't quite brave enough to fight through your throng of admirers.' He bent to pet Hotspur. 'Hello, you magnificent creature.' He looked up at Dido again. 'Is this the understudy or just your body-double?'

There was a ringing silence as assorted bystanders held their breath. But Dido flung back her head, exposing miles of long white throat, and pealed with laughter. 'Abominable man! I have a feeling we're going to get along *famously*.'

She bore him off to see the shrine to Sir Terry in the study. Nick and I trailed behind as they philosophised on *Pericles* and doubling in Shakespeare.

'It was *Pericles'* setting that gave Kash the idea,' Adam was saying. 'Syria and Lebanon. North Africa too. All the conflict hot spots. I mean, the plot's batshit, but the themes had natural crossover. Sex-trafficking, assassins, refugees ...'

'Had you done much Shakespeare beforehand?'

'Shamefully little. I'm a stage-school brat.'

'Ah yes – that's how you know Lily. Though I'm having a hard time picturing *you* among the jazz-hands and leg-warmer crowd.'

'It can give you a bit of a complex. I always thought iambic pentameter was a RADA prerogative. But Kash sent me on an intensive immersion course with the RSC and now I've caught the bug. Still scares the hell out of me, mind.'

'That's exactly as it should be! I feel the same. All great art is inherently terrifying.'

It was increasingly hard to tell who was greasing up who.

When Adam was taken off by my stepmother, Dido gripped me by the wrist. 'Lily, you really *are* full of surprises. I'll admit I assumed he was just another dim pin-up. But he's got real depth, hasn't he? A young Alain Delon ... with a dash of de Niro.'

Nick snorted. 'And a splash of gigolo.'

I extracted Adam from the kitchen and the collectively heaving bosom of my stepmother and her opera-singing pals.

'Dial the smarm back to eleven, why don't you.'

'What, are you jealous?'

'No, but I think Nick is.'

'Nick?'

'Dido's husband. Sarky-looking bloke with the stubble.'

'Sounds just my type. C'mon … Let's show them what they're missing.' He pulled me in for a kiss – deep and warm and languorous. I tasted gin and lemon, felt the prickle of stubble against my cheek. I closed my eyes, just for a moment. Just for a moment, I let it feel real.

'Are you going to be in *Star Wars*?' a small voice piped up at my side. It was Milo, the older of my two half-brothers. Aged eight, he has the genial portliness of a merchant banker and Pa's weak chin. A born character actor.

'Mummy said it will be full of rudie bits, so we can't see it.' This was Sebastian – dainty and sly-eyed. I could map out his trajectory too: after a couple of years in posh-twat roles, he'll move on to sexually ambivalent psychopaths and other varieties of gilded youth gone to seed.

'The show's set in space but it's not *Star Wars*,' I told them.

'And Lily doesn't have any rudie bits,' said Adam, giving my hair an affectionate tweak. 'I should know.'

CHAPTER SEVEN

The night of Pa's birthday, I did my usual web search.

Adam Harker gay

Adam Harker boyfriend

Adam Harker drugs

So far, none of these searches turned up anything significant. In fact, old *Wylderness* slash-fiction sites remained pretty much the only source of speculation about Adam's sexuality. There was one new gossip-blog discussion of the subject, but it was fairly low-key. The comment that gained the most 'likes' was: 'A.H. gay? It's always hard to tell with the Brits. Guess it's because they're so refined, lol.'

Next, I typed in *Adam Harker Lily Thane*.

Adam's most popular fan-site had been set up by someone in the US. It was fairly amateur looking but had a committed base. From what I could tell, they hated everyone he allegedly dated, but for some reason my *Hollow Moon* casting had sent them even more round the twist. I keep returning to the comment threads all the same.

Wow that is one thirsty trick

UGLY AF

So ppl take advantage of adam becuz he is the most humble, down to earth guy. He has been so broken ever since cassy dumped him, now this bitch has wormed her way in, playing sweet and nice, when all the time she is out to ruin him. WHY CAN'T HE SEE?!?!?!?!?!?!?

She looks mentally slow? Maybe she isn't but she sure looks it.

Her face annoys the hell out of me

WTF skank

Basic-ass bitch

C'mon. Everyone knows child 'stars' aren't supposed to have talent. They exist for real actors to play off. Once they grow up it's just the casting couch. Bet Little Lucie has learned some wicked blow job skills. Why is Adam doing this crap? Dump her, pay her off. Hire a hitman and GET RID!!!!!

Desperate ugly dead-eyed wannabe

Fameho

I told myself that the more viciously you were trolled, the closer you were to making it. There was even a sick sort of pleasure in reading this stuff. Like when you scratch an itch hard enough to bleed.

Ironically enough, the day before we flew out for the film festival, I came face to face with one of my likely trolls.

I was in a crowded coffee shop, reading through some scripts, when I became aware of somebody staring at me. I looked up to see a young woman standing in front of me, shifting from foot to foot and breathing hard.

'Hello,' I said.

She stared – if it was possible – even harder. 'You're Lily Thane.'

'Can I help you?' I said it pleasantly, but without warmth. Her pale stare was unnerving.

She swallowed painfully. 'I've been … waiting … for this.'

OK, maybe she was just shy and wanted an autograph. 'What's your name?' I asked, like one would to a child. She was probably about my age but seemed very young in her awkwardness. And there was something sloppy, shapeless about her that wasn't just because of the excess weight. She seemed … unfinished, somehow.

The girl hesitated. 'Zalandra.'

Ah. Zalandra was the name of Adam's love interest in the *Wylderness* movies, the one played by Casilda Fernandez. Now I realised the incongruous eyebrow piercings and cropped hair, dyed an unflattering black, had probably been chosen as a tribute. I felt a twist of pity as well as disdain. But Adam Harker groupies made me nervous.

'Well, it was nice meeting you.' I pointedly returned to my coffee. Unfortunately, 'Zalandra' didn't get the hint. In fact, she edged closer. She was trembling.

'You're dating Adam Harker.'

Oh boy.

'I read about it,' she said. 'I saw the photos. You're going to be in a new TV show, too. You're really lucky.'

'I know.'

'Lucky,' she repeated insistently.

I was already wondering if she'd been typing poison into the Adam Harker fan pages late into the night.

She took a deep breath. 'He'd better watch out.'

'Excuse me?'

'Adam. He doesn't know the real you. Someone should warn him.'

'Right, I think we're done here.' I got up, sweeping my stuff into my bag, and looked around for a security guard or manager.

But the girl just stood there, biting her nails and blinking. Her voice was very soft. 'A cunt like you doesn't deserve any of this.'

I went home and gorged myself senseless on stuffed-crust pizza and fondant fancies and pints of Coke. Then I purged until it felt like my throat was bleeding. But I didn't tell Adam about his manic fan. At that point, I didn't want anything to take the shine off our adventure. His adventure.

Tyre was, of course, Adam's last significant role.

The protagonist – unnamed in the film but listed as *Prince* in the credits – is a young officer from an upper-crust US military family. Dishonourably discharged from the army, we see him revolt against civilian life as he descends into mania. Flashbacks to his time in combat and on peace-keeping duties are interspersed with the Shakespearean dream sections. Here the warlords, sex-slaves, assassins and refugees he encountered in the theatre of war are recast as players in a grimy orientalist fantasy.

Not all critics thought this mash-up of PTSD and *Pericles* was an unqualified success, and *Tyre* wasn't one of the award season's big winners. Still, industry influencers were impressed, and the box-office returns exceeded expectations. This was more than enough to relaunch Adam as both a Serious Thespian and an action hero pin-up.

Subsequently, the film's attained an unwholesome kind of cult status, on account of the lead's death. Doomed talent, damned beauty. There's a still from the movie that was used in most of the obituaries. Adam's in military fatigues, leaning against a burnt-out jeep. His eyes are narrowed against the desert glare. A cigarette dangles nonchalantly from his lip. On his head, a lopsided gold crown. It's a little bit *Lawrence of Arabia*, a little bit Brando, a little bit Prince Hal.

I try to remember this, rather than the last image I have of him. The pallid corpse in a swimming pool.

But I'm getting ahead of myself. The film had made its mark, and it was time to party.

Telluride marked a turning point. Adam and I got closer, but in uglier ways. Press tours and festivals are a gruelling political campaign dressed up as an exotic holiday in which you're pampered, chauffeured, primped. Wined and dined. Interrogated. Feted. Assessed. You're at once bored out of your skull and permanently buzzing – from the stimulus overload, the jangled nerves. Then there's the exhaustion, the jet lag, the daily introductions to hundreds of strangers expecting to be charmed …

In London, waiting for everything to begin, Adam had been restrained. He was still careful – he wasn't stupid and he knew what was at stake. He didn't get wasted, or at least not in public.

He showed up to every junket with glad eyes and a ready smile. He was warmly personable to everyone from PR execs to hotel porters. But after a long day of back-to-back interviews Adam was ready to let off steam. After red-carpet events he wanted to celebrate or drown sorrows. The booze, the pills and I all had the same job to perform. We were each a little something to take the edge off.

At first, Adam's need for me was flattering. He was being true to his promise to make our relationship so much more than a business arrangement. Best of pals! Partners in crime! In front of the cameras, our chemistry crackled. Behind closed doors, we kicked back and cut loose. I was the Cool Girl sidekick, ever-ready to down shots and dish dirt. I was also the dutiful wifey, serving up the aspirin in the morning, applying an ice-pack to the head. Fielding calls, packing bags. On escort sites, I told him, they call this the Girlfriend Experience.

'Yeah, I see you more as an emotional support dog,' said Adam. 'Bitch.'

'Bitch *goddess*, if you please.'

Our barbs were still mostly playful at this point.

'Fine.' Adam passed over the joint. It was close to five a.m. in another anonymous hotel, this time in Berlin. Adam had been filming a segment on a German chat show. One of the other guests, a musician, had invited him clubbing afterwards with some friends-of-mutual-friends. It wasn't excessive – we'd had maybe half a gram of coke between us and a gram of MDMA. 'And I'm the Prince of Pricks. Match made in heaven.'

'OK … what if you meet someone who really *is* a match?' I was emboldened by the dozy warmth between us, even if this was mostly thanks to the codeine we'd sipped along with the weed. 'How long are you going to keep this –' I gestured at the two of us entwined on the bed '– up?'

When it came to hotels, Grace, the publicist, would instruct a minion to phone shortly before we were due to arrive and change the booking to a twin or else request another bed be put in the room – 'Adam's girlfriend is feeling under the weather.' Once or twice this didn't work out, and I slept on the couch. ('I need my beauty sleep more than you,' said Adam.) But sometimes, spare bed or no, we fell asleep in a companionable tangle.

Adam adjusted his pillow. 'Where's this coming from? I thought we were having a good time.'

'We are.' He was stroking my hair. It felt nice. Peaceful. 'I'm just curious, I guess. You told me you believe in The One. What happens if you meet him?'

'So what if I do? So what if I have? I already told you: this is the plan till I'm too big to fail. Or until I fail utterly. And in the meantime, it's not like I live like a monk.' He laughed a little to himself. 'There's a fair amount of fun to be had in sneaking around, let me tell you … What about you? Pining for cock?'

'Hardly.'

He put his finger to my mouth, traced the line of my lips. 'Why not, Lily-pet? Some bastard break your heart?'

'No.'

The finger moved down my throat. 'You frigid?'

'Piss off.'

He rested his hand against my breastbone. 'Did a dirty old man tickle Little Lucie places he shouldn't?'

I batted him away. 'No. God. Why do people love to assume I've been kiddy-fiddled?'

'Well, it happens, doesn't it? Maybe you give off a vibe.'

I felt myself go rigid, despite myself.

'Sorry,' he said, reaching for my hand. 'No offence. I happen to like your vibe.'

'I know. That's what worries me.'

'How so?'

I turned to look at him with as much focus as I was able. 'If I'm the "troubled ex-child-star", then you're the "boy wonder living a lie". There's a vibe there too.'

'Sure … but can't you find me a better back story? C'mon. Use your imagination. Tormented childhood. Casting-couch trauma. Tragic love affair.'

'Are any of those things true?'

He shrugged. 'Even if they were, it wouldn't make a material difference. Not to me.'

'Then why are you …?'

'What?'

I searched for words but could only find the obvious. 'Sad.'

For a long while, I thought Adam wouldn't answer. He stared up at the city lights sliding across the ceiling. 'Because I fake everything. All of the time.'

'You're an actor.'

'This is different. And I'm not talking about being closeted. Even if I was the loudest, proudest, campest queen of them all, I'd still be faking it. I'm so good I frighten myself some-times.'

He began to stroke my hair again. 'Your turn.'

'For what?' The chemical haze was receding; I was starting to feel cold.

'Your turn to say why you're sad.'

'I'm not sad. I'm – wrong.' I began to cry. 'What's *wrong* with us?'

He shushed me, then kissed me, full on the mouth. 'It doesn't need to be real,' he murmured. 'We can still make it true.'

'Are you faking it now? With me?'

I was kissing him back. The tears on my cheeks weren't all mine. 'I don't know,' he said as he held me in the dark. 'Like I told you. I don't even know.'

CHAPTER EIGHT

That was the last time, more or less, I took Class As with Adam.

I woke up to find myself soaked through with an achy, twitching misery. The anxiety over what I had revealed of myself, and how dangerously easy it had been, jittered through my bones for the rest of the day. It felt as mortifying as if we'd actually slept together. Both of us avoided the other's eyes.

I've always had bad comedowns, to be fair. Maybe it's a good thing. It's why I generally avoid anything stronger than weed. Plus, I'm painfully aware of the clichés – 'Little Lucie is a Crack Whore!' is a headline that haunts my dreams. Even so, I knew I'd miss the narcotic sparkle behind so many of my and Adam's public appearances. That invincible feeling of being lit from within. The numbing of whispers and shadows.

Desperate ugly dead-eyed wannabe

Fameho

It was hard to be sure how much of a problem Adam had. We spent a fair amount of time with the *Tyre* tribe, and Adam was hardly the only cast and crew member to indulge in a toot or two. If he and a couple of others slipped off to the toilets with increasing frequency over the course of an evening, it wasn't my job to chaperone. Or was it? Victor Green would certainly think so. Adam was always on his best behaviour whenever anyone from his management team was around. When they weren't, Victor would call me up, ostensibly to compliment me on an especially flattering photo or to check on the logistics of some engagement. 'Anything else to report?' he'd ask. 'No,' I always said, 'everything's great, everyone's well.'

It was simpler that way.

I told Adam, as breezily as I could make it, that the coke and its accompaniments were making me cranky, and so I was going to stick to unadulterated booze for a while. Adam nodded, but he didn't like it. He was watching and waiting for me to flag. To turn into a flake and a bore … So I chugged energy drinks like water. I snacked on caffeine tablets. I started smoking again and downed shots like a frat-boy on a bender. Sometimes I even pretended to take a pill, squirrelling it out of sight like a cut-price magician. Anything to make it look like I was still the life and soul of the party.

Adam had epic reserves of stamina. It shouldn't have mattered that I did not: unlike Adam, I had most of every day to recover from the ravages of the night. Even so, I found it hard to relax, let alone nap, as my thoughts jumped and stuttered in fretful loops. A lot of my expenses were paid for but I wasn't earning; alone in hotels in unfamiliar cities, I lacked the will or resources to venture out and entertain myself.

Instead, I lay in bed and tried to read the seven enormous tomes that made up the *Hollow Moon* chronicles. It appeared my own comeback was going to be launched on the back of turgid space-porn with literary pretensions. Better hope those boasts of 'Twenty Million Copies Sold!' translated into similarly stellar viewing figures.

There was a lot of waiting, a lot of hanging around. A lot of eating junk and binge-watching TV. A lot of purging. One time, in New York, Adam came back early and caught me in the act.

'I took a sleeping pill by accident,' I told him as he stood in the doorway and surveyed me crouched over the toilet, fingers fresh with the glisten of being stuck down my throat.

'Uh-huh.' His face wrinkled with distaste. 'Seriously, though, isn't bulimia for teenage beauty queens? It hasn't been a thing for grown-ups since Princess Di.'

'Piss off,' I said wearily, getting up to reach for my toothbrush.

'Oh, I'm not judging. If a daily puke got me out of hitting the gym, I'd probably be doing it too.' He came into the bathroom to peer at my face. 'You should be careful, though. You're starting to get that swollen cheek thing. I don't want people thinking you've had work done.'

Adam was right. My face was looking puffy. My eyes were bloodshot. I remembered the appearance clause in my contract. But that's what I was doing this for, wasn't I? Laid out on the bed was the latest garment bag, fresh from the courier. The dress inside was the usual sample size.

My event outfits were, like the wearer, hired for the night. Or else they were on loan; as photos of Adam and me became something of a social diary fixture, I got promoted from smaller up-and-coming designers to more established names. The première we were attending that evening was for a movie Adam had made pre-*Tyre*; his part had been cut down post-production and was now more of a cameo, but it was a big-budget international thriller, starring assorted A-listers and European heartthrobs. The frock I'd borrowed was in keeping with the company: an eye-wateringly expensive wisp of lace and silver beading.

By the evening, it was clear the rawness in my throat wasn't from the purging. I had hot and cold chills and a band of increasing tightness around my head. The make-up artist knit her brows after the final blot of powder and exchanged looks with the hair stylist. Adam's publicist pursed her lips. 'Take this,' she said, rummaging in her bag and handing over a couple of white capsules.

'Flu medicine?' I asked.

'Something like that,' she said blandly.

Since I'd already taken ibuprofen, I decided against mixing. This was probably a mistake: Grace Tang had a fix for everything. But she made me nervous. Although her scepticism about me was as exquisitely polished as the rest of her, I knew she could have hidden it if she'd wanted to.

Up close, the red carpet is as rich and velvety as the Wicked Queen's cloak in a fairy tale. That night, all I wanted to do was lie down on its soft, deep nap and pull the enveloping folds over my head. Instead, I waited brightly at Adam's side and tried not to stare at the famous beauty in front of us. I was in touching distance of her backless dress, which showcased the bones of her spine, poking up from under her skin like a line of tiny clenched fists. But her face, when she turned, was luminous, the curve of her cheeks as luscious as a peach.

It was an icy November evening. The screaming hordes behind the barriers were padded out in parkas and scarves; in my flimsy lace I was pulsating with cold. It was almost a relief when the fever swept through me, except I could feel a sickly sheen of sweat forming under the layers of cosmetics. Ahead of us, lights flashed and flared. Like a crime scene, but festive.

Grace gave the signal and we took our turn in front of the photo pit. 'Adam! Adam!' clamoured the press pack. 'Over here, over here!' Then, 'Lily, Lily!' 'Gissa smile!' 'Gissa kiss!' One arm on the hip, elbow slightly bent. Shoulders up and back. *Smize*. The Momager had been practising this with me since I was three; I could do it in my sleep.

Ten seconds done. Our turn to move on. But my legs were suddenly limp as old tit-tape and I stumbled, so that Adam had to hold me up by the arm. He steadied me with a smile. His breath frosted the air. 'You look like shit,' he told me, still smiling. 'Don't ever do this to me again.'

'You looked tired,' the Momager told me over the phone the next day. 'Time for a Botox refresher? Lovely dress, though. Very slimming.'

I was recovering in bed and feeling so terrible I was almost relieved to hear from her. Almost.

The Momager called most days to run through the tweets and Instagram captions she'd drafted and to update me on my online ranking on the various movie databases. She told me she was making a print-out folder of all my press appearances 'so you'll have something to look back on'.

'Once Adam's kicked me to the kerb and I'm a nobody again?'

'No, *silly*. Once you're back up where you belong! It'll remind you of how it all began.' There was a sudden and suspicious pause. 'Why should Adam kick you to the kerb? I do hope you're keeping him happy, sweetie.'

'We're getting on fine. Adam's ... tired, that's all.'

'Poor boy. He must be under *all sorts* of pressure. Don't lose sight of the fact it's your responsibility to lighten his load. Adam needs to know that he's your first priority, that you'll always be there for him. Always. This is *critical*, darling. I mean it. Has Judy called?'

Judy was my agent.

'Um, a day or two ago. Yeah.'

'And ...?'

'She said there've been a few more requests.'

'What for?'

'Some interviews. Some fashion stuff. I have to run them past Grace.'

'But no scripts?'

'A couple. I haven't had a chance to consider them properly.'

'Darling! Honestly. Where's your focus?'

'I'm *trying*,' I said pettishly. 'There's a lot going on.'

'Oh, Lily.' I could almost feel my mother's exasperation vibrating through the phone. Then her tone changed as she tried another line of attack. 'Listen. You probably don't remember much about your granny and grandpa and how much they doted on you. Doting was what they *did*. That's why they always said yes to me, to everything. Ballet school, my move away from classical dance, my marriage, my divorce ... Every decision I made, they applauded! And although that unquestioning support was marvellous in many ways, it has also led me to believe that *questioning* support is far better in the long run. So that's what I'm doing here. Questioning. And my question is: are you doing everything in your power to make the most of this opportunity?'

82

'No stone of potential will be left unturned by the hand of success. I promise.'

I ended the call. I hadn't looked at any of the scripts. My current role was so all-consuming I couldn't imagine playing anything else.

'You looked wasted,' said Nina, who phoned a mere fifteen minutes after my mother. 'Rumour has it you're on drugs. It's all over tinseltattles.com. I mean, it's a blind item, but barely. Hang on ... OK. Here it is: "Which fallen angel has developed an increasing fondness for snow? While escorting her handsome prince to a recent première, this Little Starlet was so coked up she couldn't even walk the red carpet straight." Not exactly subtle.'

'I have the *flu*. Jesus.' I didn't much like the escort reference either. But if Nina had picked up on it, she didn't say anything.

'How is the Happy Prince, anyhow?'

'Handsome,' I corrected her. I brought the blind item up on my iPad, just to make sure. Nina's Oscar Wilde reference was most likely unwitting, but everything about this conversation was making me jumpy.

'Tell me something I don't know. Seriously, Lily. I'm tired of following your adventures on gossip blogs. *Obviously* I want to believe that you're a miserable coke-slut who's throwing away her one shot at the big time. But I'm open to other narratives. Tell me something fun. Or shocking. Or silly. Sod it – tell me something that'll warm my cold old calloused heart.'

I wasn't feeling much of a raconteur but managed to dredge

up a few anecdotes. I wanted to keep Nina happy; I couldn't afford for somebody else to be disappointed with me.

'How much longer are you in New York?' she asked towards the end of the call. 'Talia's in town for the weekend; maybe you should look her up.'

I groaned.

'You don't sound like yourself, Lily. Maybe seeing a familiar face would do you good.'

'Seeing some familiar plastic, you mean.'

'*Miaow*,' said Nina, delighted. 'That's my girl. I was starting to worry.'

The fever was sharp but short. After several days of bed-rest and a couple of sessions hooked up to an IV vitamin drip (prescribed by Grace), I was well enough to report for duty at the latest gala. And as luck would have it, Talia was one of my fellow guests.

'Omigosh, Lily! Omigosh!'

The charity auction was over and Adam had vanished en route to the bar. Talia was perched on a banquette with a couple of WASPy blondes. The ballroom was ice-bright with mirrors and chandeliers; an improbable tonnage of crystal hung airily over our heads. 'So. Crazy. Beautiful.' She bounced up to greet me. 'Look at you! An actual real-life goddess!'

I was trussed up in a mint-green tulle midi-dress with feathered trim. (Alas, the style blogs didn't agree with Talia: ''80s prom meets bargain-bucket mermaid,' sniped one; 'Ugh, that colour makes her skin look like dishwater,' bitched another. And another: 'Hard pass. No wonder Adam looks embarrassed.') I smoothed down a stray feather, feeling self-conscious. 'You look great too.'

Talia was in some kind of deconstructed white panelled sheath that flashed a peek of aggressively taut stomach.

She clasped her hands. 'That's so lovely of you. *Thank* you.' In the US, she sounds like a jolly-hockey-sticks Brit, whereas in London, she has a transatlantic drawl. 'Everyone here's madly gorgeous, aren't they?' Her head swivelled to survey the room, as if for the first time. 'It's funny. This side of the red rope, you get used to the idea that everyone in the world looks like a model. And then you step outside, and you realise that, actually, most people have wonky teeth and bad eyebrows and are wearing acrylic.'

I remembered Adam saying the same thing. Life in the bubble. The girls Talia had been sitting with let out long tinkling laughs. But Talia looked sad. She lowered her voice to a whisper. 'I guess this should make us feel lucky. Powerful. I don't, though. Why is that?'

'Maybe you're not as shallow as your friends.'

'Oh, but I am,' she said seriously, Daisy Duck eyelashes blinking away. 'Listen … where's Adam?'

'Canoodling with A-listers.'

'As he should be! Honestly: his new film, it blew my mind. Shattering. It should *rain* Oscars on that boy. And as for the two of you – wowzers. I should've known I'd see you tonight. You guys are *everywhere*.'

'It's been quite the rollercoaster.'

She linked arms and, wobbling slightly on her vertiginous heels, drew me off to one side. 'So it's serious between you two?'

'Well, it's still early days.'

'You really like him, though?'

'Of course.' Talia was so hopeful it made it hard to lie to her. 'We have a connection.' It's possible I sounded a touch lacklustre. I infused my face and voice with all the buttery sincerity I could muster. 'You know I'm not the gushing type, but Adam's different to the other guys I've dated. It feels special.'

This didn't elicit the response I was expecting. Talia looked pained. 'I can see that. In all the photos and so on, the way you look at him ... you're *radiant*. That's why ... I don't know ... this is really awkward ...'

I felt a chill. 'Talia, what's all this about?'

'I'll tell you but you mustn't hate me – promise you won't? Promise?' I nodded. 'OK then. A friend of mine, Tintin – you met him once, he's the one with the hair, obviously – he was dating this ballet dancer, a boy dancer, at the Royal Ballet I think it was? And one of the dancer's friends there, *he* said he once had a fling with ... Adam.'

At least the dramatic build-up had given me some warning. I forced the sincerity to flush through me again. I put a hand on Talia's arm. I looked deep into her eyes. 'Thank you for telling me. You're a true friend. But you don't have to worry. Adam's adventurous, that's all. I know he's ... experimented ... in the past. I mean, so have I. That's what your twenties are for, right?' I laughed a breezy little laugh. 'Who *hasn't* had a little girl-on-girl fumble after one too many shots? It's really no big deal.'

'Oh,' said Talia, her whole face collapsing with relief. 'I'm super sorry if I made it sound like it was, like, a thing. I just worried ... well ... I didn't like the idea that Adam maybe wasn't being honest with you. For whatever reason.'

'We've always been completely open with each other. But I'm sure you understand why he has to be discreet about this sort of stuff. You know what the tabloids are like. They'll try to make a scoop of shit out of anything.'

I knew that Talia's mother had been a victim of phone hacking back in her modelling days, as well as a nude-photo leak. She nodded vigorously. 'It's evil what they do. Pure evil.'

'So I don't have to tell you to keep this to yourself.'

'I won't mention it to a soul. Cross my heart and hope to *die*.'

'A pinkie swear will be fine.' Then, as casually as I could make it: 'What about this gossipy dancer, though?'

'Apparently he only told his friend when they were really drunk. And he's, you know, basically a civilian.' Talia pulled me into a patchouli-scented embrace. 'Not like *you*. That's the thing with red ropes. They keep you separate to keep you safe.'

I found Adam at the bar, being chatted up by an older redhead. Or perhaps he was doing the chatting-up; it was hard to tell. I held back, taking a proprietorial pride in watching him work his magic – the subversive look from under his lashes that promised, yes, he could be yours; that he was fantasising, hotly, about that very possibility, even as he was exchanging meaningless remarks about the weather.

The redhead was reclaimed by her date, and a svelte blonde took her place. As she gave her order to the bartender and caught Adam's eye, I expected a replay of the redhead encounter. Instead, they both did a slight double take of recognition. Adam raised his glass, as if in greeting. The girl, however, looked startled – unpleasantly so. She backed away almost at once.

'What was all that about?' I asked, intrigued.

'What?'

I settled in beside him. 'The blonde just now. You gave her quite a fright.'

'Ah.' He laughed a little to himself. 'That's because the last time we met was in very different circumstances.'

'Who is she?'

'These days, by the look of things, she's a Park Avenue princess. Five or six years ago she was a hooker … Did you see the rock on her ring finger? Inspiring stuff. Maybe you should consider taking your escort duties up a notch.'

I glanced at the bartender. Adam had lowered his voice but he wasn't exactly being discreet. 'I'm not a *prostitute.*'

He brought my left hand up to his mouth and sucked, lasciviously, on my ring finger. 'Potato, pot-tah-to.'

Back in the hotel, I related my conversation with Talia. 'Oh yeah, the ballet dancer,' Adam said, yawning. 'The rumours are true. They're very bendy.'

'You're not worried?'

'I wasn't as careful then as I am now. Still, the guy's a nobody. Is Talia likely to shoot her mouth off?'

'No. She really admires you. And she thinks we're close friends.'

'God. She's even dumber than she looks.'

I resented this. 'Talia's not an airhead. She's just a bit lost.'

'Poor little rich girl.'

I resented this too. According to general standards Talia's hot, and by all standards she's rolling in it. As far as poor little rich girls go, I reckon she's doing fine.

But Adam wasn't having any of it. 'I mean it, Lily: you need to hang out with a better class of people. That Nina character's even worse – I told you before, the two of you are a car crash waiting to happen. People like that will only drag you down.'

'Lay off Nina. You don't know anything about her.'

'I suppose you're going to try and pretend she's got hidden depths too.' He lay down on the bed and pulled out an unmarked bottle of pills. 'Get me a drink, will you?'

'Get it yourself.'

'Don't be pissy.' He threw over one of the little pills. 'Here.'

'What is it?'

'Xanax.'

'I'm sleeping fine.'

'No, you're not. You shout in your sleep most nights. Something about doughnuts and roses. Very *violent* doughnuts and roses.'

'You're talking nonsense.'

'Pfff. A pill will relax you. Take that sour look off your face. C'mon,' he coaxed. 'Take off that God-awful dress and lie down here with me. Have a drink.'

'No, thanks.'

'Damn, Lily, when did you become such a bore? A bore and a nag.' Here was the coke comedown, right on cue. 'A *drag*.'

'And you could do with a night off the Charlie. Your nose is all rabbit-y.'

It was the first time I'd ever called him out on his habit. I calculated that an appeal to his vanity was my safest best.

'I don't care,' he said, sulky as a child.

'You will if your management notice. I don't recall getting bundled off to rehab being part of your grand comeback.'

I'd gone too far. Adam sprang off the bed and pushed his face into mine. His breath was rancid, eyes rimmed in red. 'Are you fucking with me? Seriously? Are you aware of how much you have to lose here? Are you?'

He grabbed me by the arm but I wrenched myself free. 'I'm not *threatening* you. All I'm saying is that maybe you should take it easy for a while.'

'Or what – you'll go tattling to Victor? Might as well suck him off while you're at it. Even then it's doubtful he'll remember your name.'

'This is the coke talking. You're being disgusting and delusional.'

I turned and walked away. I was still in the absurd feathered dress. Out in the hotel hallway, I realised it was two a.m. and I had nowhere to go.

But Adam came after me.

'Lily, wait. I'm sorry, OK? I was out of line. Way out of line. Shit. Maybe you're right. Maybe I have been overdoing things, let the whole circus go to my head. Ignore all that stuff I said. You know it's bollocks – it's not the real me. Shit. Don't go, stay with me. Lily-pet …'

I rubbed my arms, considering. I would find a bruise there the next morning.

'I don't want to be alone,' he said. 'I want you. I need you. You're the only one keeping me sane.'

Did Adam need some kind of intervention? If he had a problem, it wasn't common knowledge. The blind gossip items were all about me.

And if Adam was shut up in rehab, that would be the end of our contract. Especially if he blamed me for putting him there.

So I kept quiet. I got on the bed with him, like he wanted. We had a drink, like he wanted, and held hands, and eventually we drifted off to sleep. Adam didn't need help, I told myself. Not yet. We both just needed a little more time.

CHAPTER NINE

Back in London, I was introduced to Adam's family over tea in the private salon of a fancy hotel. 'There's my boy!' boomed his father, slapping Adam so soundly on his back he stumbled a little. 'I swear you've grown again,' cooed his mother. His younger sister, Sarah, gave him a perfunctory peck on the cheek.

'We already started on the bubbles,' Mr Harker informed us, summoning a waiter to replace the empty bottle of Bollinger. 'After all, it's a special occasion, meeting this lovely young lady who we've heard so much about.' He bared his teeth in a yellowing grin.

'*Read* so much about, more like,' said the sister. 'These days, we only find out about your adventures from the tabloids.'

Adam returned her thin smile. 'I'm here now, aren't I?'

Sarah shared Adam's more distinctive features – the bruised eyes, the sulky mouth, even the faint sprinkle of acne scars. But the quirks that made his face so arresting were more pronounced on hers. She was wearing a lot of make-up and a tight lace dress, and was watching me narrowly.

Tea and a tier of tiny iced cakes arrived and I made stilted small talk with the two women while Adam and his dad necked champagne. I asked about Mrs Harker's family in Ireland and

Sarah's job as a paralegal. ('Adam got the beauty, and our Sarah got the brains,' interjected the dad. 'Haw, haw!') Mrs Harker, a pretty woman sagging complacently into flab, asked a couple of questions about *Hollow Moon* but didn't seem particularly interested.

'Did you ever meet Casilda Fernandez?' she asked when Adam went away to take a phone call.

'No. I know she's very well thought of, though.'

'We met Cassy at the première for *Wylderness*. No airs at all. So glamorous! I'm not surprised she's gone on to do incredible things.'

'Having that incredible body can't hurt,' said Mr Harker with a wink.

'Mike!' His wife slapped his knee.

'Our Adam's always been able to attract the hotties. Like flies to honey. Takes after his old man that way.' He winked again.

Another squeal, another teasing slap.

Sarah took a swill of champagne. 'We thought it was funny how the papers make out you and my brother are such old friends. I don't remember anything about you.'

'I suppose Adam's always been quite private.'

'He's an enigma, all right.' She glanced at her parents, who were bickering over the last cake, and moved her chair closer to mine. She wasn't as good an actor as Adam: her expression was concerned, but under their thick spidery lashes her eyes were sly. 'He likes to act the ladykiller, but I have to say, there's times I feel his heart's not in it … Of course, I'm sure it will be different for *you*. But still. Look after yourself, yeah?'

'Thanks for the warning,' I said drily.

She squeezed my arm. Her grip was uncomfortably tight. 'Us girls have to stick together.'

'Your family are nice,' I said dutifully, once we were safely away.

'No, they're not.'

I checked the screen between us and the cab driver was pulled close. 'Well, I think you might need to be careful of Sarah.'

'Oh, Sarah won't do anything to upset the gravy train – it's my name on the deeds to her flat because it was me who paid the deposit. Just like I paid off my parents' mortgage. Having a film star in the family's got to be good for something, right?' Adam snorted. 'Though, fair play to her, Mum fought my corner when it came to stage school. Dad was dead against it.'

'He didn't want you to act?'

'He pretended it was about the money, even though I got a bursary. No, the real issue was that he didn't want his son – and I quote – "poncing around in musical theatre with a load of faggots". Now, of course, all he does is boast down the pub about his son the Hollywood stud.'

'I'm sorry.'

'Don't be. Most of the time I'm able to forget those people exist, let alone that they're related to me.'

'I wish I could do that with the Thanes.'

'C'mon. Sure, your family can be on the overbearing side, but I'd still choose *Easy Virtue* over *Abigail's Party*.'

'That's only because Noël Coward characters have better clothes.'

Adam smiled. 'That's what Dido said.'

94

'Dido?'

'We've hung out a few times. What's with the face? I'm hardly shagging her behind your back.'

'I'm a bit surprised, that's all. What do the two of you, uh, talk about?'

'Noël Coward versus Mike Leigh.'

'Seriously.'

'Oh, this and that. Connections, ideas. People … She claims to have no interest in doing TV or film. What's that about?'

'Pique, mostly. Dido did a splashy TV drama once and it bombed.' Or rather, one critic called her performance 'over-wrought'. 'I don't think she's ever gotten over it.'

'It's funny – on the one hand your cousin's clearly ridiculous. That dog! The hair, the Pseud's Corner chat. But she's also the real deal. On stage she's *electrifying*.'

'Well, she's very clever.'

I remembered going to visit Dido in Oxford. I was guesting on a glossy US teen show at the time and feeling pretty pleased with myself, with my Californian tan and newly whitened teeth and perfect nose. When I arrived at Dido's college, I caught sight of her striding across the quad. She was wearing baggy old man's trousers, tied up high on her waist with some grubby bit of string, and what looked like a Victorian lace blouse. Her hair flowed and nostrils flared. Her hands gestured – every movement oversized yet precise. Trailing after her was a gaggle of youths, plus tweedy professor, all hanging on her every word.

'And that,' I told Adam, 'is when I knew she was a Dame-in-waiting.'

'And your nemesis.'

I laughed. 'No, Dido's welcome to her mad queens and corsets. I've never been jealous of her. She's not like –' I stopped.

'Who?' he asked, intrigued.

I saw a swish of strawberry-blonde hair, the flash of a sugar-'n'-spice smile. Silver-blue eyes, bright with malice. I blinked the image away. 'She's ... not like any of the actresses I've ever gone up against. We're apples and oranges, I guess.'

'Fairy cakes and sea urchins.'

'Me being the urchin?'

'Obviously.'

I wasn't jealous of Dido's thespian skills, it's true. But I *was* jealous that she and Adam had been having cosy little get-togethers without me. It sounded as if he'd talked to her about his family and I wondered what he'd said about me. I wondered, too, what Nick would make of it.

We plunged back into another round of press and promotion. From here on, much of my time with Adam turned into a groggy blur of interchangeable hotel suites and airport lounges and SUVs. The constant chill of air-conditioning. The burn of stomach acid in my throat. The prickle of champagne, the tingle of coke-numbed gums. Good times, bad times. The day a famous writer–producer called off their meeting at the last moment, without apology, so that Adam was wasted by noon and called me a useless whore, hurling a whiskey glass at my reflection in a mirror. When he won Best Actor at the Los Angeles Film Critics Association Awards and thanked me in his speech. *To my muse, my love, my Lily.*

Or the happiest time of all, when *Tyre* was nominated for Best Picture at the Golden Globes. It didn't win, but that was OK – it had always been the outside bet – and Adam took a week's holiday in LA after the event. He knew – we all did – that with time, and a little bit of luck, plenty more dazzling prizes were bound to fall in his lap.

A friend of his lent us her house in Camelot Grove. It was a gated community built in the Mediterranean style; the ice-cream-coloured villas were accessorised with matching balconies and giant ferns. As a mere entertainment lawyer, Adam's friend had one of the smaller villas, but it still had the obligatory two-storey entrance hall with sweeping staircase and chandelier. The décor was ivory silk drapes and milk-white carpets, lights that blushed rather than glowed. I padded about in a sateen dressing-gown and felt like a 1940s starlet.

That evening Adam told me he was in the running for a superhero movie.

It wasn't in the Marvel or DC franchises, but they were losing steam as well as credibility – everyone knew that. This would be the first adaptation of the Lord Vanquish comics – a stylishly bleak superhero universe that was the crowning achievement of cult graphic novelist Hank Finlay. A couple of big names were also up for the part. But just the fact he'd got to the final stage of casting was a sign. He'd turned the corner.

And he had a present for me. A green amethyst half-moon ring, made from an Art Deco brooch he'd found on the Portobello Road. It was to bring me luck, for when *Hollow Moon* started shooting next month. 'The perfect fit,' he said, sliding it on to the third finger of my right hand. 'Just like you.'

Afterwards, Adam swept me into his arms and waltzed us across the foyer. There was nobody to see us. It wasn't for show. He sang 'I've Got You Under My Skin' as he twirled me across the marble, and I found myself blushing with pleasure and relief.

From there we went to a party at a producer's mansion high in the hills. Its walls were black granite and glass, with criss-crossing stairs that appeared to go nowhere. This party was different to the galas or the premières or fashion shows. No press. No civilians. And though most of the guests were famous or glamorous and usually both, there were anonymous faces too. These were insider faces, male for the most part, with heavy jowls and pouched eyes and coarse skin. They wore their power like the other guests wore their beauty: lightly, but still tilted towards those who were least in thrall. Here was the red rope behind the red rope.

And Adam and I rose to the occasion. Our conversation was all flirt and fizz. We were apt and witty and shiny bright. We were, I promise you, a *delight*.

Our return to the villa felt like a homecoming. The pent-up pressures of the evening had left us raucous, though we were only tipsy at most. Waltzing into the garden we stripped down to our underwear and plunged into the pool for a midnight swim. Adam lay on his back and floated in the water. In the moonlight, his body looked like something carved from marble. Now and again he still made me catch my breath.

Afterwards we lay on the lawn and shared a joint while looking at the stars. They blurred in my mind with the hundreds of candles that had glittered in every nook and cranny of the party and the net of lights flung over the valley below. 'I don't care that it's a cheap trick,' I said drowsily. 'I still love this city. I'll take fake enthusiasm over real indifference every time. Give me citrus groves and cobalt skies, and I'll swallow any candy-coated bullshit you want.'

'Same,' said Adam. 'I can definitely see myself here, with all the trimmings. A wife, a couple of brats, a house in the hills. An Oscar in the crapper. And a *really* hot pool boy.' He passed me the joint. 'Play your cards right, and maybe I'll give you a real ring the next time.'

I'd just inhaled and nearly passed out thanks to the resultant coughing fit.

'Hey, take it easy. What's the worst that could happen?'

Although Adam's tone was teasing, I was ashamed of the wave of longing that swept over me as, just for a moment, I indulged the fantasy. Wife of a movie star. That's what a superhero gig would mean for Adam. He would become wealthy in a way that meant personal assistants and multiple homes. And the door that had opened a crack with *Hollow Moon* would keep on opening for me. Wider and wider.

But … *What's the worst that could happen?* 'I can think of a few things,' I croaked, wiping my eyes.

'"If you can't handle me at my worst, then you don't deserve me at my best."' It was one of Adam's rare parodies of camp.

'Damn. Marilyn's an even more terrible role model than Lord Vanquish.'

'She still made a good point. Because we've already seen each other's worst.'

Had we, I wondered. I looked down at the half-moon ring. It was lovely, but in truth the fit was a little tight.

'And we're still here. Still pals.' Adam started laughing. 'Be honest … if we had a kid … and it took after you … would you let it keep the nose?'

A baby. A *baby*. Childbirth is, obviously, repulsive, and I've always been faintly alarmed by children themselves. But for the rich even the indignities of procreation can be avoided: a superhero could afford a surrogate. I tried to picture a child with the Thane nose and Adam's blue eyes, still wide with innocence. The Momager might like grandchildren, I thought.

I passed back the joint. 'You're just winding me up.'

'Maybe. We'd be in good company, though. Think of tonight's party – Mr and Mrs Oscar-Bait and their photogenic progeny. You know who I'm talking about.'

'I've heard the rumours,' I said, though I hadn't.

'There are always rumours. About everyone.'

This spoiled my mood a little. I'd visited tinseltattles.com repeatedly in the weeks that followed Nina's introduction. Whoever ran it – their identity was a subject of much debate among the commentators – seemed to have taken against me in a disconcertingly personal way. I thought of the girl, Zalandra, in the coffee shop. *A cunt like you doesn't deserve any of this.*

But Adam continued, dreamily. 'We'll install a personal trainer for me, a tennis coach for you. Imagine. We'll get rich and famous together. Throw outrageous cocktail parties. Grow some babies in the orange groves.'

We blew smoke towards the stars, trailed our toes in the water.

'As long as there's a pool,' I said, my head on his shoulder.

CHAPTER TEN

Superheroes notwithstanding, there was another reason for Adam's burst of benevolence: he had someone on the side.

It wasn't his first dalliance, of course. There'd been a waiter in Berlin. A bartender at the Toronto film festival. An ex-castmate during our first trip to NYC. Adam wasn't coy; he liked telling me about his hook-ups. He'd send a message telling me not to wait up or to make myself scarce ('SCAT'). The first time, I absented myself in the hotel bar; on another occasion I went to an all-night cinema; once I slept in our hire car. Mostly, though, Adam would disappear for the night and swagger back to our hotel or apartment rental early in the morning, rumpled and smug. 'Don't worry, Mum, I used protection,' he'd say, waving the envelope of an NDA.

I found it hard to tell how risky this behaviour was. Even with the threat of legal action, there are always rumours, as Adam said. The trick is to restrict them to a faint background hum, running at a frequency most people don't tune into. In my increasingly obsessive scans of the gossip sites, I only found two new discussions of Adam's sexuality. Maybe he just wasn't famous enough to attract the gossip-hounds. In which case, I couldn't understand why *I* was in their sights – according to which site you believed,

I had a drug habit, was mentally unwell or was blackmailing Adam over some unspecified teenage indiscretion. One blind item suggested I'd only got the *Hollow Moon* part because the casting director had abused me as a child and I'd used this as leverage. Another insinuated I'd been a 'yacht girl' (hooker) at Cannes.

Compared to all this, Adam's boy-toys seemed pretty tame. The new one, however, was different. The day after the party, Adam was away at meetings until late. I came down for breakfast the following morning to find a strange man sitting and smoking in the kitchen. He wasn't Adam's usual type, which, as far as I could tell, was slight, fair and twenty-something. This one was older; handsome, obviously, but strongly built, stocky even, his peroxide bleached crop in striking contrast to his inky dark eyes and brows. There were amateur-looking tattoos up his muscular arms.

'Good morning,' I said, a little too brightly.

'Morning,' he replied after a pause. There was a trace of accent.

'I'm Lily.'

'Yeah. I know who you are.' He continued smoking and staring.

Awkwardly, I set about making coffee. My offer of a cup was declined with a terse head-shake. At last Adam came in, wearing a T-shirt and briefs and whistling 'I've Got You Under My Skin'. 'What's for breakfast? Oh, hi, Lily. I see you've met Rafael.' He ruffled my hair, ending with a tug. 'Any chance you could kindly piss off for the day?'

So I went window-shopping on Melrose Heights, though I was too distracted to take anything in. Rafael was the name of Mr Bad News, the one Victor had warned me about. I was heading for brunch, lost in various uncomfortable thoughts, when I realised someone was blocking my path to the restaurant. For a moment I thought she was a tourist who had stopped to ask for directions.

But it was the groupie from the coffee shop. Zalandra.

'Boo,' she said. And smiled.

'Wh-what are you doing here?' This was insane. Had she been following us the whole time? 'How –?'

In the Californian sunshine, she looked paler than ever, layered in thick dark clothes wholly unsuitable for the heat. A squat dark blot, sweating malice.

'You and Adam. You're not so special. Because I know your secret.'

'Wow.' I managed a cracked little laugh. 'Couldn't you think up something a little less cheesy?'

I moved determinedly on.

'Don't you walk away! Don't you *dare*.' She seized me by the arm. Now her face was only an inch from mine. Her eyes were bulging, her cheeks blotched with emotion. 'You're going to get what's coming to you, you know that? You think you're successful. Safe. You're not. There'll be a reckoning. Whenever you least expect it, I'll be there –'

I shook her off, my heart banging painfully against my ribs. 'Get away from me, freak.'

Other pedestrians had stopped to stare. Several were filming the confrontation on their phones. I looked around for an escape route, my breaths coming short and fast, but it was a security guard from one of the nearby boutiques who came to my aid. 'Excuse me, miss, would you like to step inside?'

'I see through you,' the girl howled after me as the guard

hustled me to safety. 'I always have. *Destroyer* –' A little while afterwards, though, she was trudging stolidly down the street.

Inside the shop, the sales assistants hovered around me, making sympathetic noises, fetching a glass of water, urging me to sit down. I saw my reflection in one of the mirrors: the designer accessories, the moneyed tan. I looked like Someone and that's why I'd been rescued. Here I was, safely behind the rope again.

Back at Camelot Grove, I let myself into the villa and headed out to the backyard. I could hear voices and laughter.

I paused at the sliding doors to the pool. I knew I was intruding. Adam and Rafael were entangled on the grass amid a clutter of beach towels and magazines.

'What's up with you?' Adam asked as I made my entrance. 'You look like you've seen a ghost.'

'Close. One of your fans tried to attack me in the street. She calls herself "Zalandra" and is convinced I'm out to ruin your life. So she's out to ruin mine.'

'Ah.' He grinned. 'Beware the Wylderbeasts. I thought they were an endangered species these days.'

'What beasts?' asked Rafael, frowning.

'C'mon, Raffo, you remember – it's what the hardcore *Wylderness* film fans used to call themselves. All five of them, that is. Still, nice to know one or two are still keepers of the flame.'

'Adam, this is serious. I first met her in London. Now she's in LA. She's a lunatic stalker with time and money on her hands. If she can afford to fly out here to follow you …'

'That would be immensely flattering if it were true. But it's not. Listen – no, shut up and listen. The *Wylderness* movies might not've set the world alight, but the original books are still a big deal. The author's launching the prequel this weekend in LA. It's basically a fan convention. Hell, her PR even sent me an invite. This Zalandra wannabe will be in town for the book party. Randomly bumping into you was just bad luck.'

'She was outside that brunch place! Our regular spot, the one I posted about on Instagram.'

'OK, then stop posting tacky shit that's basically an invitation to nut jobs.'

I shivered. 'This isn't a joke. She said there was going to be a reckoning, that I wasn't safe. And she told me she "knew our secret".'

'C'mon. How likely is that? It was just some line.' Still, Adam frowned. 'What did she look like?'

'Youngish. Piercings, cropped black hair. A bit goth. Fat.'

'Then you're fine,' said Rafael tersely. 'Nobody listens to girls like that.'

'He's right. Poor little Lily-pet, though. I'm sorry you had a scare.' Finally, Adam got up to pull me into a hug. He was still wet from the pool and oily with sunscreen. It smelled faintly of coconut. 'Fear not – the Lord Vanquish fans will all be hipster nerds who only want me for my action figures. And, listen, I know what'll pep you up. The three of us, out on the town tonight. Cocktails at the Sky Bar. It'll be fun.'

I met Rafael's eyes. He didn't look as if this was his idea of fun at all. Quite the opposite. Adam, however, seemed oblivious. He stretched and smiled. 'Fuck, it's hot. Who's up for a mojito?'

While he went off to mix them, Rafael and I stood and looked at each other. The breeze ruffled the palm trees; the pool glistened in the sun.

'I'm sorry for interrupting,' I said at last. 'I was just a bit shaken up.' I was still feeling faint. *You're going to get what's coming to you …* The words throbbed blackly in my head.

'Yeah, there're a lot of crazies out there.' Rafael picked up a towel and began to dry off his torso. 'But I guess that's the price you pay.'

'For what?'

He laughed shortly and said something under his breath in Spanish. 'For being seen on Adam's arm.'

It was a strained evening. For one thing, I kept looking over my shoulder for Zalandra's baleful form. I couldn't get her out of my head. There was something increasingly familiar about her and I had a sick, nagging feeling this was because I'd half-glimpsed her in other settings at other times. But our night would have been awkward in any case. Adam was irrepressibly buoyant and – wilfully? – oblivious to the incompatibility of our threesome.

'I thought you wanted to be careful,' said Rafael at dinner, when it was pretty clear some serious footsie was going on under the table. 'It's fine,' said Adam. 'We have our magic charm right here.' He chinked his glass against mine. Then he ordered another two-hundred-dollar bottle of wine.

In the beginning I'd made some efforts to pay my own way, but Adam had generous impulses and increasingly expensive tastes, and the gesture only seemed to annoy him. It was true he'd made good money over the years. I knew he'd helped his parents with their mortgage and he owned an apartment in a smart modern development in the London Docklands. But the fee for an indie like *Tyre* would have been modest, his Broadway earnings considerably smaller. Now, of course, he was on track to have real money coming in again, big money, a future.

Rafael made his own contribution to the evening. Quite early on, he made a call and slipped outside shortly afterwards. When he came back, he and Adam disappeared to the toilets and came back with a tell-tale sparkle around their nostrils. It was the first of multiple trips.

I didn't know what to make of Rafael. His stare was pugnacious and his tattoos were scratchy, but he seemed entirely at home in the overpriced Asian fusion restaurant and fancy bars we went to and was warmly greeted by a couple of fellow diners.

'So what's his story?' I asked Adam, in an interlude when the two of us were alone. 'How'd you meet?'

'Health and fitness, baby.'

I remembered our midnight conversation by the pool. 'He's a personal trainer?'

'He's a VP for a chain of gyms. Fancy ones. For basic blonde bitches like yourself.'

'Oh.'

'You thought I picked him up off the streets, didn't you? Racist. Hey, Raffo,' he said, as the man himself made his way back to our table, 'Lily wants to know about your gang-banging past in the slums of Puerto Rico.'

Neither I nor Rafael found this nearly as amusing as Adam did. Sometime later, we had our own tête-à-tête. We were on the rooftop terrace of a bar, and Adam had just told me to move aside, as the light I was standing under made me look haggard. 'And that,' he said, 'is not a good look for me.'

'Adam treats you like crap,' Rafael said, as the man in question headed off towards the toilets. Again. 'You don't care?'

'He isn't being serious. It's … banter.'

'Whatever you call it, I wouldn't take that kind of shit from him. Or anyone.'

I believed him. I didn't care how fancy his job title was. The man only had to hunch his shoulders to look like the kind of person who'd make you cross to the other side of the street.

Rafael eyed me through his cigarette smoke. 'Must be paying you good, I guess.'

'That's not how it works.'

'No?'

'You know, you're being quite offensive. Adam and I are partners; we have an understanding. The two of us go back a long way.'

'I know Adam a lot better than you, *gringa*.' He didn't say it boastfully or insinuatingly. He was stating a fact. I'd already got the sense that whatever the two of them had was something more than an occasional hook-up. There were in-jokes. Understandings. A physical ease that comes from more than just sex.

How long had they known each other, I wondered, and how deep did the connection go? Adam the closeted gay man was also Adam the closet romantic and that – in his own words – made him weak.

I glanced over to where Adam was chatting away to some random fan, giddy as a glitter-ball. I turned back to Rafael and lowered my voice. 'OK, then maybe you should tell him to ease off the nose candy.'

'He's a grown man. He makes his own choices.'

'They're not doing him much good.'

'That's too bad. Because in my opinion, *chica*, neither are you.'

I flushed. I had a feeling that these '*chica*'s and '*gringa*'s were performative. Rafael was mocking my presumptions about him. I was wrong-footed, again.

I left the two of them together after that. I'd had enough. But once I was back in the villa, I couldn't sleep. My thoughts kept circling back to Zalandra. How frantically she loved a person who didn't exist. How much she hated me, who was even more of a mirage.

Adam and I had both been launched by fantasy: me, with a Christmas fairy tale, he with his dystopian fable. And now I was boldly going into space and he was joining a universe of superheroes. Even *Tyre* was mostly magic realism. I was gripped by the thought that if either of us had been primarily known for realist dramas, we wouldn't be where we were now. Adam and I had become too familiar with the promise of improbable transformations, the seduction of other worlds.

At some point I got up and decided to get something to eat from the kitchen. My room was round the corner from Adam's; when I reached the turn, and just as I was about to switch on the lights, I saw Adam at the top of the stairs with Rafael.

They were too absorbed in each other to notice me. In a stumbling tangle, they lurched as one towards Adam's room, their progress punctuated by muffled laughter. Outside the room,

Rafael pushed Adam against the door and bent to kiss his neck. Adam let out a long murmuring sigh. Then he began to kiss him back, messily. Urgently. His hands were on Rafael's hips and waist, sliding up under his T-shirt. His own shirt was half off. As Adam felt for the doorknob, I watched Rafael unbuckle Adam's belt and slide his hand against skin. The sigh turned to a groan.

I crept back to my own room. I'd been afraid to move in case they saw me. But I was mesmerised, too. I crawled deep under the bedclothes and hugged a pillow to my chest. Then I slid my hand between my legs.

CHAPTER ELEVEN

Over the next few days I tried to be out of the house as much as possible. It wasn't just about giving Adam and Rafael their space. I heard raised voices more than once, and Adam's mood swung between sky high and sullen. If there's anything more uncomfortable than sharing your living space with two people having a lot of hot sex, it's sharing your living space with two people in the midst of a bad row.

I only had one other meaningful exchange with Rafael. There had been shouting, the sound of something smashing. Shortly afterwards, I came upon Rafael sitting on the back step and scowling into his phone.

It was an opportunity to make peace. I didn't take it. 'Trouble in your mutually respectful paradise?'

Rafael didn't take the bait, just looked at me sidelong. 'Adam won't admit to hurt. Only anger because anger lets him be strong.'

'Then you should leave him alone,' I said. 'Friends don't hurt each other.'

'You'd like that, huh? Me leaving. The two of you, playing house.'

'Maybe it would be easier. For all of us ... but mostly for Adam.' I moved past, shrugging. 'You know it's true.'

A couple of days later, I came down early to find Adam sitting at the breakfast bar in his dressing-gown and pouring himself a measure of Scotch. He was sporting an impressive black eye.

'Adam! What happened?'

'A gentlemanly disagreement.' He knocked back his drink, halfway between a smirk and a wince. 'Don't worry. You shoulda seen the other guy.'

I lowered my voice. 'Is he … is he here?'

'Long gone.'

'I'm sorry. God. I don't know what to say. I can't believe he *hit* you.'

'Relax. I deserved it.'

'You sound like a battered wife.'

'Yeah, well, I wanted him gone.' Adam poured out another generous measure. 'Trust me, this way was easiest.'

'I'm sorry,' I said again, uselessly.

'Christ, Lily. Stop looking so tragic. This isn't Brokeback bloody Mountain.' Another long swallow. He shrugged. 'Easy come, easy go.'

The Oscar nominations came out the next day. *Tyre* was, as they say, snubbed.

Outwardly, Adam took it well. I overheard him on the phone to various members of his team, agreeing with the predictable platitudes. We flew back to London that night. On the plane, Adam took a Xanax washed down with a large glass of red. His eyes glistened. His palms were clammy. As he fell asleep he clutched my hand and smiled beatifically. 'Lily, Lily, Lily … I'm so glad you're mine.'

He passed out for the duration of the flight and had to be propped up through Arrivals. I was pretty bleary-eyed too. London seemed even more dank and dismal than when we'd left. 'Shall I come up?' I asked when the taxi got to Adam's Docklands high-rise. I found the district depressing; so anonymous and modular, its towers blankly gleaming above the sullen river. I thought he maybe shouldn't be alone.

'I think we've seen more than enough of each other, don't you?'

I didn't hear anything from him for the next week. He didn't answer my messages or return my calls. In just a few weeks, our contract officially ran out. I heard nothing from Victor Green or Grace Tang either.

The silence was humiliating. Possibly Adam's management assumed he'd already sorted everything out with me and were just waiting for him to confirm before pressing 'print' on the new contract. It seemed unlikely. They were details people; they choreographed and plotted with obsessive control-freakery. Was Adam *ghosting* me?

I told myself I was being paranoid. I was sure our midnight conversation by the swimming pool hadn't just been castles-in-the-air for Adam. And, OK, I had reservations about renewing, of course I did, but I reasoned our next six months together would be very different from the first. Adam would be away shooting something super-starry. I was about to start filming *Hollow Moon*. It would be a long-distance celebrity relationship, with all the perks and none of the slog.

Oh yes, I'd got used to life behind the rope. That tightening in the air, the new alertness every time Adam entered a room.

The ripples of interest in his wake. And of course I saw myself differently, too, in other people's eyes. Like when you look into the camera, right down the lens, and see the little rainbow reflection in the big black hole.

Me, exactly, but not. Upside-down.

A distant rainbow.

I told the Momager that I was staying at Adam's apartment. We were not to be disturbed, I said. He needed all my attention and support right now in preparation for a big audition. No, I couldn't tell her what it was. It had to be very hush-hush. (She was, naturally, thrilled. 'Oh, darling! Can't you give me the *teeniest* hint? It's not – could it be – is it *Bond*?') Then I checked myself into a low-budget chain hotel, under a fake name, like somebody on the run.

On Monday, I set off for the table read, all of a jitter. A read-through isn't supposed to be a full-blown performance, but everyone is on alert for potential casting or script problems. Executives from the network would be watching and taking notes. My biggest source of anxiety was that this was the first time I'd be face to face with Cal Knightly, the Australian actor cast as Lys's love interest.

Cal came over to introduce himself as I was pretending to browse the refreshment table. His looks were rakish, not unlike Adam's, but his hair was dirty blond and his smile a sunny one. When he moved on – after giving my hand a quick farewell squeeze – I found I was blushing. The woman next to me, who played the evil Xebian High Priestess, laughed. 'Looks like chemistry isn't going to be an issue for you guys.'

The rest of the cast included a couple of theatrical grandees who'd not be out of place in Dido's kitchen and a sprinkling of household names. Maybe it wouldn't matter that the script was stuffed with such gems as 'Time to activate the solar probe and set course for Sn'ar! The ice canyons of Agazat await!' Afterwards, everyone exchanged smiles and applauded. 'Nice work, people,' said the director. 'I think we've got something really special here.'

How did it go? My first communication from Adam for nearly a week. *Good, I think,* I messaged back. *Tell you about it tonight?* Three hours later came the reply: *Busy, sorry. TTYL.*

I was pissed, but also emboldened from the success of the table read. So I decided to try and ambush Adam at home. I arrived the next morning just before nine a.m. He didn't answer the bell, but on the off-chance he was simply lying low, I got into the building by following another visitor as they were buzzed into the foyer.

I exited the lift just as somebody came out of Adam's apartment. A young guy, hunched and dishevelled in low-slung jeans and a hoodie. The hood was pulled down low over his face. He hurried past, fists balled in his pockets, and practically shouldered me out of the way to get into the lift before the doors closed.

Dealer or hook-up? I waited a moment, then rapped on the door.

'Did you forget –?' Adam began as he opened it. Then he saw it was me. 'Oh.'

'Morning!' He didn't invite me in but I pushed past him none the less.

I'd only been here once before. It was a high-end apartment but despite Adam's surface clutter hadn't felt particularly lived-in. Now its sleek lines and polished surfaces were overlaid with a scum of disarray. Stuff from the LA trip spilled out of luggage and was strewn all over the floor. The place stank of cigarettes and weed, and both the coffee table and the kitchen counters were a thicket of bottles and takeaway cartons. Adam was in his bathrobe and didn't look much better than his flat.

'Must've been quite the party,' I said.

'A pity party. I didn't get Lord Vanquish.'

That brought me up short. 'Shit. Really?'

'Yeah. Found out the other day. It went to one of those Swedish arseholes.'

A Skarsgård brother, I assumed. It wouldn't be the first time Adam had lost out to one of them. 'Well, you'll have the last laugh. You're being showered with offers.'

He muttered something under his breath, then slumped down on the sofa, pulling at his nose.

'The right project's out there,' I continued soothingly. 'Something mainstream, big budget, classy. Like that family drama you were telling me about. The one adapted from the Pulitzer-prize novel. Didn't the author say you were her dream casting for the lead?'

'You're talking to me like I'm some kid who dropped their ice-cream cone. I don't need babying.'

I gritted my teeth. 'So what *do* you need me for?'

'Hey – it was your idea to come barging in uninvited. But since you ask … Fine. What I'd really like is for you to get fucked up with me.'

'Jeez, Adam. It's nine o'clock in the morning.'

'C'mon. Don't be such a pussy. We'll go a bit Amber and Johnny, but without the aggro.' He smiled, and it wasn't his bared-teeth, lupine grin. It was the other one: the smile that

116

promised to make you rich, fall in love, throw all caution to the wind. He poured the dregs of a champagne bottle into two dirty tumblers. 'A toast to our happily-ever-afters.'

I could guess what Adam had in mind: coke, booze, a couple of oxys. I'd excessively binged and purged yesterday, in response to the pressures of the table read, and was already feeling a touch light-headed. But I'd have two days to recover before filming began on *Hollow Moon*. And I could pace myself. Adam would be so out of it he wouldn't notice how enthusiastically I was or wasn't partaking. I'd do a line, drink some wine and pull a fast one when the pills came out.

I knocked back the flat champagne and managed not to wince. 'All right,' I said, shrugging. 'Why not?'

But he was still staring at me. 'Huh. Interesting.'

'How so?'

'Why haven't you told Victor I'm using?'

I blinked. 'What?'

'He asked you to keep an eye on me and my partying. Don't bother with the denials – it's the least any reputable manager would do.'

'Good for Victor. But I'm not a snitch. Or a babysitter.'

'Is that what you told him?'

'I said that we were friends. You're an adult – you make your own choices.'

'Yeah, but what if those choices are going to screw things up for me?' Adam was ashen faced and greasy haired … and also suddenly, disconcertingly, focused. '*Do* you think I need some kind of intervention? Could my express wish for another epic bender actually be a cry for help?'

He spoke mockingly. But his eyes were fixed on mine.

I licked my lips. 'Look. You always said you'd cut back after awards season. I believed you; I encouraged you. I called you a dickhead when you were high. Remember?' I spoke lightly. None the less, my mouth had gone dry. 'At the same time, I'm not here to judge you or whatever if you want to cut loose. That's not my job. This is *your* life.'

'Uh-huh. Whatever I say goes. Just as long as I sign on the dotted line and lock in another six months of our fauxmance. Right?' Adam still sounded entirely sober. 'The truth is, you like me better when I'm off my head. That way I don't see what you're up to.'

'You can't be serious. You cannot seriously think I'm, what, some … some evil Svengali pulling your strings. To what end?'

'To have me all to yourself.'

'That is the most paranoid crap I've ever heard.'

'You told Raffo to leave.'

Shit. 'What did he tell you? Believe me, that's not how it went down. I think he was maybe threatened by me and –'

'Sounds more like the other way round to me.'

'I was looking out for you. Victor said –'

'Yes! I knew it!' He actually punched the air. 'You *are* his spy. A shit-stirring double agent.'

'Screw Victor. This is about the break-up, isn't it?'

'Oh, Lily-pet. From TV's least-convincing lawyer to the world's lamest psychologist.'

I was embarrassed by my own stupidity. I should have taken Rafael more seriously. Mr Wrong, The One. Mr Right Bad News. Mr One Bad Wrong.

Everything had got back to front.

'Adam, I – you have to trust me here. I know it's been a terrible week, but whatever you think I've done, I never meant to upset you. Or get between you and Rafael. You're my friend, you've always had my total loyalty and I've never gone behind your back. I swear –'

'A true friend would have my best interests at heart. It seems increasingly clear to me that you don't.' He lounged back again and lit a cigarette. 'Thank you for your service. Now get the fuck out.'

I didn't move. The situation was too sudden, too brutally irrevocable, to be anything but absurd. 'I don't understand. I don't understand why everything's changed. Just a couple of weeks ago we were talking about *marriage*.' And babies, for Christ's sake. 'I know we were only messing around but we – you – the two of us –' My throat caught. 'You told me I was the perfect fit.'

It came out as a shamed whisper. Adam laughed. 'Wow. For a fake break-up, you use some real clichés. Just remember: it's not me, babe. It's you. All you.'

The next morning, I had a call from my agent. She was sorry to say that the people at *Hollow Moon* had had a change of heart. After the table read, they'd decided that Cal Knightly and I weren't a good match. The chemistry wasn't there.

It was all very bad luck. They thanked me for my hard work and wished me every success in the future.

CHAPTER TWELVE

'I blame myself,' said the Momager bitterly the Morning After. 'All those years of always putting you first ... I've spoiled you, and this is the result. Spoiled children turn into selfish adults. Because it seems to me the moment you had to dig a little deeper, move just *slightly* out of your comfort zone, you wanted out. Consciously or not, you chose to sabotage everything we've ever worked for.'

'Fnnrgggggahhh,' I said from where my head was buried under a bed-pillow.

'Let's not forget the last time you were dropped from a high-profile project like this. You were only a young girl then, so of course one made allowances. Too many allowances, perhaps, because all the warning signs were there. The self-absorption, the heedless disregard for –' Her voice caught. 'I can't help but wonder if part of the reason you did this was to punish me.'

'It's not about you,' I mumbled. 'None of this has ever been about you.'

But my voice was so muffled I doubt she heard.

What was the point, anyway? The Momager was quite certain that my unreasonable behaviour and/or expectations had driven Adam to cut me out of his life. Nothing I could say or do would change her mind.

It's true, my expectations probably *weren't* reasonable. I had expected to be able to maintain a friendly yet professional fauxmance with a vindictive, paranoid coke-head.

Though I'd covered up for his drug use. I'd shared in some of it.

Was I an enabler?

Had I betrayed him?

No. It was Rafael who was the enabler. That's what Victor told me. Warning him off was the responsible thing to do.

(Not that a man like Rafael would give a monkey's for the opinion of a girl like me.)

This is not a real break-up, I kept telling myself. This isn't real loss. And the guy was a jerk anyway.

You don't need closure from smoke and mirrors.

You can't mourn something you never had.

I probably wasn't supposed to spread the news without official sanction from Grace Tang. No doubt the whole thing would be expertly stage-managed, with some helpful 'insider' quoted as saying how the break-up was entirely amicable, how we'd always be supportive of each other. Blah de blah.

Who would I tell, in any case? I have people I do Pilates with, people I brunch with, people I drink with. When I first got together with Adam, some of these part-time friends were suddenly a lot more anxious to 'reconnect'. I was careful to brush them off politely, though we weren't in any case close enough for them to bear a grudge. That meant we weren't close enough for anything else either.

I had Nina, of course. We'd been comparing rejections our whole lives; it was a competition she generally won. But the secret between us was still Adam's, not mine.

By now I was overflowing with self-pity. I rolled my head out of the pillows to see if the Momager was still there. I could hear she was taking deep, slow breaths. Centring herself. She sat down on the bed next to me and patted my hand.

'All right. That's enough. It's time to pull yourself together, sweetie, and focus your energies on finding a solution to this mess. As your manager –'

'As my *manager*? What about just being my parent for once?'

We stared at each other. I found I was trembling.

'You are not a child any more.' She spoke in chips of ice.

'Yeah, that's the trouble, isn't it? You always preferred Little Lucie to the real me.'

My mother's neck arched and breath hissed. The Dying Swan was preparing to strike. But there was no snapping beak, only a tragic smile. 'If you wanted to wound me deeply, Lily, then congratulations. Job done. As for my own position, I can see it's untenable.' She rose from the bed. 'Please consider this my resignation.'

She glided serenely, sorrowfully from the room.

That left me with Nina. And Talia, I suppose. (Dido couriered round a tub of homemade chicken soup – delicious – a pair of brogues – hideous – and a note quoting Chekhov on learning to love bare fruit trees.)

'So … on a scale of one to eleven, how murderous do you

feel right now?' Nina asked, two drinks in, in the darkest corner of the dive-iest bar I could find.

'A solid ten. Mostly towards my mother, to be fair.'

'Well, I divorced mine. I can recommend it.'

I shook my head. Nina couldn't be expected to understand my relationship with the Momager. Or know how much I depended on her to voice my own worst instincts, which allowed me to ostensibly chafe against them before giving in. I'd go crawling back. I always did.

'If it were me,' Nina continued, 'Adam had better hold onto his knackers. Because I'd be coming for them with a rusty spoon.'

I'd told her that Adam was doing too much blow, I'd confronted him about it, and he'd dumped me as a result. This was definitely breaking our contract's no-disparagement clause, but I wasn't in the mood for crying over spilt small print.

'I still can't believe he got you kicked off *Hollow Moon*. That's some seriously vengeful shit.' Nina sounded almost admiring. But then, Nina loves a grudge match.

I stared at the table. As my mother had pointed out, it wasn't the first time I'd been ditched by a project after I'd been cast. It seemed to me I could feel the heat of both humiliations, beating under my skin. Admitting to this would only make it worse. 'I guess it's possible the execs really didn't think Cal and I made a good match. I'll never know for sure.'

'Huh. It sounded like a douche-y show anyway. Spacebilge with tits. But whatever you do next, you need to rub the tosser's face in it. First off, you should sign up to Raya and upgrade to online-dating an A-lister.'

'You overestimate my pulling-power.'

123

'Fine, a B-lister then. But a bona fide one this time.'

'Adam's bona fide.' Funny how defensive I felt about this.

'Just wait till he crashes into rehab.' Nina gestured to the barman for another round. 'Seriously, though. What's the plan?'

Good question. My agent remained upbeat. Whatever his listing, dating Adam meant that a lot more people knew my name, or had at least been reminded of who I was.

Trouble was, I'd begun to need reminding too.

The little rainbow ghost in the lens ...

'I might go travelling, actually. Take a sabbatical, whatever. I like the idea of finding a scenic wilderness with no Wi-Fi and disappearing for a while.'

'Sounds terrible. *Eat, Pray, Love* meets *Heart of Darkness*. Or – even worse – that Reese Witherspoon film about hiking.'

'At least Tinseltattles will be off my case.' I tried to look Nina full in the face as I said this.

'Mm. They were really gunning for you.'

'It felt personal, yeah.' I paused. I was still waiting for her to catch my eye. 'As if I was the punchline to all these sick jokes. Some of it was obviously crazy – like how I was an escort, a junkie.' Those, I could blame the likes of Zalandra for. 'But sometimes it felt as if they must've had someone on the inside.'

'What, like a mole?'

Nina had got her fringe cut extra blunt and short. It made her eyes look unexpectedly round and childish under the over-exposed brow. I didn't know if I could trust the look of cartoon innocence she gave me. Maybe I was just projecting, anyhow. Nina didn't *do* innocence. She did truth or dare or bare-faced lie.

'Right. Like the "inside source" who told the website about

the time Adam had a nosebleed, wiped the blood off on his co-star's Hermès scarf and hid the evidence in my handbag. Nobody could have known about that unless I told them.'

I waited. Nina was still holding my gaze.

'And,' I said, 'the only person I told was you.'

'Piss off.' She sounded entirely cheery.

'I'm serious. Nobody else knew about that incident. That's why I knew it had to be you who passed it on, along with the other personal stuff.' I shook my head. 'Why'd you do it? For laughs? A dare? Or just to take me down a peg or two?'

'OK. Pay attention, cos I'm only gonna say this once,' said Nina, one finger held dramatically aloft. 'I. Have. Never. Spread. Or. Invented. Gossip. About. You.'

'Bollocks! It's one of your hobbies – posting made-up shit to gossip sites. Look, I'm not going to give you a hard time. But I still need you to be straight with me.'

Or maybe I was just minded to burn everything down.

Nina sprang to her feet. 'The only thing you need is to get over yourself.' The air between us crackled. 'Aww, so you've been dumped? Aww, so you lost a job? Big deal. You'll get over it, and you'll be fine. People like you always are. Little Lucie bought you a flat. Your nose job bought you a load of crummy TV shows. Mummy and Daddy buy you everything else – except for some fucking self-respect, obviously. Otherwise you'd never've turned tricks for a creep like Harker in the first place.'

I shrank back. 'Is this how you really feel? About me?'

'It doesn't matter what I feel or what I say. You won't believe me.' Nina looked at me hard and straight – the way I'd looked at her when I said I knew she was Tinseltattle's source. 'There's times I think you only keep me around so's to feel better about yourself.'

I had never felt so shrunken, so ashamed. So alone.

(Actually, that's not true. But the other occasion was a lifetime ago.)

At least I still had Talia.

Her care package was certainly an improvement on Dido's. Ladurée macarons, a vintage Alexander McQueen scarf and a glitter-spangled greetings card with a quote about difficult roads leading to beautiful destinations.

Even so, she struggled to come to terms with my back-packing plans. ('You know I adore *Eat, Pray, Love*, but these days it's practically a historical novel'.) Instead, she tried her best to persuade me to check into a luxury Mexican wellness retreat she'd done some promotional Instagramming for. As a last resort, she offered to go travelling with me – 'We could go find ourselves together!'

I told her this was something I had to do for myself. I needed, I said, to find my own beautiful destination.

This was at the airport, where Talia had come to wave me off. She was sniffling a bit at Departures. 'God. Look at me! Ugh! I *knew* I should've worn waterproof mascara … I'll miss you so much, Lily. *Everyone* will. But I know you'll get over this and come back stronger, more radiant, than ever.' She clutched at my hands. 'And Adam will always, *always* regret losing you.'

If he had regrets, he didn't dwell on them. When I got back from my travels, three months later, it was to find that Talia was his new beard.

PART TWO

CHAPTER ONE

'Shameless, trashy, back-stabbing *wench* …'

'Good luck to her,' I said tartly. 'She'll need it.'

The Momager continued to look tragic. 'Well, it's true such grotesque attention-seeking can only be a cry for help. I just don't understand why poor Adam would want to be associated with some brainless socialite. Not after *you*.' She sighed. 'Though, to be fair, the unwashed hippy look is unlikely to win him back. Boho can be tricky to pull off past your twenties.'

I'd only been back a day after three months off-grid in Southeast Asia. I'd taken photographs on disposable cameras rather than posting to Instagram, read serious books and stayed in low-budget rentals. I was thin and brown without recourse to spray tans and purging, and my hair was its natural mouse. I'd even dreamed up plans to reinvent myself as a screenwriter. I felt lighter and therefore liberated.

Wanting to be magnanimous, the first act of my return had been to follow up on my postcards and voicemails and make peace with my mother. Now it was starting to feel as if I'd never left.

'Ask Nina what's going on, sweetie. She'll know the inside story – she always does.'

Invoking Nina was a sign of how seriously the Momager was taking the matter. She wasn't to know that Nina had cut me out of her life.

I blamed Adam for this as well as for everything else. Sure, Talia's move was a shocker. But Adam shacking up with her was a calculated provocation. He'd called her a loser, sneered at her, sneered at *me* for being her friend, and now he was using Talia to stick in the knife. Grace Tang and Victor Green were no doubt all smiles: Talia, spawn of a supermodel-turned-activist and a retail tycoon, was much better connected than a third-rate Thane.

Victor had phoned me post break-up to remind me of my contractual obligations, serving up his poison pill of threat with a sugar-coating of commiseration. At that point I hated him even more than Adam. But at least I wasn't scared of Adam.

My travels had been meant to draw a line under that part of my life. But this was impossible now. As soon as the Momager had left, I did what I was supposed to have sworn off forever, and looked Adam up online.

'Hot New Couple Alert!' yelped the gossip sites, which variously described Talia as a socialite or heiress or influencer. (With a pang, I remembered Nina: 'That girl couldn't influence her way out of a colostomy bag.') So here were she and Adam strolling hand in hand in Central Park, heading out of London's celebrity restaurant *du jour*, frolicking on her dad's yacht. There was even a snap of them hanging out with Nina at an ice-cream stand, the two girls laughing over their lollies like poster-girls in a tampon advert. That hurt.

Adam appeared the same as ever in this montage. Talia looked genuinely thrilled. Awestruck, in fact, as if she couldn't believe her luck. Was it possible she didn't even *know*? Or was she a better actress than I imagined?

I tried to take comfort from the trolls, but so far their antipathy was tepid. *Lol so our boy's got himself a suga mama.* Or *Adam's type = real basic bitches amirite?*

I wondered what Zalandra thought of it all.

(For a mad moment, I thought I'd spotted her in a street market in Senegal. There were times *I* felt like the crazy one.)

And here I was, late at night, down the rabbit hole again.

I looked up from my laptop to the mirror above my desk. My bare face, with its childish new freckles. The straggling eyebrows and limp bob. Who was I kidding? My mother was right. This wasn't what liberation looked like. This was defeat.

I plugged on with my new life goals all the same and started filling in applications for various screenwriting courses. I was browsing the creative-writing section of Foyles, when who should I bump into but Nick, with a stack of literary magazines under his arm.

He peered at me dubiously. 'Lily?'

'Nick! Hi!' It's possible I overdid the sprightliness.

'You've been away.'

'Travelling! Yeah –'

'Trying to get over your toxic ex.'

I glanced around in case of witnesses. 'Oh, it was fine. The break-up, that is. All for the best! I'm feeling good about it – we're all good. Everything's great.'

'You don't have to put a brave face on it,' he said, putting a hand on my shoulder. The smile that followed was more condescending than consoling but, being Nick, was probably the best he could manage. 'Adam Harker's your classic narcissist. And that bimbo he's dating – the new one – she's just a cover.'

I was taken aback. 'What?'

'He was screwing Dido most of the time he was with you. Still is.'

'Ah. No. No, definitely not.'

He laughed hollowly. 'Christ, Lily. I wouldn't have thought you were so naïve. Mind you, Dido's almost as bad. She actually believes that Adam's going to fix her up with Kash Malik and turn her into a film star.'

Since when did Dido want to be in the movies?

'I'd got a bad vibe from your blue-eyed bimboy from the off. Still, Dido was convinced he wanted to help her. He took advantage of that. Strung her along, then made his move.'

'I really don't think –'

'All the signs are there. Late-night phone calls. Unexplained absences, odd receipts. Some guy's sweatshirt left in the car. And Dido's not herself. She's distracted, dreamy. Even Hotspur's picked up on it.'

I suppressed an unkind urge to laugh. Nick's eyes were puffy and he'd lost weight, along with his trademark sneer. Dido was definitely cheating on him, poor sod. It just wasn't with Adam Harker. But I couldn't be bothered to protest Adam's innocence any further. Why should I?

'I'm very sorry to hear that, if it's true. I hope the two of you can work it out.'

'What I can't get over,' he said, ignoring me, 'is how someone of Dido's intelligence could be taken in by a pseud like Harker.' The sneer was back. 'Even you, Lily, must've known he's a vacuous little prick. But since the camera apparently *lurves* him, everyone else is falling over themselves to gush what a great talent he is. What an inspiration, what an *artist*.'

This, I realised, was the real sore point.

'Someone needs to expose him for what he is.'

Two weeks passed. I sent in my writing-course applications, got my hair done and went to a couple of castings, one of which seemed to go well. In the meantime, Pa fixed me up with his former agent, who's in his eighties and retired but needed someone to type up his memoirs. Nina was probably right to jeer at my cosseted lifestyle, but the residual cheques were getting smaller and my Southeast Asian adventures had made a hefty dent in my savings.

I swore off news sites and social media after finding myself on the *Daily Mail* online. There was a deeply unflattering picture of me trudging along in my gym kit with a bag of groceries. ('From Morrisons, of all places!' wailed the Momager.) 'Lily Looks Downcast as Adam Says He's "Never Been Happier"', opined the Sidebar of Shame.

The next day, I came home from work to find Talia waiting for me on the doorstep.

As soon as she saw me she burst into tears.

'I'm sorry, I'm sorry,' she eventually choked out. 'Do you hate me? Please don't hate me. I totally would if I were you.'

My first thought was that she'd come over because things had already come unstuck with Adam. But no, everything there was still peachy – except for the guilt. Talia couldn't sleep, she said, for worrying about me and what I was thinking. God, she was *the worst* –

To shut her up, more than anything, I invited her in.

Once in the flat, she perched on the sofa and covered her face with her hands. 'I don't expect you to forgive me,' she sniffled. 'All I want is for you to understand.'

I folded my arms across my chest. 'Fine. Explain it to me, then.'

She took a wavering breath and launched into a stream-of-consciousness account of running into Adam at Annabel's, shortly after our break-up. How she'd confronted him for being a loser and a dirt-bag for letting me go, and how he'd laughed at her, and that made her really mad, so she hit him, actually *hit* him, and everyone saw, and she thought he'd be crazy angry but instead they went into a corner and talked, about everything, for hours, and then met up and talked again. At first, she thought this was because Adam wanted to come to terms with breaking up with me, and maybe even think about winning me back, but it ended up being a completely different kind of conversation, well, more of an *unburdening*, for both of them, a heart-to-heart the likes of which Talia hadn't had with *anyone* before. And Adam explained the truth about his relationship with me and how he'd always be so thankful for it, even though he'd come to feel the two of us weren't the right fit, which made him really sad. Heartbroken, in fact. Talia didn't know what to think at first but mostly she was just so moved, so honoured, he'd shared his secret with her. (Many of her closest BFFs were out-and-proud LGBTQIA, of course, but she totally understood that, as an aspiring Leading Man, Adam was

134

up against the heteronormative industrial complex.) And then they met up a couple more times, as friends, but now there was this new and beautiful feeling of trust between them – so when Adam suggested that maybe she might like to go on a few dates with him, it seemed natural to say yes.

'Obviously, if the two of you had been genuinely, you know, *in love* I would never have gone anywhere *near* him. But I figured … well, you were away travelling … nobody even knew when you'd be back … maybe you'd be *pleased* Adam was with me rather than some, you know, random model or actress type? But then you came home, and the tabloids were saying all these mean things about you. And Nina said the two of you weren't talking any more, though she wouldn't tell me why. And I realised I'd been kidding myself the whole time because, actually, I'd gone behind your back, and that was a totally disloyal thing to do, and it made me a shitty friend. Because however much I like Adam and want to help him – and I really do – he's still not worth sacrificing our friendship for. So I'm here to say I'll end it, right this minute, if you want me to. Just don't hate me. Say you don't hate me. Please?'

It was all very exhausting. Talia looked so ridiculous, with her nose red and her cheeks wet and her eyelash extensions half falling off because she kept scrubbing her eyes … Adam wasn't my ex-boyfriend; he was my ex-business-associate. And at least I'd signed our contract with my eyes open. Talia was clueless, otherwise she'd know Adam was only with her for her trust fund. His tastes, not to mention predilections, had got hella more expensive during the time we'd dated, and until the movie megabucks came in, he was no doubt in the market for a sugar mama. Like the trolls said.

Plus, I was consumed with curiosity. How was Adam treating his new boo? How was he treating himself?

So I fetched a bottle of wine and a couple of glasses and sat down next to Talia and told her that, actually, it was fine; I'd just needed to get over the shock. 'It's kind of a relief to know that you know. There's nobody else I can really talk to about Adam because of the NDA.'

'You didn't even tell Nina?' Talia blew her nose, trumpeting, and reached gratefully for the wine.

'No. It can be lonely, keeping someone else's secret. Living a lie with all your family and friends.'

Talia looked sad again. 'My parents *love* Adam. They keep saying how much better he is than my other boyfriends. They'd be so disappointed if they knew the truth.'

No wonder. Talia's exes include a fifty-year-old nightclub owner and an ex-con covered in gang tattoos.

'I suppose nobody knows the truth of anybody else's relationship behind closed doors.'

'Right? Why shouldn't my relationship with Adam be "real", just because we're not sleeping together? I mean, loads of married people don't have sex. Are they all fakes, too?'

I topped up both our glasses. 'How *is* Adam ... behind closed doors?'

'Oh gosh, just so sweet, so funny. We have *such* a giggle.'
Huh.

'That's good to hear. I know he can be a bit of a bastard after a bender.'

'Oh? We haven't been partying that much.'

'But you know he's got a dependency.' I framed it as a statement, not a question.

Talia's eyes widened. 'I wouldn't go *that* far. I think the pills are more of a fallback when he gets a bit overwhelmed or frustrated. It's something we've been working on together – along with the three Ms.' Then, when I looked blank, 'Mindfulness, Meditation and Manifestation!' She blushed. 'Look, I get that it sounds hokey. I used to be a total sceptic too. But what's so laughable about trying to stress less and create more? It's about taking ownership of your life, that's all.'

'OK. That sounds … positive.' Perhaps Adam and I really had brought out the worst in each other.

Talia swilled the wine around her glass. 'Remember, in New York, I was telling you about how we were all behind the red rope, and how I worried I didn't feel the same as everyone else? Almost like I didn't fit in?'

'I remember.'

'Now that I'm *truly* pretending to be something I'm not, I actually feel more like my real self. Isn't that strange?' She hugged herself, smiling. 'The way I see it, if someone like Adam's faking it, then *everyone* is. And that's liberating, right?'

Some days later, I got a phone call at midnight from an unknown number.

'Lily-pet, Lily-pet, don't hang up,' said Adam, his voice sleepy and slurred.

'We have nothing to say to each other.'

'But I'm calling to abase myself.'

'There are chat lines for that.'

'Mmm … I'd like us to have a happy ending. Wouldn't you?'

'Too late.'

'Don't be over-dramatic now. We had some good times, didn't we? Best of times, worst of times. I'm sorry I turned it all to shit.'

I pursed my lips, à la Momager. 'Are you.'

'Yes. I miss you, Lily.'

'Funny – I heard you'd "never been happier".'

'That's what happens when you're dating a Care Bear.'

'A Care Bear with a platinum credit card.'

'Ha. Share Bear always *was* my favourite. Are you jealous?'

'Don't flatter yourself. I'm still pissed at you, though. Using Talia is a dick move but throwing me off *Hollow Moon*? That was a whole new world of spite.'

There was a pause. I could hear heavy breathing. 'Yeah. I know that was bad. But it was all Victor, I swear.'

'Uh-huh. I'm sure you fought him tooth and nail.'

'I only found out after the event –'

I made a scoffing sound.

'I want to make it up to you, Lily-pet. I really do. That's why I'm calling. I can still put things right, if you'll let me.'

'I wish that were true. But I don't think we're good for each other, Adam.'

'You're being melodramatic again. Listen, I'm throwing a party in a couple of weeks. Talia's dad bought this mad house down in Norfolk and then basically forgot about it. It's the perfect venue. I'm not planning anything too wild – just a few creative types gathering for a sniff of country air. Come and join. As mates. As we were always meant to be. You can yell at me in person if you like, give me a good slap round the chops. Get it out of your system.'

'That's not how it works.'

'We can *make* it work. I want you in my life again. I screwed up, and I'm sorry. I miss you.' His voice wasn't slurred any more; it was artful, coaxing. 'C'mon. Don't make me beg.'

'I'll think about it,' I said.

CHAPTER TWO

I fully intended not to go. I didn't believe Adam when he'd laid the blame for *Hollow Moon* at Victor's door. I didn't believe his offers to make it up to me, either. He'd drunk-dialled me at a sentimental moment, that was all. Or else he'd called to jerk me around, reeling me back into the drama and the messiness. For kicks.

I had work, too. Finally. *The Other Women* was a glossy revenge drama about the mistresses of three powerful men (a politician, mob boss and film star) and one woman (a fashion editor) who meet by chance in a posh hotel. A pact is made, conspiracy plotted, high-jinks ensue. The first series had been a big hit for the streaming service, and I'd snagged a three-episode story arc in the second, as a blackmailing tabloid journalist. The girl originally cast got pregnant and had to pull out, so it all happened very quickly. Filming was already well underway and the series was scheduled to air in September.

All the same, it's possible I wasn't as set on extricating myself from Adam as I liked to think. Amidst all the emotion of Talia's visit, she'd managed to leave her scarf behind, and after filming finished on Friday, I used this as a pretext to drop by her house. Thanks to her obsessive updating of social media, it was easy to pick a time when she'd be home alone.

My flat's the first floor of a Victorian terrace house in Kilburn. Talia lives in kitsch-y Art Deco-inspired splendour just off the King's Road. She professed herself thrilled, *thrilled* to see me, but when she invited me in for coffee, I got the feeling it was mostly from a sense of obligation.

A large rose-gold-framed photo of the lovebirds was prominently displayed on the drawing-room mantelpiece. I smiled at it benignly and mentioned that Adam had phoned to apologise.

'Aww! That makes me so happy! I know he hated how he left things with you – it was really eating away at him.'

'It's the ninth step, isn't it? Making amends.'

'What step?'

'On the road to recovery. From addiction. Who knows … maybe one day Adam will circle back and try steps one to eight.'

Talia bit her artificially plumped lip. 'Don't take this the wrong way, but maybe you shouldn't joke about this stuff? The position Adam's in – the secrecy, the hiding … It's been brutal for his self-esteem.'

I nearly spat out my coffee. 'If Adam's self-esteem was any healthier it would be doing burpees on a vegan yoga mat.'

'Maybe you don't know him quite as well as you think you do.'

Talia had turned red all over but she held my gaze. There was an uncomfortable pause.

'So,' I said abruptly. 'This house party in Norfolk. Adam invited me. Do you think I should go?'

'Gosh. I – well – it would be a teensy bit awkward, wouldn't it? The two of us there? Especially after you made such a big deal about moving on.'

'I didn't make a big deal of it.'

'You left the country for three months …'

'And now I'm back.'

'Oh,' Talia exclaimed, covering her face with her hands. 'You're still angry with me, aren't you? I should've realised. Of course my stupid explanation wasn't enough. You're hurting, and I'm being an insensitive *bitch*.'

'I'm not and you aren't. I swear it's –'

'You and Adam have known each other *forever*. Of course the two of you have this incredible bond. I'm never going to get in the way of that. I just think … well, me and Adam, we're on a journey too.' She lowered her voice. 'Adam told me that one day he wants marriage and babies. Babies! He actually asked me what I thought about it. Can you imagine?'

'Wow,' I said weakly. 'That's … big.'

'Obviously it's pie in the sky.' Talia giggled, tossing back her hair. 'But some day … who knows?'

'You're not serious? Surely you want all that with a real partner?'

'Oh, absolutely. I mean, that's the dream.' She was all pink-cheeked and shiny-eyed. 'It's ironic, that's all. Because, like Adam says, the two of us are basically the perfect fit.'

The final straw was the news, via Pa, that Dido was set to star in Kash Malik's latest, an as-yet-untitled film featuring the ghost of Dorothy Parker. I remembered Kash talking about the screenplay over dinner, back in the day. It had been written by his ex-girlfriend and would be a real departure for Kash: a tragi-comedy, set in Manhattan, extra-talky – 'a feminist Woody Allen movie'. Naturally, it hadn't crossed either of our minds that the likes of him would ever consider casting the likes of me. Now I learned that Adam had scrapped my TV-show comeback at the same time as pushing my cousin towards bona fide Oscar-bait.

I was *definitely* going to that sodding party now.

Adam had been messaging me, though I was yet to respond. It was usually late at night and usually just one line.

I miss you.
What are you wearing?
Partypartypartypartycomecomecomecome
cum
?? ·
do you miss me
sorry
sorry
Please?

After I finally responded, asking for details of the upcoming weekend, he did his usual trick of not replying for ages. Then:

YAS queen!
Be just like old times
The good ones I mean
Old loves, new friends, Barbies, Kens. Care Bears.
Oh and you can meet my latest recruit ha ha
It's a surprise

I don't like surprises, I messaged back. And, later, *Don't make me regret this.*

No regrets, he said.

I regretted it as soon as I reached the house. The journey itself was surprisingly smooth, even though it involved a five-hour trip by rail and bus (I've a driver's licence for work purposes but am too nervous to use it much). Just after three, the bus left me on the outskirts of a flint-and-brick fishing village. The venue was a little over a mile away, so I set off along the road, trundling my overnight bag behind me. Even on a bright June day, the flat landscape looked windswept and, to my mind, underwhelming: land and sea and marsh all seeping into each other in smears of bronzy-grey.

Adam had told me to arrive early, 'before the ravening hordes', so we'd have the chance to talk properly. Come for tea, he said. Or gin. Whatever you want. Just the two of us. But when I'd messaged him to say I was on my way, hoping for the offer of a lift, I heard nothing back.

Talia was right to say my presence at the party would be awkward. Unwelcome too, probably. That wasn't going to stop me. I had plenty of professional experience of feeling exposed and humiliated. I could fake sass and sparkle as easily as Adam could feign being straight. Whether we kissed and made up, or tore bloody strips off each other, the onlookers could think whatever they pleased. Let them titter and tattle as much as they liked. I had unfinished business.

The house was set back from the coastal road, a flank of pine trees and a wall hiding it from view. Adam had pitched the invitation as a country-house weekend so I was expecting something with gables and turrets. A rose garden, perhaps, and forelock-tugging staff.

But the forbiddingly high grey walls were more *Prison Break* than country break. There was even a little sentry box by the gates, for a security guard, and a CCTV camera. Since the box was unoccupied, I pressed the buzzer. After a long wait a woman's voice said 'Yes?' querulously down the crackly line.

'Hi. Hello there. I'm here … for the party?'

'We were told not to expect anyone till six.'

'Yeah, I know. I'm meeting Adam early.'

After another pause, the gates grudgingly creaked open.

The grounds within were bare and slightly unkempt looking. I walked up the long curving driveway to be confronted with a sprawling modernist construction built of interlocking cubes clad in grey granite. It was flanked by woodland to either side, overlooking the salt marsh from its north face. It was eerily quiet and the house's windows were dead-eyed. I was relieved to see a flashy car as well as a catering van parked outside; a teenage boy and an older woman were unloading boxes of glasses from the latter.

'Hello. I think I spoke to you on the intercom just now? Is Adam about?'

'Mr Harker left. Had some errands to run.' The woman turned back towards the house. 'There's a couple of others inside.' She sounded disapproving.

Cursing Adam under my breath, I followed her. The interior of the house had raw concrete ceilings and white rendered walls. Untreated wood and floor-to-ceiling windows featured heavily. To the left of the entrance hall was a library with birch-ply shelves but no books; beyond glass double doors was a large kitchen, where the caterers were busy setting things out on slate worktops. The house reminded me of the Shoreditch gallery where I'd met Adam for the second time, and was nearly as empty. I knew this kind of minimalism didn't come cheap but it still had an oddly neglected feel. There was a film of dust on many of the surfaces and smears on the huge windows.

I was starting to get hungry but I didn't see much in the way of actual food being prepared in the kitchen. The house's cubes were arranged in a deconstructed L-shape; I wandered around the impressively blank rooms until I found my way out onto a raised patio on the shorter leg of the L. This led into two walled gardens, which had been built into the woods on the eastern side of the property. They had high cement walls and slate paths winding through sparsely planted beds. The second garden contained a swimming pool.

It was lined in steel polished to a mirrored finish and was steaming gently. A woman was languidly doing breaststroke naked while a much older man smoked by the side.

'Hi,' I said. 'I'm Lily.'

'Welcome,' said the man, looking me over with faint interest but without any sign of recognition. 'I am Jorge and this is Stassia.'

'Hello,' said Stassia, from the water. She was beautiful in that highly exaggerated, specifically model sort of way. There wasn't even anything particularly sexual about her nakedness: it seemed to come ready filtered. Jorge had the paunchy sleekness of an ageing Roman emperor.

I shaded my eyes with my hand. 'Quite some place.'

Jorge nodded. 'The architect is famous, I understand.'

Stassia climbed up the pool steps and towelled herself off in the same leisurely way she'd swum. It wasn't an especially warm day but if she was feeling the cold she didn't show it. 'The water is very nice,' she said. 'You should try.'

'Lily Thane? What are you doing here?'

I turned around to see Adam's sister padding over from the direction of the house. She was in a one-piece and a sarong, which, seeing Stassia in her tiny bath-towel, she hitched more tightly over her hips. Then she put her dark glasses on the top of her head to scowl at me better.

'Hi, uh … Sarah.' I'd momentarily forgotten her name. 'Nice to see you again.'

She rubbed her goose-pimpled arms and scowled harder. 'Does Tally know you're here?'

Tally? 'Sure.' Strictly speaking, Talia knew I'd been invited. Not that I'd said yes. 'Is she around?'

'She's with her dad. It's a last-minute thing. She'll be here tomorrow.'

OK. On balance, this was good news.

If Sarah found my presence surprising, I was even more disconcerted by hers. Adam had told me he preferred to forget his family even existed. There certainly hadn't seemed to be any sibling warmth between them the one time we'd met. Evidently a lot of things had changed over the last few months.

'And Adam? Where's he got to?'

'He said he had something to take care of.'

Finding the local county line dealer, I'd bet. Jorge and Stassia were watching the two of us curiously. I felt uncomfortable but,

147

really, it was Sarah who didn't fit in. It wasn't that she hadn't made an effort with her appearance – she was acceptably groomed, acceptably angular. But she wasn't someone who was used to people looking at her and it showed.

'Perhaps you should swim too, Lily,' Stassia suggested again to break the silence.

'Thanks, but I think I might go for a walk.'

Sarah's lip curled like her brother's. 'Don't get lost, yeah?'

It was a relief to be alone. I continued my explorations on the north-facing side of the property, where the lawn sloped down to a muddy expanse of marsh. It wasn't the kind of vista I'd choose to look out on, I thought, if I could afford a famous architect to build me a fancy house on the coast. The marsh was a maze of sandbanks and twisting creeks with no real colour or contour. No sound but the lonely piping of birds. No vegetation except for a few scratchy bits of shrub. Limpid water, glistening mud. Behind me, the house's grey boxes looked like children's building blocks, tumbled onto the ground and left to fade, then rot.

So I turned back, walking along the driveway to the main road. I spotted a sign saying 'Coastal Path' and followed it into a wood. I wandered along it for a while, enjoying the pale sun on my face and looking for a path down to the dunes. The first track I found was unmarked and overgrown, but I was feeling adventurous and set off down it all the same.

I soon realised I'd been too ambitious. The path wasn't steep but my thin plimsolls were wholly unsuitable for the loose rocky ground. I turned round, but in my hurry to get back to a firmer footing, I slipped, then skidded, and suddenly found myself on my front, scrabbling to find a grip. I slipped further and felt the crash of something craggy against my head. I lay face down on the slope, gasping from shock, my body limp. Everything felt bruised. When I put my hand to my head, I touched blood.

After a while I got to my feet. I was shaking all over but mostly undamaged. I hadn't blacked out, I told myself, so the blow to my head couldn't have been that bad. I was just an idiot who'd tripped over her own feet. Still, the walk back to the house left me faint.

I must have been away for over an hour but I got back to find Stassia and Jorge still by the pool. No sign of Sarah, thank God. Jorge was dozing under a blanket. Stassia was in a fur coat and dark glasses and reading a magazine. 'What happened?' she asked, without much concern.

'I fell … on a rock. Is Adam back?'

'I have not seen him, I am sorry. I think the sister is resting.'

Gingerly, I touched the lump on the side of my head and asked if she had any painkillers.

Stassia shook her exquisite head. 'You could look in Adam's room, perhaps. If you think he will not mind.'

'He won't. Which one is it?'

'The studio.' She pointed to a gate the other side of the pool. I suppose I looked rather disconsolate. 'I'm sure he will be home soon,' she added, as if reassuring a child, and returned serenely to her magazine.

The studio was a wood-clad annexe set just outside the garden wall. It had its own kitchenette and shower room and a deck looking out over the pine wood. Adam's stuff was strewn all over the divan bed. Despite myself, I felt a little bubble of nostalgia at the sight of his dirty socks balled on the floor.

In the shower room, I saw my reflection for the first time and was surprised Stassia hadn't recoiled at the sight. There was crusted blood on my forehead and dust and dirt everywhere else. I did an amateur clean-up job and went to look for some drugs.

It didn't take long to find Adam's goodie bag, zipped up in one of the compartments of his suitcase. It was another familiar item to me: a battered fabric pouch emblazoned with a British bulldog over the Union Jack and embroidered with hearts. (Apparently it had been gifted to him by a fan; I assume he kept it for the kitsch appeal.) I didn't feel any guilt about going through his stuff. This was a medical emergency. Besides, a minor invasion of privacy was the least he deserved.

The goodie bag's contents were fairly standard. A couple of wraps of coke, a baggie of weed and a bottle labelled Percocet, with seven or eight pills inside. The label had Adam's name on it, and the pale-yellow tablets looked legit, but I knew it was unlikely the 'perks' had been legally prescribed. Still, I'd taken them in Adam's company once or twice before and I knew his dealer was A-list. (Thirty-something and well-spoken, with branded loyalty cards, he claimed all his clients were professionals from the world of culture, media and sports.) I decided to risk it – I needed something strong if I was going to get through the rest of the day and night. My head was pounding and I ached all over.

So I took one of the tablets and helped myself to a protein bar I found in the kitchen. I hadn't eaten anything since breakfast, which was probably contributing to the dizziness. Then I stretched out on the divan and closed my eyes. All I needed was a little rest, let the drugs work their magic, and I'd be good to go.

I blacked out almost at once.

When I awoke, the sun was setting. Music thudded; the baseline to the happy roar of a party in full swing.

'My God, did somebody try to murder you?'

CHAPTER THREE

There was Adam, grinning down at me.

Waking to find a heavy male figure looming over my bed had stirred some primitive dread. I was queasy and disoriented and shrank back at first, rather than sitting up.

'I ... I took one ... one of your pills ...'

'I only get the best.'

'I fell onto a rock ...'

'Yeah, I've already heard about your misadventures. I came to check on you earlier and you seemed to be breathing. You look terrible, though.'

Wincing, I swung myself off the bed. According to the clock on the wall, it was just before nine. I'd been out for four hours.

I took a swig from my water bottle and tried to collect myself. 'Never mind my misadventures. What about yours? I got here at three, like you asked. We were going to talk. You were going to further abase yourself. Remember?'

'Something came up. Sorry. I didn't know you were going to throw yourself off a cliff in your disappointment.'

That smirk.

He looked good, though, damn him. Lean and dark and burnished bright.

I'd wanted to look good for this party too. Or at least not like a reanimated corpse. Back in the shower room, the damage looked worse than I remembered. There was still some congealed blood in my hair, I'd torn several nails, and my dust-covered blouse was ripped at the hem. I splashed some water on my face and had another go at sponging off the gunk.

'So what happened to your child bride?' I asked from behind the door.

'Daddy flew into London last-minute and demanded her presence for dinner tonight. Perfect timing.'

'Not for Talia.'

'She's got the rest of the weekend to play hostess. She's threatening all sorts of nonsense. Country walks. A hog roast. Probably a bouncy castle too.'

I came out of the shower room. 'A hog roast? Last I heard, Talia's vegan.'

'There is no dearly held belief or sacred principle more potent than that girl's eagerness to please.' He snorted. 'Imagine what the straight guys must get out of her.'

'God, you're a prick.'

'Talia doesn't think so. Maybe there's something to be said for the simple life. You should probably know that I've asked her to extend the contract.'

I can't lie: that hurt.

Adam lolled against the open doorway. Behind him, the sky over the pines was molten gold. 'Do you remember, right at the start, when I said you made me want to become a better person?'

I cleared my throat. 'It certainly sounds like the sort of deathlessly naff line you'd come up with.'

'No, I meant it. Or partly. It turns out it's easier to be Mr Nice Guy once you start getting the things you want.'

'Is that why you invited me and your sister here? The Joy of Nice?'

'I wanted to see you because I miss you. You know that. As for Sarah – my mum had a minor health scare, which opened up lines of communication. Plus, they seem to prefer Talia to you. Less prickly, I assume.'

I raised my brows but made no comment.

'Anyway, I'm in Sarah's good books because I wrote her a cheque for a new car or new teeth or whatever. So I thought I might as well let her tag along tonight.'

'How generous.'

'Don't pout. I'm going to put things right with you too, like I promised. Not with a cash bung, obviously – it's better than that. I think I've found a way of fixing you.'

'Fixing *me*?'

'Of the sadness. The wrongness.'

I shook my head. 'Spare me. I know where this is heading. The "Three Ms" and all that falafel-bean and crystal-rubbing crap. I'm not interested in joining your wellness cult.'

He grinned. 'Have no fear. The only cults I'm interested in are the sex-pervert kind.'

'Well, according to Talia, you're a reformed character.'

'Reform*ing* … I've got a drugs counsellor. Talia found him. Beardy fella – looks a bit like Santa. He's helped me cut back on the party favours.'

'Bollocks! I've already gone through your stash.'

'I said I cut back, not quit. I've gone from three perks a day to one, maybe two, max. And I'm keeping any nasal naughtiness strictly to the weekends. No more pissing about. For one thing, I can't afford to keep snorting all my winnings up my nose. Or at least, not until I start my new gig. This one's gonna be a game-changer.'

'Sounds exciting.' I wasn't going to indulge him by asking for details. Of course he told me anyway.

'It is. You're looking at the new Luke Zane, baby.' He flexed his biceps. 'I signed the contract last week.'

Bloody hell. As action heroes go, Zane wasn't quite Bond. But he was damn close. 'Congratulations. I'm sure the two of you and Talia will be very happy together.'

Adam laughed. 'Oh, how I missed that sour face … But listen, I'm serious about –'

'Adam! There you are!' A gaggle of Sloane-y girls appeared. They seemed familiar, either because they were part of Talia's crowd and I'd seen them before or – more likely – because they were generic Party Blondes. 'The DJ is being a *dick* and we need to *dance*. You *have* to come tell him off for us.'

They tugged at his hands, wrapped themselves round his chest. Giggled and squirmed and shrieked. Mock-protesting, Adam allowed himself to be dragged away.

'Later, Lily,' he said over his shoulder. 'Come and find me.'

I'd handled the reunion quite nicely, I thought. We'd bitched and bantered just like old times. There'd been the same mix of exasperation and affection and, underneath it all, an equally familiar trickle of unease.

155

For all his talk of better-personhood, Adam's idea of 'fixing' me most likely involved getting me either laid or high. Still, he'd seemed more like the Adam of our early days. Lighter and shinier. I felt a little breathless, seeing him again.

I needed to eat, I decided. Hunger was making me light-headed. There wasn't much more I could do about my appearance; I'd brought a dress to change into from my travelling clothes but this and my cosmetics case were in my overnight bag, which I'd left somewhere in the main house. One of the Party Blondes was probably about to be sick in it.

Oh well. The new me wasn't supposed to be so hung up on the trivialities of hotness v. notness. I had nothing to prove at this gathering. People could think what they liked.

Bold words, and I'm not sure how much I believed them. At any rate, I didn't go after Adam through the walled gardens but took the long way round – following the little gravel path that wound back towards the salt marsh. This way, I had the chance to appraise the party at a distance before going in.

Darkness was falling, and the house's huge windows no longer looked dead-eyed. They were glass boxes pulsing with light and colour, moving limbs, tossing hair; it was as if the building had been turned inside-out.

Adam knew a lot of people without being particularly close to any of them. Another thing we had in common, I guess. When we were fake-dating, we'd socialise with ex-castmates or industry-adjacent hangers on. But there were, in fact, people I knew at this party. People I knew very well.

I drew closer across the scrubby lawn. In one of the central rooms, a trio of laughing figures was silhouetted against the glass:

Adam, Dido and Nina. A blonde standing in the background might as well have been a placeholder for Talia.

I stayed in the shadows watching for a while. Then I looked down at myself, in my ripped and dusty clothes, my bashed-up hands. What the hell was I doing? As if on cue, I heard a low chuckle from the darkness behind me. I spun around and saw the glow of a cigarette and glittering eyes.

'So I'm not the only one out in the cold.'

It was Rafael. His muscular torso was packed into a tight, neatly torn T-shirt and his hair looked freshly bleached.

'Speak for yourself.'

He spat on the grass, an indolent, unthreatened gesture. 'Don't kid yourself, *chica*. Adam got you out here so he can play his games.' He tilted his head, considering. 'Let me guess: he wanted to say sorry, to make things up to you. He is going to explain. He is going to put everything right. And so you come running. Again.'

'It's really none of your business.'

'Business, yes. You two had a *business* relationship. So why are you still here? Still waiting in the dark?'

'Adam's my friend.'

'Adam doesn't have friends.'

I peered at Rafael's face. There was an ugly bite mark just above his jaw.

'That looks nasty,' I said. 'You should watch yourself.'

'So should Adam.' He took a long drag of his cigarette. 'Some day his games are gonna end in tears.'

I went inside. Let Rafael sulk in the dark. Our encounter had reinvigorated me; there might well be a deranged ex at the party, but it wasn't me.

My stomach was cramping with hunger but it looked as if the caterers had already left. The kitchen was empty and immaculate; the adjoining dining room housed the picked-over remains of a buffet. Adam had obviously taken charge of arrangements. If Talia had been hostessing, waiters would be flowing back and forth, circulating canapés, proffering drinks. There would be whimsical themed props and floral displays, perhaps a personalised ice sculpture or candy bar, and an event planner with an earpiece to coordinate it all. This, despite the glossiness of the crowd, had the feel of a chaotic student house party. The bar had been set up in the library, and was fully stocked with an array of premium booze, but the two pretty-boy bartenders didn't look especially professional. They were messing about with the cocktail shakers, giggling uncontrollably as the contents of one sprayed all over the plywood shelves.

I headed back to what was left of the buffet: a few folded cold meats, scrapings of a complicated couscous salad. Bits of fruit, bits of bread, some sloppy-looking cheese.

'Lily! You poor animal! What on earth have you done to yourself?'

Dido. Terrific.

'Yeah … so I fell off a horse.'

'A *horse*?'

'Uh-huh. Research for a new role – there's an equestrian angle. Sometimes one has to suffer for one's art.'

'So I can see.'

'Congrats on your Hollywood début, by the way.'

'Whatever do you mean?'

'The new Kash Malik. Uncle Felix told Pa.'

She frowned. 'Well, he shouldn't have.'

Typical Dido. If she wanted to play coy, I wasn't going to coax the information out of her. I started tearing into a bread roll instead, then reached for a sweaty clump of prosciutto.

'Goodness, what an appetite.' Dido popped a cube of melon into her mouth. 'And yet you're always so lovely and slim. What's the secret?'

'Bulimia.'

'Ha ha ha! You're *outrageous*.'

This is how I am around Dido. Dead-pan, smart-mouthed. I'm waiting for her to call me out on it, but she never does. In our duologues, Dido always plays dumber than she really is. I suppose it amuses her.

'Well, I have to say,' she continued, 'I didn't expect to see you here.'

'Same. I never knew you and Adam were such buddies.'

'Mm. It's an awful shame it didn't work out between the two of you. I suppose there just wasn't enough in common.'

'Because he's a prince and I'm a showgirl?'

'Lily, stop it. Don't put yourself down like that. On screen, you're charm personified. Always so perky and loveable. Even when you played that serial killer. I don't know how you do it.'

'Thanks. Anyway – you should probably know that Nick thinks you and Adam are screwing.'

'*What?*'

'Don't worry, I know there's nothing going on. Nick might need more convincing, though.'

159

She wasn't laughing now. I stuffed a gob of brie into my mouth and moved on.

Adam may have skimped on the catering but there was nothing budget about his sound system – I could feel my bones vibrating along with the bass. I wandered around the party for a while, looking for Adam and my bag, in no particular order. I recognised some of the other guests – an actor and an influencer here, a radio DJ and a model there – but found it hard to work out if this was because I'd met them IRL or I just knew their faces. Nobody said hello, in any case. I got several strange looks. Some people even laughed. Or was I imagining this? My head was still hurting and my vision was weirdly fuzzy around the edges. I passed Sarah at one point and she gave me a look of such loathing I almost stumbled.

On the other side of the library was the smaller of the two living rooms. It was the closest this house came to cosy in that it had a wood-burning stove and was furnished with a couple of angular mid-century settees. Plus a shit-ton of coke. It was all laid out on a mirrored glass table, pretty as you please. Jorge appeared to be the source; at any rate, he was presiding over arrangements with an avuncular air. The people gathered round were bright with the simple pleasure of anticipation.

The first to dip her head was a girl in a slinky snakeskin dress and black bovver boots. When she sat up again, pinching her nose and with her face scrunched, it took a moment or two for us to make eye contact.

For just a second, I thought she was about to break into a grin or shout of welcome. Then the shutters came down. She turned her head and got up to leave.

I intercepted her. 'Hi, Nina. Long time no see.'

'What the fuck are you doing here?'

'Adam invited me.'

'That's weird.' Nina sniffed hard. 'Anyway, you look like shit.'

'Whereas you fit right in. Ironically.'

'What do you mean by that?'

'Nothing.' I'd planned to be apologetic, placating. I hadn't realised how much it would sting, seeing her here. Like the most painful kind of homesickness. 'I'm glad that you've found some new friends, that's all.'

'Wasn't hard. My only criteria is they don't accuse me of hate crimes.'

Anger swept through me. I'd lost count of the feuds Nina had waged, the scores of people she'd cut out of her life. But I never dreamed I'd be one of them.

'Please. Your bar's a lot lower than that. You think Talia's a loser and Dido's a pseud. You've told me, multiple times, that Adam's a creep. Yet here you are, snorting lines with his entourage without a care in the world. And you had the balls to call *me* a star-fucker –'

My voice cracked. I turned on my heel before things could escalate further. On the way out, I blundered into someone. 'Hey,' he said, 'are you OK?' and the concern in his voice nearly undid me. 'Let's sit down,' he said, putting a hand out to steady me. 'Let's get you a drink. It looks like you've been in the wars.'

He was no more than twenty, a baby-faced boy-bander type.

161

One of the Ken dolls. Anxious and predatory and optimistic all at once.

I shook him off and moved on.

Here, finally, was a piece of luck – I caught sight of my bag, stuffed behind the back of a deconstructed iron armchair. It felt a bit pointless to change clothes at this point but now I'd got my cosmetics case I could at least tidy up my face. I went upstairs to find a quiet bathroom. I tied up my hair, spritzed myself with perfume and started to feel better. Then, when I was rummaging in the case for my concealer, I felt something lumpy in one of the zipped compartments. It was the amethyst ring Adam had given me, that dreamy star-spangled night in LA. I'd packed it at the last minute on a whim. After a moment's hesitation, I pushed it onto my finger. I'd always liked it even though the fit was wrong.

I came out of the bathroom to find someone waiting in the hall outside. I'd been a while, what with the primping. 'Sorry,' I said. Then I saw it was Zalandra.

It was as if I'd fallen on the cliff path again. The ground sliding under my feet, the ringing and roaring of panic in my ears. I even put my hands out in front of me, as if searching for a grip. My vision blurred.

'There you are,' Zalandra said. She gave a tiny, sly smile but her face was otherwise blank. She was still fat and pale, still dressed in her thick black layers. It was uncanny how ghostly she appeared, despite her stolid form. 'I told you I'd keep turning up. I told you there'd be a reckoning. Didn't I?'

I looked around wildly, but we were alone. 'Stay away from me,' I wheezed. I backed away on wobbly legs, half-expecting the girl to lunge at me, shouting obscenities, but she stayed where she was, hands in pockets, staring after me with the same sly watchfulness as before.

A knot of people were coming up the stairs and I pushed through them so violently they shouted in indignation. Where the *fuck* was Adam? The rest of these morons would be of no help. I'd be a joke to them: the crazy ex-girlfriend, pursued by a ghost. On the ground floor, I saw Adam's sister rolling around on a couch with some bearded guy, sucking face with sloppy abandon. She looked up as I stumbled past, her lipstick smeared bloodily around her mouth. 'I know all about you,' she hissed. 'I always did.' I was trapped in a hideous carnival where everyone was reeling drunk, manically laughing caricatures of their real selves.

Finally, I spotted Adam. He was outside on the patio with Rafael. They were having words. Or at least Rafael was – he was gesticulating and shouting, spittle flying in the air. Adam was idling against the railings, infuriatingly relaxed.

I wrenched open the sliding doors. When Rafael saw me he froze for a moment, made a furious gesture and spat out something incoherent of everything but rage. Then he shouldered past me into the house.

Adam and I were alone at last, but for a few moments I couldn't get the words out. My heart felt monstrously swollen in my chest, beating hard enough to burst out from my ribcage, squeezing all the air from my lungs.

'Za– Za– Za– Za– Za–'

He laid his hands on my shoulders. 'Whoa. Slow down. Deep breaths.'

'Zalandra,' I finally got out. 'Your stalker. She's *here*. *Now*. In the *house*. You have to call the police, *right now –*'

But Adam started laughing. 'Shit, Lily, it's fiiiine. I invited her.' He did jazz hands. 'Surprise!'

I stared at him. My mouth gaped.

''S'no biggie. After the two of us broke up, she waited for me outside my agent's and apologised for freaking you out. Said she'd been off her meds or whatever. She's kind of an impressive person, once you get to know her. So I gave her a job.'

'You *what*?'

'She's in charge of my official fan-site. She's done great work, actually. Very smart, very organised. Then I was emailing her about some promotional thingie, and I told her about this weekend and said she could come along if she wanted to.' He giggled. 'Admittedly, I was caning it at the time.'

'You are unbelievable.' I wanted to smash his face in. My fists were clenched so hard my nails dug into my flesh. 'The drugs have fried your brain. Or maybe Talia's right. Maybe your self-esteem is so pathetically low you actually *need* a lunatic stalker in order to feel good about yourself.'

Adam looked at me calmly. 'That's not what this is about. Zalandra is an interesting person. I think she's important. And how she acted towards you –'

'Shut up. Just shut up, OK? You did this to mess with me. You lured me out here, made all those promises, just to humiliate me. Again. What did I ever do to you to deserve this?' He started to speak but my voice rose and flowed, swelling with fury. 'No, really. You treated me like crap, ended our contract in the shittiest way possible and got me thrown off a job – at the exact same time you were presenting Dido to Kash on a silver platter.'

'Now, hold on –'

'Shut up. You schmooze my cousin and my best friend, fake-date my other friend and tell her you want her babies. And then you ambush me with the freak show who tried to physically assault me the last time we met! You're a sociopath, you know that? An actual sociopath. A user and abuser and –' My voice choked.

'Takes one to know one, Lily-pet. It's why the two of us were meant to be. I told you that, right at the start.' He gave a rueful shrug. 'But it's different now, because I understand you. *Really* understand you. That's why it's going to be OK. If you'll just calm down a minute, I can explain everything, and then we're going to put things right, together. I can help you. I promise.'

He put his hand out, as if to stroke my cheek. I jerked away. 'Fuck you.'

Adam smiled. It was the smile of someone who could not only get away with anything, but made you long for him to try. I looked at him for the last time and saw, in spite of it all, moonlight on marble. Superheroes and presidents. The man of my dreams.

'You're dead to me,' I said.

CHAPTER FOUR

I needed to get out of that insane asylum. I needed untainted air and space and silence. Another minute among those people and I would combust.

I grabbed my bag and forced my way back through the party and out the main entrance of the house. The driveway was jammed with luxury cars; more vehicles were parked haphazardly on the grass surrounds. I started walking down the drive, fast and hard, needing the reassurance of hearing my footsteps on the tarmac. *Slap, slap, slap.*

A dark figure suddenly straightened up in the shadows by the side of the drive. My insides lurched. But it was the boy-bander I'd stumbled into earlier. He'd been rummaging in the front of his car, which was parked on the slope.

'Sorry,' he said, holding up his hands. 'Didn't meant to startle you. I was just getting my charger … Hey! It's you again. You know, you really don't seem OK.'

I stared back blankly. 'It's been a bad night.'

'Has it? I'm sorry. I know who you are. You're Lucie. Lily, I mean. Lily Thane. You and Adam used to date.'

I did a half-shrug of acknowledgement and started to move on.

'No, wait. Please wait. I'm only saying this cos I'm wasted, but *Snow Angels* used to be my all-time favourite film. Seriously. It wasn't just a Christmas thing for me. I'd drive my parents nuts because I'd watch it all year round. I was, like, obsessed.'

Eurgh. A fan-boy. I squinted at him. 'What are you, twelve?'

He gave a happy laugh. 'I'm twenty-one! I'm an actor too. That's how I know Adam. Well, I don't really *know* Adam. We worked on this fashion campaign a while back, and then …'

On he burbled. His name was Tig, and he looked just Adam's type: fair, slim, pouty. But straight, given the hopeful way he was appraising me.

'Can you give me a lift?'

Tig flung out his arms. 'Where to, milady?'

Good point. It was midnight and I was stranded in a salt marsh. 'There must be a hotel somewhere. Or a B & B.'

'There's only one local hotel. A bunch of us are staying there – Adam said the house wasn't really equipped for sleepovers.'

I thought of the bare echoing rooms and that ridiculous iron chair. 'No.'

'It's just down the road. I think there's supposed to be a shuttle bus?' He looked around doubtfully, then belched. 'I mean, I'm delighted to be your chauffeur, but to be honest, my fine motor skills are *fuuucked*.'

'Give me the keys,' I said brusquely. I felt bruised all over, inside and out, but I was also as sober as I'd ever been in my life.

We squeezed into the car, a beaten-up Toyota, and I – slightly nervously – pulled into the drive. When we reached the gates at the bottom, I saw there was now someone on sentry duty. He had got out of his little cabin to have words with a driver waiting to be let through. 'Cool ride,' said Tig. It was. A vintage 1970s Porsche 911S in hunter green. I recognised it because I knew the owner.

'Lily!' Nick called, leaning out of the car. 'Thank Christ. I could do with some help here.'

I rolled down my own window. Close up, I saw that the security guard was the same spotty teenager I'd seen unloading glasses from the catering van a few hours earlier.

'I'm trying to get to the party but this moron won't let me in,' Nick fumed.

'There's a password,' said the youth sulkily. 'I was told not to let anyone in without the password.'

'Lily,' said Nick, trying to sound matey. It didn't suit him. 'Help me out, would you? I really need to talk to Dido, and I know she's here.'

'I don't actually know ...'

Tig stuck his head out of the passenger window. 'It's "vanquish",' he called out helpfully.

'*Thank you.*' Nic revved the engine with unnecessary force. 'Vanquish it is.'

The sulky youth looked considerably sulkier. In the end, however, he merely pointed to the CCTV camera, in what he no doubt imagined was a threatening manner, before returning to his box to press the button for the gates. I reversed – cursing and stalling – into the verge so that Nick could drive through.

Without so much as a wave of acknowledgement, he tore up the drive and then came to a screeching halt outside the house, boxing in all the other cars. As I inched back onto the road, I started laughing to myself.

'What's so funny?' asked my new friend.

'Adam's night is about to get a lot more complicated.'

The hotel was the other side of the village and chintzy as hell. 'Night cap?' Tig asked, predictably, as I was being told, predictably, by the yawning concierge that they were at full capacity. So we went up to Tig's room and raided the mini-bar. I'd already decided I was going to have to sleep with him, which meant I was going to have to have a drink. It wasn't the worst idea in the world. I hadn't had sex for over a year, and as aspiring models-slash-actors go Tig wasn't so bad. Soft skinned and puppy-ish and eager to please. In bed, he kept calling me 'Lucie', but he was hardly the first, and at least he was drunk enough to make the slip borderline acceptable. I writhed about and made the requisite sounds and faces, and let him spoon me afterwards, so I suppose he was happy enough.

I couldn't sleep. The hot meat of Tig's body was uncomfortably packed against mine, my head pulsed, and my mouth tasted as fetid as my thoughts. After a couple of hours of fitful dozing I woke up for good.

I lay listening to Tig's bubbling snores and let the self-loathing wash over me. What had I been thinking, coming out here? How could I hate on Adam's machinations when I was – *literally* – tripping over myself in my eagerness for humiliation? I wasn't just a dupe; I was a masochist.

All I'd had was a couple of drinks but I was crashing hard: hollowed out and twitchy, suffused with dread. I had a looming sense of having made an undefined yet soul-shredding mistake.

169

And I couldn't shake the idea that some kind of retribution was coming.

Dawn was breaking; I reached for my phone to check the time. Half-past five. Then I saw a message from Dido, sent two hours earlier.

I want to talk to you.
I did something dreadful
Are you still here?

It was almost a relief, knowing my foreboding was justified. I remembered seeing Nick drive furiously up the drive, and how I'd laughed. My thoughts were foggy – the flickering shape of my fears was just out of reach – but I was now gripped by the certainty that a catastrophe was coming. Or had, in fact, already arrived.

I called Dido but her phone was switched off. I didn't have Nick's number. I hesitated, then tried Adam. No answer. I lay in bed for a minute or so more, heart racing. Tig let out a slobbering groan and burrowed himself deeper into the bed.

I got up and gulped down some water. I didn't stop to shower or brush my teeth, just pulled on some clothes and stuffed the rest of my things into the bag. The house was only a couple of miles or so away; if I walked fast, I could be there in half an hour.

It was a beautiful early summer's morning, the sky limpid with the promise of brightness to come. The village streets were deserted, and so was the bus stop where I'd disembarked. I've never trusted the quiet of the countryside, and now I was thinking of horror movies – that shot filled with sunshine and birdsong and waving grasses, just before the zombie hordes burst out of a wood.

The walk took longer than I thought and it was just past seven when I reached the house. The teenage guard had left his post but someone had helpfully propped the gate open with a traffic cone.

The light was growing richer by the minute, but the shadows were still cold and blue; walking under the trees, the air felt liquid. A number of cars were parked in the driveway but I didn't see Nick's Porsche. I didn't know if this was a good or bad sign. (What, even, was I expecting to find – smashed windows? Shell-shocked bystanders? Dido wringing her blood-spattered hands?) I tried the front door but to my surprise it was locked. The place seemed even more lifeless than when I'd first arrived.

No matter – I knew another way in. I walked around to the salt-marsh side, following the little path to the studio by the pine wood and the garden gate. The door to the studio was wide open, so I decided to risk putting my head round. It was unoccupied and in the same sort of disarray as the hotel rooms I'd shared with Adam – scattered clothes, bottles, glasses. The bottle of painkillers lay empty on the threshold; I recognised the label.

My foot crunched on something in the deck. A couple of little yellow tablets lay on the wooden slats. I picked one up and slipped it into my bag for later, just in case. The headache had receded to a distant throb but I liked the idea of having something knock-out in reserve. Adam's amethysts glinted on my hand. I'd had a notion of hurling the ring into the marsh, but maybe it was best to keep it as a reminder: All That Glisters Turns to Shit.

Now I was here, it should've been easier to dismiss my fears. Dido was prone to theatrics. She and Nick were probably long gone. It was hardly surprising there were no signs of life: the last of the revellers had likely only just gone to bed. Which was just as well, because I definitely didn't want to run into Adam. Or Nina. Or Zalandra. Or anyone. I'd take a quick peek inside, then head back to the bus stop.

How sensible this train of thought seemed. Yet it failed to distract me from the thread of fear that was winding its way, tighter and tighter, around my skin.

I pushed open the gate to the walled garden.

The swimming-pool enclosure basked in the morning sun. The paved surrounds bore testament to a successful party: more empty bottles, more glasses; an upturned trilby used as an ashtray. A black lace thong was puddled on one side, next to a curiously neat pool of vomit.

And there, in the water, the body.

A man in briefs and an open shirt.

Not floating, but suspended in the depths, face down.

Later, I learned that dead bodies only float once they start to decay. It's the putrefying gases that make them buoyant. There was no breeze that day and the water was perfectly still, so when I found Adam, he was more like something encased in ice or glass. His skin was pearlescent; the frozen billow of his shirt was pale; the frozen drift of his hair was dark. The mirrored lining of the pool meant he was hanging over his own distorted reflection. I could see his shadow in the sides of the pool, too; indistinct as an echo.

My first impulse was to dive in. Not to rescue Adam – he was clearly beyond that. But the water was so beautiful. It must be peaceful to be held, gently and silently, in its shining depths.

My second impulse was to walk away. I had come through the briars and found the enchanted castle with its sleeping prince. I didn't want to be the one to break the spell.

I didn't want this to be my story.

For a long time, I stood beside the water and wept. My cries sounded thin and trivial, swallowed up by the landscape and the stillness of the morning. After a while I grew ashamed of the sound.

Then I walked through the second garden and slid open the doors to the dreaming house. There were six or seven bodies passed out on the ground floor. I realised that the front door had never been locked – an iron coat stand had simply fallen across it. I righted the stand and felt a brief glow of accomplishment. *There.*

I wiped my wet cheeks.

I could just go, I thought. I could just walk through the door and forget I'd seen any of this. I could head straight to London or back to Tig. He probably wouldn't even know I'd been gone. A warm body in a soft bed wasn't such a bad prospect right now. And I was so, so, so tired.

I went back to the main reception room. The blinds were drawn and it was comfortingly dim. Sarah and her beardy hook-up were entwined on the couch, half-unclothed and snoring gently in their sleep. Stassia's fur coat was in a chocolatey heap by the fireplace.

I lay down on the floor and curled myself into a ball under the coat. It was perfumed and silken yet unmistakeably animal. I closed my eyes, gripped Adam's ring and held it to my quaking chest, and despite it all, despite everything, I fell asleep.

CHAPTER FIVE

You're dead to me.

And now he truly was. To me, to everyone. A tabloid cliché, a cautionary tale. Another sad little entry for the listicles: 'Top Twenty Celebs Killed By Drugs!'

The official cause of Adam's death was accidental drowning, but according to the coroner's report, the major contributing factor was 'mixed drug toxicity' from the fentanyl, cocaine and alcohol found in his system. Most likely Adam had started to feel unwell shortly before going to bed. He would have experienced chest pains, dizziness and difficulty breathing. He would have then stumbled out of the studio and towards the house in search of help, but suffered a seizure at the side of the pool. Water found in his lungs indicated that he was alive when he hit the water. However, the inquest concluded that unless he'd received immediate medical attention, his level of drug intoxication was likely lethal in any case.

Police said an investigation into who supplied the drugs to Adam was ongoing. Evidence of drugs and drug-taking paraphernalia had been found at the property where the fateful party took place, but no arrests had been made so far.

I accept that the image I have – the sleeping prince in the embrace of water – is false. It didn't represent Adam's last moments: sluggish, stumbling, alone and terrified, as his skin sweated ice and the breath squeezed from his lungs. But when I try to picture the moment of his death, my mind confuses two swimming pools. The mirrored basin in a pale Norfolk dawn. The scoop of turquoise shimmer under Californian stars. And I see Adam's face reflected in both pools as he falls to his ruin, eyes widened at his own tragedy and bluer than both waters had any hope to be.

All the same, it could've been worse. He could have been found in dirty bed-sheets, slumped in a pool of his own sick, with purple lips.

I know he would have wanted to leave a beautiful corpse.

I don't know who, exactly, of the other party guests found him, but I woke up to screams. Sarah was on her knees, half-naked and crying and vomiting with equal vigour, as her bearded friend held back her hair. Even so, there was a split-second, before I remembered, when it could have been the aftermath of any averagely regrettable night. I'd already woken up once that day, disoriented and aching, with a rancid taste in my mouth and a foggy sense of doom. I sat for a few moments, huddled in my borrowed furs, rubbing my face, as strangers rushed around crying and wailing and shouting at one another.

When I'd first re-entered the house, the sleeping bodies had seemed like courtiers under an enchantment. Smooth faces, languorous limbs, soft sighs. Now they looked as crumpled and seedy as I did, their panicked faces still creased from sleep.

Zalandra wasn't there, thank God. Neither was Nina, nor Nick. Dido stumbled in at some point and I suppose it was a testament to the gravity of the situation that she didn't appear as the Great Tragedian Lamenting a Death. She was just another shaken, upset woman with a hangover.

'I got your text,' I said, in one of the strange, small lulls. 'Is everything OK?'

She blinked at me. Maybe she thought the question was inappropriate, given the circumstances. 'I was a total bitch to Nick. Did he tell you?'

I shook my head.

'In spite of everything, I wish – I wish he was here.'

She began to sob. I'd only ever seen her do it on stage before.

Talia arrived just as the paramedics were moving Adam's body into the ambulance. It was a little after nine; she'd set off from London early to surprise us, loading up her car with crates of breakfast pastries. She's there in one of the photos some dickhead leaked to the press, flying towards the body on the stretcher, arms outstretched, mouth open in an animal howl. If you look closely, there's a smudge of white powder around her upper lip. This was the subject of much unkind speculation online. Actually, it was confectionery sugar from one of her vegan croissants. This detail struck me as particularly sad and absurd and very Talia, somehow.

Before the emergency services arrived, efforts were made to remove some of the evidence of the night's hedonism. The air churned with the sound of flushing toilets. Yes, I told the police officer who took my statement, I was aware Adam used drugs, though he had told me he was cutting down. He had not overdosed in the past to the best of my knowledge.

Had I witnessed him taking drugs during the party?

I hadn't. When I'd talked to him, Adam had seemed disconcertingly sober, in fact. I told the officer about the goodie bag, though. I knew my prints must be all over it. I went through the stuff, I explained, because I was looking for a painkiller for my headache.

Did I take anything from the bag?

No, I said. I couldn't find any paracetamol.

I'm not entirely sure why I lied about this. I hadn't done anything wrong. I guess I just wanted to keep as much of a distance from the whole horrible mess as possible. I'd already lied about not finding the body for the same reason.

I was staying with a friend in the hotel, I said, but couldn't sleep. I decided to walk over to the house for breakfast and to say goodbye to Adam. When I got there, the blinds were drawn and it was clear everyone was sleeping off their hangovers. I myself drifted off while waiting for others to wake up or arrive.

I was asked about the cut on my head and mentioned my argument with Adam of my own accord, in case the other witnesses brought it up. Rationally, I knew I wasn't a suspect, and in any case this was the scene of a tragic accident, not a crime, but I felt so guilty about so many things I fretted I was acting out a parody of innocence. Hamming it up, like a bit-player on some naff cop show.

I explained I was still upset at how Adam had ended things. He wanted to apologise to me, but I was feeling too emotional to hear him out. That was when I left the party. With my new friend.

I blushed despite myself.

The police officer was middle-aged and broad-bosomed, with one of those no-nonsense, Nanny-knows-best faces. I had to suppress the mad urge to ask her for a hug. 'You're an actress?' she said, as she checked over my details. She sucked her teeth. 'There's a lot of it about.'

I spent the days following Adam's death hiding out in Aunt Naomi and Uncle Felix's holiday cottage in Brecon. The Momager stopped by my flat to collect some things and told me, gleefully, that the entire street was besieged by the press.

Dido's parents do their virtue-signalling through the rejection of worldly comforts. The cottage was furnished with a few spindly bits of furniture and a great deal of ugly abstract art; even the magazines in the loo were relentlessly high-minded. The broadband was negligible, which, apart from not being able to watch anything on my laptop (obviously there was no TV), suited me fine. I had no desire to check the news or refresh my inbox. There was an unironically retro shop in the village, and I binged on Vesta curries and Angel Delight and went for bracing walks in Dido's oversized galoshes.

The only person I tried to contact was Talia. Every morning for a week, I trudged up to the top of a soggy hill behind the house in search of a signal so I could either message her or check for a reply. She didn't respond except for this one line, the first I'd received from her that didn't have a single emoji.

why didn't you look after him

Pa visited on week two, trailing the air of befuddled benevolence he puts on when he wants to avoid talking about anything difficult.

It was a relief when he left. Shortly afterwards, though, he returned with the Momager. It's hard to say which she despises more – country living or her ex – so making the trip was a mark of how seriously she was taking the situation. She'd come to inform me in person that Adam's funeral had been delayed by the post-mortem, which had at least given the powers-that-be plenty of time to coordinate a suitably starry guest list. I hadn't made the cut. However, she'd somehow managed to find out all the details anyway. It was, she said, my duty to gatecrash the event. 'You *deserve* to be there. Poor Adam would have wanted it, I'm convinced. You *earned* the right. And besides, if you stay holed up here, you might as well be in your own mausoleum.'

I looked out to where Pa was waiting in the car in the muddy yard; the surrounding trees were misted with drizzle. It was July, but I still had the single-bar electric heater on. We were sitting on a sofa as bony as Aunt Naomi's chest; a battered copy of the *Collected Works of Bertolt Brecht* awaited me on the side-table. My mother had a point.

I dressed for the funeral with care. I couldn't afford a repeat of my beaten-up bag-lady/crazy-ex-girlfriend cameo. My black dress was discreetly form-fitting, my make-up subtle yet flattering. Still, my face in the mirror looked wan. *Tired is halfway to old*, I mouthed to my reflection. My heart clenched. *But old is still better than dead.*

Adam's funeral was held at a big Catholic church in North London. There were actual security guards at the churchyard gates. I'd assumed slipping in at the back wouldn't be such a big deal, but now I had cold feet – what if Victor Green and/or Talia were sufficiently pissed at me to circulate an 'access denied' mug shot? A knot of photographers was already in position – getting thrown out of my ex-boyfriend's funeral would make for some gnarly headlines. I loitered on the pavement some way down from the church, pretending to check my phone, but I guess my uncertainty was a giveaway. 'So you aren't on the list either,' said Rafael, suddenly appearing at my side.

'No.'

We looked at each other.

'I'm sorry for your loss,' I said formally.

'Adam was always lost to me.' Rafael was impassive. 'I think you were right, out in LA. You told me friends don't hurt each other. Adam and I ... we were not friends at the end. And I wished him a world of pain.'

'I can understand that.'

'Maybe so.' He cocked his head towards the bouncers. 'We shall go in together, huh? In the clubs, they always let in the man with the pretty girl.'

It was the first time I'd seen a glint of humour in him. He was right, too. We didn't have any trouble. In the church, he gave me a slight nod of acknowledgement before parting ways.

I had arrived early but there were already plenty of other people eager to get front-row seats. Adam would have approved of the turn-out; it was a good-looking crowd with more than a sprinkle of famous faces. One profile in particular caught my eye.

'Hi, cuz.' I slid into Dido's pew, forcing her to budge up.

'Oh ... Lily...' she said vaguely, as if she needed to take a moment to remember who I was. 'I'm so sorry. How are you bearing up?'

'OK, I guess. I still can't quite believe it.'

Dido nodded. She looked more obviously bereft than I did. She's always pale but today her face was positively greenish, and she was wearing a severely belted monastic outfit that looked as if it had come straight off her stint in *Mourning Becomes Electra*.

'I'm sorry,' she said again. 'I meant to be in touch. I should have been in touch. It's just … not been a good time.' She looked down at her hands. 'Nick and I are separating.'

'That's very sad news.'

'It seems rather inconsequential on an occasion like this.' Her hands were fidgeting and she stilled them with visible effort. 'But you should know our marriage difficulties didn't have anything to do with Adam. There have always been a number of incompatibilities. Nick wants children, for one. As for the rest … well. It's for the best.'

I murmured some vague commiseration.

Everyone was now in their seats, and the organ music was swelling in a gloomily climactic sort of way. It could have been the soundtrack to my walk back to the house by the salt marsh. That sunny June morning, saturated with impending doom.

'So that text, the text you sent me the night Adam died … about doing something dreadful?'

She frowned. 'I already told you, didn't I? Nick gatecrashed the party and I got very angry and told him, in front of everyone, that it was over. So I publicly humiliated him, on top of everything else. It was very wrong of me. I don't know why I reached out to you in the aftermath. I suppose I thought you might help calm him down … Nick's always been rather fond of you.'

This was news to me. Still, the coffin was about to make its grand entrance. The audience got to its feet, rustling with anticipation. Even Dido brightened. 'Showtime,' she said.

I'd already mourned for Adam. I'd wrung out the last of my tears beside the swimming pool. I spent his funeral and its aftermath dry-eyed. Watchful.

Adam's sister was got up like a Mafia widow, in defiantly slutty black. The mother was glazed and probably drugged. His dad just looked angry. His popping eyes darted here and there, shoulders squared belligerently, face red. Talia was also sitting in the front row, though across the aisle from the family. She was with her mother, the aristo-model, who looked about her with a brightly social air, nodding to people she recognised and occasionally giving a queenly wave. Talia looked pale and shrunken beside her. If anyone came up to her, she was like a rabbit in the headlights. No wonder. This hadn't been in the contract.

The reception was just for immediate family, which meant that after the service ended people were not quite ready to disperse. Laughter, insider chat and lots of enthusiastic air-kissing gave the churchyard an oddly festive atmosphere. Victor saw me and pursed his mouth before pointedly turning away. Grace Tang and Kat Knightly, Adam's US agent, whom I'd met several times, looked straight through me before going back to efficiently working the crowd. I even spotted Zalandra, talking to one of the Penfold Green PAs.

That gave me pause. Zalandra hadn't been in the house when Adam's body had been found. Which was just as well – there would probably have been some kind of confrontation between us, and the police would have turned up to find us mid-brawl. Finding her here, I wouldn't have been surprised if she'd launched herself at Adam's coffin, tearing her hair and beating her breast, while bawling out gobbets of the *Wylderness* script. Instead, she was making conversation like a normal person. Her black garb didn't look out of place for once and her cheeks had a bit of colour in them; she seemed almost animated.

She'd been invited to the funeral and I hadn't. I was the ghost now.

I turned to leave before Zalandra could spot me, only to feel pointy nails digging into my arm. Sarah had her brother's blue eyes; their bloodshot glare was disconcertingly reminiscent of how he used to look at me when things got bad. 'Don't expect an appearance fee,' she hissed.

'I beg your pardon?'

'That's the only reason you're here, isn't it? To get a pap shot in the papers.'

'That's not true. I cared for Adam very much. He was –'

'He was a fag,' she said savagely. 'And now we find out he was a junkie as well. They –' she jerked her thumb at her parents '– won't admit it but they've always known, same as me.'

'I don't think we should –'

'All the deception, all the lies, and he still acted like God's gift. Even as a kid. Treated us like shit. You too, I'll bet. Traded you in for a younger, dumber model. That's Adam. My brother played us all for fools. My *brother* –'

She was crying. Proper ugly crying, with snot and running mascara and gasps that turned to howls.

'I'm so sorry,' I said, and fled.

CHAPTER SIX

Maybe Zalandra had spotted me at the funeral after all.

I answered the door to a delivery the next morning. It was a florist's box. I opened it to find a bunch of rotting vegetation, crawling with flies and stinking of decay. The sender hadn't skimped: there were the remains of roses, lilies and some kind of fern, tied up with a glossy ribbon. Now it was just a box of rot. There was a card: *Death Is Not the End*.

I took a photo as a record, then threw it in the bin and phoned the courier company. They were predictably useless. So were the florists who'd originally supplied the bouquet. Not that it took a genius to work out who'd sent it. But if Zalandra was moving her attentions from Adam to me, I knew I needed proof of harassment. The really scary thing was that she'd found out my address.

The Momager's arrival was a welcome diversion. She'd come to gloat over press coverage of the funeral. 'If anything, you were a little bit *too* composed, but you looked positively Hepburn-esque in that dress. I don't know what Talia was thinking. Obviously, she's milking her fifteen minutes, but couldn't she do it in a more dignified fashion? At the very least she could have brushed her hair … And Dido! I don't care how many Oliviers the girl has. That nun-on-the-run costume was indefensible.'

It was a red-carpet fashion blog come to life.

'Dido could've been in character.' Might as well get it over with. 'Before he died, Adam helped her sign up to Kash Malik's new film – it's about the friendship between a bereaved alcoholic and the ghost of Dorothy Parker. Dido's the alcoholic,' I added unnecessarily. My cousin is not known for her comic timing.

The Momager let out a muffled groan. 'Please don't torment me with the opportunities you squandered. Your failure to persuade Adam to take you seriously –' She pinched the bridge of her nose, sighing. 'I'm sorry. The man was an addict. Of course his judgement was impaired; why else would he date that ridiculous Bratz doll? Besides, recriminations are pointless at this stage.' She stuck on a bravely determined smile. 'We need to look ahead. *The Other Women* airs in a couple of weeks. You can still have the last laugh.'

At who? Dido was unlikely to be threatened by what the *Radio Times* described as 'a campy yet addictive melodrama'. As for Adam … I'd already had the last word, and it wasn't a laughing matter.

'I'm in three episodes.'

'Of an international hit – and you're the major plot twist, for goodness' sake. *And* you're in negotiations to join the main cast for the third season. All we're waiting for is the series to be officially renewed. Which everyone's clearly banking on, given the final cliffhanger.'

Fine. OK, so *The Other Women* wasn't a multi-million-dollar, genre-bending juggernaut like *Hollow Moon*. Or an angsty auteur masterpiece with a comic edge, à la Kash Malik. But there was a time when I would've been more than happy to be part of a mainstream TV show again. This was my level, wasn't it? Light entertainment. A guilty pleasure.

'And I have another opportunity for you,' the Momager said brightly.

'Not that ITV beauty-salon thing? Judy already sent me the script. It stinks.'

'Oh, this isn't an acting job, or not acting *per se*. Remember my friend Maddie? Well, she's like a *sister* to Danny Bowers. You know – the Olympian. Rowing, I think it was. Though he's more famous for his TV appearances these days.'

I nodded. I was familiar with the gold-medallist host of *The Danny Bowers Show*. Everyone was.

'Obviously you've had other things on your mind lately, so you may have missed the scandal, but his wife only went and ran off with this *builder* person. He was supposed to be renovating their house! It was very humiliating. The press went *mad*. Dan is heartbroken, according to Maddie. Utterly devastated. It's almost been like a bereavement.'

'Mm. Poor him.'

'Well, I can't help thinking that the two of you have quite a lot in common at the moment.'

'I'm really not looking to date anyone right now. I need to focus on getting my life back on track and –'

'Silly girl!' The Momager let out a peal of laughter. 'I'm not trying to set you up, you goose. Not *romantically*. Dan is in need of a different kind of companionship. Someone to cheer him up, be a plus one to events and so forth, to show the world that he's moved on, that he's doing *really well* for himself.'

Oh. 'Another fauxmance? Wasn't the last one enough of a dumpster fire?'

'Ah, but *this* will be completely different. Poor Adam was a very troubled soul. So many demons. Dan's not a homosexual, thank heavens. Or an addict. He's a lovely, lovely man, and I think the two of you would get on like a house on fire. No dumpsters in sight.

'Maddie says he is absolutely not looking for a relationship. He just wants a safe space, really. A change of narrative. You can relate to this, surely? It would make for such a nice story. How the two of you comforted each other in your darkest hour. How a friendship forged from mutual loss blossomed into –'

'Enough with the Mills & Boon tag lines. Why me?'

'Oh, well, it was Maddie's idea. Or practically hers. I *may* have given her a little nudge.' The Momager looked mischievous. 'In any case, she says Dan's always admired you from afar. Don't forget: whatever his personal failings, Adam did raise your profile in a very flattering way.'

I closed my eyes. 'So we'd aim to start dating when *The Other Women* drops?'

'Exactly! It will create a lovely buzz for your new project at the same time as distracting the press from Dan's marital meltdown. Everyone wins.' She sighed happily. 'And unlike with Adam, of course, there's always the possibility that a union of convenience could grow into something more …'

'Don't go there.'

'Just meet with him, sweetie. See what the chemistry's like. That's all I ask.'

———

Going into the house where I would meet Dan Bowers for the first time, I thought of Adam. *This is how all relationships start: first an audition, then a performance.* And the look he'd given me – a match struck behind his eyes.

All those air-conditioned SUVs and five-star hotel rooms. Red carpets and ropes and lips. Flashing cameras, clapping hands; a sea of faces that were envious, enthralled … The finery was borrowed and the glory reflected. But it had still been my biggest role. I'd played my heart out for it.

Adam had liked to talk about fame. Not just about how to get it, but what it meant. He once compared it to when people stroke parts of bronze statues for luck. 'It's kind of a fetish. And it's probably not great for the statues – it causes erosion or whatever. But the idea of all those thousands of sweaty, hopeful hands rubbing away till your dark outer layer's worn off, and there's this patch of shiny gold … who wouldn't want to be that kind of talisman?'

I hadn't been the casting director's first choice for *Hollow Moon* or *The Other Women*. The first opportunity had been manipulated. The second was a fluke. I hadn't even been accepted onto the screenwriting course I'd wanted (my sample pages had been dismissed as 'emotionally immature'). But Adam had chosen me, and Dan Bowers would choose me too. I was suddenly set on it.

We met at my mother's friend Maddie's house, in the company of our agents, though it was the Momager and Maddie who were running the show. They presided over the introductions with arch smiles and roguish twinkles, like a couple of cut-price Mrs Bennets.

I'd have been intrigued to meet Dan in any event. After his Olympic success, he'd done stints on the usual sports-based panel and game shows. He was an ambassador for various good causes and regularly co-presented charity telethons. But for the last two years, he'd been the host of his own Friday-night chat show, an unexpected ratings hit. He wasn't charming so much as warmly straightforward, free from the insider smugness of other celebrity hosts. Viewers thought he was one of them, despite the medals and the CBE and the public-school education.

It didn't hurt that he was handsome. Not Adam handsome: something more lived-in and approachable. Pushing forty, he had one of those craggy yet boyish faces, with tufty blond hair only just beginning to fade and humorous crinkles around his eyes.

Introductions made, it was agreed that Dan and I be left alone to 'get acquainted' in Maddie's over-stuffed drawing room. We'd got through the initial chit-chat easily enough, but as soon as the door shut behind our various representatives there was a crashing silence. We both avoided the other's eye. I had to fight the urge to giggle.

'Well. This is awkward.' Dan cleared his throat. 'You ever done something like this before, Lily?'

My insides clenched. 'God, no. I've, uh, heard about this kind of arrangement, though. Friends of friends and so on.'

'My agent assures me it's a lot more common than people think.' He grimaced. 'The last few months have been a steep learning curve – turns out I've been hopelessly naïve about a lot of things.'

'Yeah, it must have been really rough.' I sat down on a chair and put on my best chat-show-host face. One part sympathetic to two parts inveigling.

Taking his cue, Dan sat down opposite me. His shoulders slumped. 'I never saw it coming. That's the thing. People this

190

happens to often say, oh, there were signs. Not me. I thought Jenny and me were solid. Better than that: golden.'

I nodded. His wife was a former model turned sports psychologist; they'd been together for fifteen years. I'd looked up photos of the family in happier times: hunky husband, gorgeous wife, adorable two-year-old. There was even a dog – a frolicsome golden retriever, straight out of central casting.

'Everyone thinks I'm the nice guy. It's my brand. So when my wife runs off … That makes me *too* nice, right? That makes me a loser. The press … it hardly seems to matter that they've taken my side. Five months on, it still feels relentless. They've ambushed my cleaner. Dredged up old girlfriends. Doorstepped my mum. They're pushing this narrative that I'm humiliated and broken and alone. And the takeaway is shit like this shouldn't happen to studs like me. So, you know, "What must be wrong with Danny Bowers?"'

'That's awful.'

He shook his head. 'No, I'm sorry. I shouldn't be making this all about me. You've gone through such a lot yourself, and the press have been stalking you too. I understand you were at the actual party where your – where Adam died. That must have been unbelievably traumatic.'

He sounded sincere. Everyone did. The cast and crew on *The Other Women*, my extended family, random strangers at the checkout. Everyone seemed genuinely upset for me. It only made my standard response feel even more stagey. 'Obviously we weren't together at the time, and I knew Adam had his struggles. But I still cared for him deeply. I mean, we first met back at school. We meant a lot to each other. It's been very hard.'

I felt more of a fraud in the aftermath of Adam's death then I ever had during his life. Which was stupid, really. Like Talia said, just because we never slept together didn't mean our relationship wasn't real.

The trouble was, I was still furious with him. For the way he'd treated me and the way he'd treated himself. Carelessly. Wilfully. With cruel abandon.

It took a momentary effort to refocus on Dan. 'What do you want from this?' I asked, more bluntly than I intended.

'I want people to stop thinking of me as some loser who couldn't keep his wife.' He paused. 'And, yeah, I want my ex to be pissed. Without me having to go through the drama of plunging into a potentially messy new relationship. I think …' He laughed shortly. 'I think my management team are worried I'm going to run off to some club and get blind drunk and shag one of those *Love Island* slags. Ruin the brand.'

Shag. Slag. The words were curiously old school. They didn't suit him.

'Basically, I'm looking for an ally. Someone to help keep my life – or my life in the limelight – upbeat and uncomplicated. Is that a cop-out?'

'Not at all. It makes a lot of sense.'

'And you, Lily? Why are you doing this?'

I paused. It was important I got this right. 'Adam and I … his death … I'm feeling a little raw, I guess. I'm not ready to date for real either. But I want to change my story all the same. I want to be associated with positive things.'

'No more pity?'

'No more pity.'

My meeting with Dan Bowers took place the same day as the coroner's verdict at the inquest into Adam's death. I was doing my best to ignore it. I knew my witness statement had been read out as part of the evidence on Adam's drug-taking, and part of me felt like a narc. We all knew what killed him; I didn't need to hear it made official.

But there was no escaping the verdict – it was on the radio in the taxi home. 'Counterfeit pharmaceutical pills are especially dangerous because users are unable to be sure of what they're taking,' the newsreader intoned gravely.

I visualised the little yellow tablets in Adam's goodie bag. It turned out they'd been laced with fentanyl. I'd thought my dizziness, and the reason the painkiller had knocked me out for so long, was because I was part-concussed. Now I realised how lucky I'd been. If I'd had any other drugs or alcohol in my system it could have been a different story. I shivered and huddled into my coat.

'You all right, miss?' asked the driver, eyeing me in the mirror.

'Sure,' I said, pulling my hat lower down over my face. The radio programme was recapping Adam's career, culminating with the news he'd been cast as Luke Zane – 'the thinking person's action hero' – in the week before his death. Of course, it made an even more piquant story for Adam to die on the cusp of stardom. As far as cautionary tales go, it would make the perfect Lifetime movie. If the writers got a move on, I could even play myself.

We didn't hear from Dan Bowers for over a week. Apparently he was meeting two other candidates. This depressed me far more than was reasonable. I was in need of distraction: too long on my own and my thoughts circled back to the rotting floral bouquet, and whether I was going to wake up one night to find Zalandra standing at the foot of my bed. But that Friday evening the Momager came round to give me the happy news in person. 'The other girls were never serious contenders – a couple of wannabes dredged up by his agent. Maddie assures me *you* were always the front-runner. Dan's feeling very happy, very positive about the arrangement.'

'That's good. So am I.'

'Though the feedback was that you were looking just a teensy bit tired when you met …'

'Dan said that?'

The Momager placed her fingertip on the space between my brows. 'It's this little line here. Easily fixed. And maybe it's time for you to go a shade blonder, hm? The ex is a brunette, of course. Good to play up the contrasts. You'll make such an attractive couple.'

I nodded. I'd be safe with Dan. His vulnerabilities weren't razor edged. His hurt was soft, like bruised fruit. Everything else about him was reassuringly solid. I thought of the way he reddened slightly when he caught my eye, and I smiled in spite of myself.

The Momager was determined we should celebrate: 'A girls' night out, at the Savoy, just like the old days!'

It used to be a tradition of ours, dating all the way back to *Snow Angels*. Every time I booked a job, my mother and I would get dolled

194

up and go to the Savoy for afternoon tea. Later, this became drinks at the Beaufort Bar. We hadn't done it for ages. The last time I'd gone to the Savoy it had been in the early days with Adam, and we'd drunk Hanky-Panky cocktails and done lines in the loos. Thanks to the magical powder, I'd found the alcohol tasted even better – more refreshing, more *crucial* somehow. Breathing became intense on cocaine, like I could really *feel* the air being pulled into my body. Throw a cigarette into the mix, and it was perfect. Like new life for my lungs! I remember telling Adam this, very excitedly, and him laughing at me. Then he'd kissed me on the nose and told me I was the bestest, prettiest, funniest Girl Friday a guy could have.

'Go on, sweetie, put on your glad rags,' the Momager urged. 'I want to show you off. My gorgeous, talented daughter. My daughter the *star*.'

On one hand, I knew this was every kind of pathetic. A fake relationship and a cheesy TV show weren't anything to boast about. Still, I couldn't remember the last time I'd felt carefree enough to dress up for drinks at a swanky hotel. And then there was the way the Momager was looking at me – her whole face lit up, joy and pride glowing from every pore. Nobody else has ever looked at me this way, except for Adam, and he was pretending. The Momager could have been performing too. But that still made it an act of love.

So I went into my bedroom and set about selecting a dress. I also decided I'd wear Adam's ring. It had symbolised a lot of things over the short time I'd worn it; as a memento mori, it could be liberating.

I spent some time rummaging through my jewellery box before remembering I'd put the ring in the shoulder bag I'd

195

worn at Adam's party and shoved them both on the top of the wardrobe. I hadn't wanted any visible reminders of my time in Norfolk. I recovered the bag and tipped out the contents over the bed. The green amethysts glittered in a wad of receipts, chewing gum wrappers, tissues and lint.

But there was something else there too. A yellow pill.

It was the tablet I'd picked up from the deck outside Adam's studio, thinking it was an ordinary painkiller. I'd saved it for later and then completely forgotten about it.

A little dose of poison, lying on my bed.

I shrank back, as if it might bite.

Counterfeit pharmaceutical pills are especially dangerous because users are unable to be sure of what they're taking.

Percocet is an American drug, a powerful prescription-only combination of oxycodone and paracetamol; I was familiar with it because Adam used the pills to manage his coke comedowns or take the edge off his day. So when I'd helped myself to his stash, I'd felt confident I knew what I was taking. After all, the pills had looked exactly as they should: pale-yellow, oblong tablets. The brand name had been stamped in capital letters on one side, the dosage (10/325) on the back. When the autopsy disclosed they were actually fakes, the extent of the risk I'd taken left me shaking.

But there was something different about this pill. Something that pulled me closer and compelled me to pick it up with infinite care, despite all my instincts telling me to grind it into dust.

It was the colour. The colour had caught my eye because it was wrong. It was a warmer, almost orangey yellow. Close up, I saw the imprint of *Percocet* was at a slight angle. The dosage stamp was so shallow it was hard to make out. The tablet seemed fatter, too, although it was hard to be sure.

But I *was* sure of two things.

One, this pill was an obvious counterfeit.

Two, it was not the same pill as the one I'd taken.

The pill I'd swallowed had looked exactly as it should because it was, in fact, the real thing. The pill I'd picked up from outside the studio was something else entirely.

Not that you'd notice the difference between the two if you were drunk and coked up at the end of an all-night party. Or exhausted and on edge and about to find a dead body in a swimming pool.

I was trembling all over now. Clammy, dizzy, short of breath … they were all the symptoms of a fentanyl overdose. Except my heart was racing rather than slowing down.

I grabbed my phone and brought up images of Percocet, both real and faked. I read that counterfeit painkillers usually came from Mexican drug cartels or China, that fentanyl is an opioid up to fifty times more powerful than heroin, that in some cases people had overdosed and died after taking just one bad pill. But I knew most of this already. It had been part of the chatter around Adam's death. And, like most aspects of his death, I'd deliberately avoiding thinking about it too closely.

Adam was trying to ditch his habit. He'd told me he'd cut back to one or two perks at the most. There had been seven or eight pills in the bottle when I'd helped myself to one. I'd seen the bottle was empty when I came looking for Adam in the morning, but there were a number of pills fallen on the deck. I'd stepped on a couple and picked up one. It was unlikely he would have taken more than two.

How stupid I'd been. I should have known that if I'd really taken one of the pills that had contributed to Adam's death, I wouldn't just have felt a bit woozy or blacked out for a few hours. I would have fallen dangerously ill, even without any other stimulants in my bloodstream.

But I'd taken real medicine, not fentanyl, and I'd been fine. That meant the medicinal pills had been replaced with their deadly counterparts at some point after I'd left the studio.

Adam hadn't overdosed on dodgy pills sold by a dodgy dealer. He'd been deliberately poisoned.

'Sweetie! You're not even dressed! What have you been doing all this time?'

I stared at my mother as if from very far away.

'Adam was murdered,' I heard my voice say, and it too sounded as if it came from a great distance.

'Adam! Ugh. Haven't we had enough of that wretched man? Honestly, *I* could have murdered him after the way he betrayed you. But we have to move on, darling. That's what this evening is about, that's why Dan –'

'*Let me speak.*' This time, something about my face or my voice made her fall silent. I showed her the pill and then the photos on my phone, trying to order my thoughts and slow down my words so that I sounded reasonable, in control of myself and my story.

'Well?' I said at the end. 'Do you see?'

My mother sat down abruptly on the bed. 'I ... I don't understand. I don't understand any of this ...'

'It's for the police to make sense of. What should I do – make a phone call? Or do I go into a station? Should I talk to a lawyer?'

'The *police*?' She stared at me. 'Have you lost your mind?'

The yellow pill was lying on my dressing table. Before I could move, my mother swept it up and crushed it under her heel. All that horror ... reduced to a smear of yellow dust on my floorboards.

'What the actual fuck? That's evidence!'

'The only evidence it provides is of your own poor judgement.'

'Were you even listening to what I just told you?'

'Yes,' she said, rousing herself, the light of battle in her eye, 'and what I heard was a ridiculous conspiracy theory based on a half-baked memory of some illegal medication you can't be sure you took. You were *concussed*, for goodness' sake. You can't be sure of *anything*.'

I shook my head. 'No. That day, that night ... they're burned into my brain. Indelibly. I'm absolutely certain of what I'm telling you.'

'Oh, darling. Even if you're right – and I'm not saying you are – what real difference does it make? In the end, Adam's predilections would have caught up with him one way or another. These things always do.'

'Unbelievable. You're talking as if he was some hopeless smack-head. Adam was cleaning up his act. He'd got a drugs counsellor, he'd just been cast as Luke Zane, he –' I stopped. I'd been about to say *he had everything to live for*, a line straight out of a Lifetime biopic.

The Momager was in any case unimpressed. 'Mm. I heard the reason he lost out on that superhero was because rumours had got out that he'd fallen back into bad habits.'

'This is insane. Whatever his "habits", Adam didn't deserve to die –'

'And *you* don't deserve to lose everything you've ever worked for. There are rumours on the gossip sites that you aided and abetted Adam on his binges. Did you know that? It's anonymous tittle-tattle at the moment. But if you come forward, publicly admit to taking drugs with him at this party? You'll be *crucified* by the press. Your reputation will *never recover*. And neither will his – because a murder investigation will rake all over his private life. Yes. Think about that for a minute. Adam Harker will be exposed as a queer: a queer who hid his true self, who *sold his soul* for a run at the limelight. And where will that leave you?'

'It doesn't have to be like that,' I said, but my voice trembled.

'I can't bear this.' My mother put her hands over her eyes. 'It's too much. Another act of self-sabotage … *just* when things are finally looking up for you again. You've got Dan, this wonderful man, so keen to form a happy partnership with you, *and* the chance of joining the main cast of an established show. And you're about to throw it all away on some sordid drugs-and-murder scandal! Sweetheart, please. Why are you punishing yourself like this? There's nothing to be done for Adam now.'

Tears sprang in my eyes. 'Adam … Adam … Adam and I …'

'Adam was his own worst enemy. Don't get sucked back into his dysfunction. Don't get dragged through his squalor. Don't you dare. You *have* to be free of him.'

'How can I? How can I ever be free of something like this?'

'I'll tell you how.' Her mouth crooked. 'Go wash your face. Put on some make-up and some pretty clothes. Then we'll go out to drink some champagne and toast your success, and you will smile and laugh and pretend you're having a good time. Until you and I and everyone else believes it. You're a good enough actress for that, my darling.'

CHAPTER SEVEN

I did everything my mother suggested. I put on a cute little dress and heels, I went to the Savoy and drank cocktails. I posed for a selfie with the Momager and posted it on Instagram – #GirlsNightOut #LikeMotherLikeDaughter – along with some drivel about learning to #LiveLaughLove again. (Dan Bowers was among the first to ♥ it.) I smiled gaily at the pap loitering at the exit, as if he was there for me rather than waiting for a legitimately famous face to emerge.

Then I came home and ordered a family-sized takeaway of fried chicken, fries, Cherry Coke, doughnuts, the works. It tasted of stale grease and sawdust. I ate until I was bloated, gassy, my mouth and fingers shiny with oil, my stomach curdling. I threw up for what felt like hours.

My habit has never really been just about keeping the weight off. That's only a part of it. The cycle itself is addictive, the high more satisfying than any of the drugs I've dabbled in. First, there's the blackly delicious moment when you stop fighting and give into the urge. Then the visualisation of the treats to come. The drive and desperation of the execution: exhausting physical effort, climaxing in the final release. The numbness that comes after. Renewal, relaxation. My favourite kind of little death.

I didn't feel any of this this time. I felt the same. Still soiled, just even more empty.

I had my first date with Dan a few days later. His show was on a break until November, which he was relieved about, since it meant he could 'put all my energy into doing this right'. Despite his relaxed public persona, I soon realised he was a worrier. 'I'm not an actor,' he fretted. 'I don't know how convincing I'll be. I mean, you're great company and an extremely pretty girl, so it's not exactly hard to imagine dating you. But this whole set-up is so bizarre … I just worry people will catch on and we'll become some hideous meme.'

We were at Maddie's again, prepping for our first public appearance. I assured Dan we wouldn't have to put on too much of a show. Hand holding, a touch of light nuzzling, heads resting on shoulders … that was more than enough. We weren't a couple of *Love Island*ers. The key is to be relaxed in each other's company, I told him, build up a good rapport and not overthink things.

'You're a real pro,' he said, then laughed. 'Sorry. Maybe I should rephrase that.'

The joke was a little too close to the bone. All the same, this time around I was determined to be nothing but professional. Part of the service was tailoring my look to my new beau. Accordingly, my wardrobe was updated to something sweeter, sunnier and a touch preppy, to go with my newly lightened hair. 'A little less Holly Golightly, a little more Holly Willoughby,' as the Momager put it.

Everything progressed according to plan. I went for drinks with the biggest gossip in *The Other Women* cast and dropped coquettish hints about a fledgling romance, how I was finally getting over the shock of Adam's death, what a relief it was to be with someone who understood life in the eye of a media storm … The PR elves seeded 'insider' gossip and updates in the press, alongside meticulously staged photo ops in which Dan looked bashful and I looked smitten. 'The Tender Kiss That Says "I've Moved On!"' gushed the *Mail*, juxtaposing a starry-eyed photo of the two of us with a grainy picture of Dan's ex scowling at the wheel of her car.

I was still avoiding gossip sites and celeb news, but the Momager assured me I was polling very favourably with the school-run mums who were 'Danny's' key constituents. I just nodded and smiled. If Dan had a Zalandra, I didn't want to know about it.

I had received some more flowers, too.

They arrived the day after Dan and I first appeared in the press. It was the same fancy arrangement. This time, however, the flowers weren't rotten. They were just chopped up. The note read, *When You Know, You Know.*

Should I go to the police?

But where to start? What did I know about *anything*?

Every time I put my keys in the lock, I looked around me, heart jumping, half-expecting Zalandra to burst out from the shadows.

And every day, the first thing I thought of when I woke up and the last thing I saw as I closed my eyes at night was that little yellow pill.

A poison pill and mangled flowers.

———

I went back and forth over my mother's warnings but I couldn't reason all of them away. Thanks to the concussion and the drugs I *wasn't* a reliable witness; what's more, I'd lied about the pill I'd taken and I'd lied about returning to the house and finding the body. And I'd waited nearly three months to come forward with my suspicions.

I would look flaky at best, unstable at worst. But if the police did take me seriously and opened a murder investigation, then Adam's sexuality and my part in disguising it would have to come out too.

Was I prepared for this to be the role I'd be forever known for?

If I was going to risk everything to question Adam's death, then I'd like to be certain an answer would be found.

Whoever had switched Adam's painkillers knew about illegal drugs: what made them dangerous and where to source them. They also knew Adam and his habits – intimately.

'Solstice aspires to be the final word in workout luxury, offering its clientele state-of-the art equipment, a range of science-based, high-octane group classes and world-class trainers …'

I knew the blurb from Solstice Fitness's homepage off by heart. I knew the location of its gyms in California and New York and I'd read their user reviews. I knew that they were a great place for celeb spotting, but only for those prepared to hand over the exorbitant membership fees. I knew that Solstice's Vice President of Business Development was one Rafael Delgado.

I knew, too, that Solstice was opening a flagship gym in London's Soho. It would boast a swimming pool and spa area as well as a private members' lounge where, according to the *Evening Standard*, 'if you're lucky, you might just bump into one of the brand's A-list clientele'. The launch party was the first week in September. I suggested to Dan that he get on the guest list.

I'd underestimated Rafael from the start. Victor Green had represented him to me as the pill-popping bad boy who'd led Adam astray, and when I'd met him, he'd looked the part. In point of fact, he was a corporate high-flyer. But just because he had an MBA didn't mean he couldn't be a pill-popping bad boy too. Or something worse.

We arrived at the Solstice party late, because Dan had a meeting that overran. Drinks were served in the gleaming black and gold lobby by outrageously jacked-up waiters. We'd missed the raw food canapés – no great loss – but we'd missed the speeches too. I scanned the crowd for Rafael. Was it possible he was back home in LA? But no, the man was in charge of business development. He'd have to be present for Solstice's first European launch. I went up to one of the PR girls. 'Hi. I'm looking for Rafael. Is he around?'

'I think he had to take a call in the office.' She was trying to work out how important I was. 'I could go check?'

'Thank you. Tell him it's Lily. Lily Thane. I'm an old friend and … anxious … to talk.'

I went to find Dan, who was propping up the juice bar in the members' lounge, together with a couple of members of the England rugby squad. 'Sorry, babe, but I'm going to have to duck out for a bit. I've just had a message to phone my agent about a role I'm chasing.'

'Bit late for a work call, isn't it?'

'She's on American time.' I blew him a cheery kiss though my heart was racing. 'I'll be back ASAP.'

Back in the heaving lobby, the PR girl beckoned me over. Rafael had temporarily left the party to send an email but would see me in his office. Although the opportunity to talk somewhere private was even better than I'd hoped, this felt disconcertingly formal. In the event, I found him standing ready to receive me in a roped-off lounge area at the top of the stairs.

Rafael looked better than he had at the funeral: more bronzed, less drawn. His hair was no longer bleached. The suit was sharp. But he still looked like a man who spent his spare time lurking in dark alleys.

'So we're old friends, huh?'

I was glad of the noise from the party. The lights were switched off, so the area was lit by the soft glow coming from a large viewing window on the wall to my right. It overlooked the swimming pool, which was set in black marble with gold accents. The pool itself was deep cobalt. I found it hard to drag my eyes away.

'Great party,' I said lamely.

Rafael folded his arms across his chest. 'Yeah. I saw your name on the guest list. You're dating a TV sports guy now.'

'Dan. Yes.'

'Is it love?'

'It's early days.'

'Or it's a contract.' He came up very close, so close that we were almost touching. I felt that to back away would be an admission of something so I stayed motionless as he looked me over, inch by languorous inch. At one point I thought he was going to smell my hair. 'No,' he said finally. 'You're not having sex.' His lip curled. 'Aren't you tired of this half-life? Always playing pretend?'

I didn't know which stung more: the contempt or the pity. 'I'm not here to talk about my sex life. I'm here to talk about Adam.'

Rafael turned to rest his arms on the sill of the viewing window and stared down at the water. 'Isn't it time to let the dead rest?'

'I wish I could.' I licked my lips. My mouth had gone very dry. 'But I can't. Because I have a confession to make. I – I was the first person to find Adam's body, and I walked away.'

That got his attention. He was very still while I told my story. At the end of it, he was silent for a long while. 'You'd had a blow to your head,' he said at last. 'You'd taken a strong narcotic. You hadn't slept. It doesn't sound to me that you can be sure of anything.'

'So you don't think I should go to the police?'

'I didn't say that.'

He didn't say anything further, though. He was watching me, impassive again. But I could sense the thoughts moving behind his eyes, like swimmers in dark water.

'If I'm right,' I said, ploughing on, 'then the perks were swapped for the fentanyl pills at some point that night, by somebody at the party. There were maybe a hundred people there. But whoever did it knew Adam well enough to know not just about his habit, but his preferred brand of oxy.'

Rafael let out a short, harsh laugh. 'So. Naturally, you thought of Adam's bit of spic rough.'

I flushed. 'It's got nothing to do with your ... background. But your history with Adam –'

His breath hissed. 'What would you know of our "history"?'

'I know it was violent sometimes.' I swallowed. 'I heard, too, that Adam only started using when he met you.'

Rafael said something short and vicious in Spanish, then pressed his palm hard against his forehead. When he spoke again, his voice was measured, though I could hear the strain of keeping the anger out. 'Listen, *gringa*. When I first met Adam, we were kids. Barely into our twenties. We liked to party, sure. We were young and dumb. The difference is, *I* grew up. I couldn't afford not to. So now I have work, and I have play, and I know where the boundary is. What the stakes are. Adam didn't. Or perhaps he did, and he didn't care. Or else he learned too late. But that is on him. Not me. *Not me.*'

I put up my hand appeasingly. 'OK. You're right. I don't know you. And maybe I've made some shitty assumptions. But I *do* know what I've seen and heard. I heard you tell me how you don't take crap from anyone. I believed you. At the funeral, you said you wished Adam a "world of pain". And he hurt you, didn't he, that night? He *bit* you. Laughed in your face. I was there, remember.' I paused. 'And I knew Adam pretty well too. There were times …'

'Times you, too, could have murdered him?'

I searched for the right words. 'Adam was … provocative.'

'He was. He was. And if he'd provoked me enough – well.' Rafael shrugged. 'A knock-out punch? A shove to the ground? These things can be fatal in the heat of the moment. These I can imagine. But the person who changed his pills – that is a calculated act. A calculated act done by a cold person.'

'And you're not cold?'

He held my gaze. 'Not cold enough to poison my lover.'

'I'm sorry.' I shifted uncomfortably. 'I had to ask. I feel I owe Adam that much.'

The sneer was back. 'So you're gonna save the day, huh? Solve the crime, find the bad guy?'

'I don't know. I don't know what to do, but I'd like to have a better idea of what I'm getting into. If I go to the police, and if – if – they believe me, then everything blows up. I don't want Adam's other life to be exposed for nothing.'

'You don't want *your* other life to be exposed for nothing.'

'That too.' No point pretending otherwise.

Rafael blew out his cheeks. 'OK. Then I will tell you this one thing. I think ...' He was frowning, trying to decide on something. 'It's possible Adam was blackmailing someone.'

I stared. 'You're kidding. Who? *Why?*'

'I don't know. I didn't take it seriously. It was to do with his new job, the Luke Zane thing. So many auditions, so much back and forth ... but Adam was confident. This time, he said, it was in the bag. Why are you so sure, I asked. And he laughed and said he had leverage. That sometimes you have to get your hands dirty. I didn't pay him much attention. Adam talked a lot of crap a lot of the time.'

My head was spinning. 'Wow. That's ... a lot to take in.'

'Actors over-dramatise – it could be nothing. Like your story about the pills.'

'But it's something I could look into.' I said this with more confidence than I felt.

'It's your world. Not mine.'

'Right.'

Rafael glanced at his watch, straightened his jacket. I thought our interview was over. Then he cleared his throat. 'How did Adam look, when you found him?

'Peaceful.' I tried to smile. 'He looked peaceful.'

'It would have been a bad way to die. Like that, alone.' He bit his lip till the flesh whitened. 'Maybe I am not as different to you as I like to think. I have never disguised who I am, but with Adam … I hid. I played pretend. He made me lesser, and I let him. That is what I could not forgive him for. As for me – I asked him for something he was afraid to give. That made *him* lesser. And he couldn't forgive me for it, however much we tried.'

When Dan came to get me, he found the two of us side by side at the window, looking down at the pool.

'So, what, you were making your phone call and this man accosted you?'

'No. I was finishing up, and he came over to say hi. I'd met him in LA.'

'Did you know he was going to be here tonight? Is that why you wanted to get on the guest list?'

We were in a taxi on the way home. Dan seemed genuinely agitated.

I touched his hand. 'What's going on here?'

'You were gone for ages. I was worried about you. And that man looked – well, he was a pretty surly customer.'

'Rafael was a friend of Adam's. The last time I saw him was at the funeral, but we didn't get a chance to speak.'

'Oh. OK. But didn't you think how it might look? First you disappear for ages, allegedly to make a call, then I find you holed up in the dark with this guy. What if somebody else saw you?'

I stared at him. 'Dan, I'm sorry for not telling you where I was. I can see you're upset. But you've absolutely nothing to worry about. For one thing, Rafael's gay. And another –'

'Sorry. Sorry.' He put his head in his hands. 'I'm behaving like a jealous prick. Which is mad. Mad! It's just ... Jenny. I was *so clueless*. She's made me second-guess everything. I can't stand it.'

'I understand, and I'm sorry,' I said gently. 'But we're a team, remember? I've got your back and you've got mine.'

'I needed to hear that. Thank you.' He sighed. 'I know I've got trust issues and I don't want them to keep messing with my head. Trouble is, you think you know someone – and then they turn out to be a lying slut ...'

I squeezed his hand, thinking of Rafael. He'd admitted he could imagine killing Adam, but only by lashing out. A crime of passion. *Could* he be cold and calculating enough to plot his murder? My instincts said not. But I've never been a good judge of character.

CHAPTER EIGHT

Four people generally have a say in the casting process. There's the casting director, the director, the producer and the executive producer who greenlit the project. If Adam did indeed have 'leverage' in the casting of Luke Zane, then he presumably had something on one of those people.

I did an internet search to see what I could find out about *Untitled Luke Zane 3*. I'd seen the first film in the spy series, which imagined a world in which Russia had won the Cold War. They were neo-noir thrillers with brains, full of moody shots of Eastern Europe in the rain. Adam would have been the second Zane, following on from Tom Hardy. (Like Bond or Batman, the character was bigger than the actor who played him.) I wondered who he'd been up against. If Adam had sufficiently cleaned up his act, as he'd claimed, then I'd have thought he'd be the perfect fit for the role.

The casting director was one of the most established names in the business. I'd met her a couple of times, a quietly efficient, seemingly anonymous woman with an encyclopaedic knowledge of talent. But casting directors don't have the final say on who gets what part. The director had worked on the *Star Wars* franchise as well as last year's splashy George Clooney thriller. The producer had been the creator and producer of a number of high-profile TV drama series, as well as several A-lister films. The executive producer, the one who financed the movie, was the president of Scaramouche Films and had received four Oscar nominations over the course of his career.

These were serious people. Powerful people. I thought of Weinstein, setting ex-Mossad agents on those who threatened to expose him. Murder, though, was a whole other level. Even if Adam *had* blackmailed somebody to get the part, was this really motivation enough to kill him? What kind of secret had he uncovered? Was this a sex thing? A drugs thing? Or a sex, drugs and #MeToo thing?

Or was Rafael just messing with me?

I needed some kind of insider track. I needed somebody who obsessively followed every hint and whiff of celebrity scandal. I needed Nina.

Nina was a sucker for conspiracy theories as well as groundless gossip. I was pretty sure she'd dabbled with QAnon. But she also belonged to various private messaging groups for ex-Disney child actors and the like. She made connections on every project she worked on, and she'd worked on a lot of scuzzy projects with scuzzy people … people who'd once been much higher up in the Hollywood food chain before their various falls from grace. It was just possible that if there were dark whispers about any of the Luke Zane execs, then Nina might have heard them.

But Nina was a girl who nursed grudges as tenderly as children. She'd blocked and defriended me in every way possible. Our last encounter, at Adam's party, had been a disaster. I thought about asking Talia to be a go-between, but Talia still hadn't responded to any of my messages either …

My only option seemed to be staking out Nina's flat. Sunday morning, I thought, was the safest bet. It was a relief when I found her name by the door – Nina rarely stays in the same place for long – but I couldn't risk ringing the buzzer, in case she refused to let me in. So I lurked outside for the better part of two hours, waiting for her to either enter or exit. As the minutes ticked into hours, I couldn't help thinking that Luke Zane would have come up with a better plan.

Just after eleven, Nina sauntered round the corner. She was in jaunty leopard print and last night's make-up, with retro dark glasses even though it was drizzly and overcast. When she saw me she came to a dramatic halt. 'Hell no,' she said, squinting at me over the top of her glasses and wagging her finger remonstratively. 'Nope, no, *nada*. That's all I've got to say to you.'

I figured I had about thirty seconds. 'Nina, I've been a whiny, entitled little bitch. You were right about me – more right than you could ever know. But now I want to explain why.'

She squinted at me some more. I'd piqued her curiosity. And for Nina, curiosity is an itch that demands to be scratched. 'A whiny, entitled bitch you say?'

'A whiny, entitled bitch screw-up who really, really misses you.'

'Huh … it *does* sound like you have some explaining to do.' Long pause. She was chewing her lip, looking me up and down. Making me wait. 'Guess you'd better come up then.'

Up we went, into Nina's dingy studio, which she'd turned into a nest feathered with colourful drapes and fairy lights.

Nina's always had a knack of making a home for herself. She learned the trick in her child-actor days, when her seedy mother would drag her around even seedier motels during pilot season. The same small collection of home comforts followed her into trailers, onto dressing tables, even the squat she once occupied in her anarchist drama collective phase. There's a plastic figurine of Ursula the Sea Witch – her favourite Disney character. A bunch of silk daisies in a jar, their sunny yellow centres now faded and wan. A snow globe of Brooklyn Bridge. A poster of Liza Minnelli in *Cabaret*. (Nina once said that the only thing more tragic than a grown woman fixated on Marilyn Monroe is a grown woman fixated on Sally Bowles. But she's never got rid of the poster.)

'So what do you want?' she asked brusquely. She put the kettle on and started shoving tablespoons of dusty-looking instant coffee into a mug.

'I – why do you think I want something?'

'Because it suits me. I like the idea of you feeling beholden. Beholden and pathetically grateful for any scraps I drop your way.'

'OK. I want to talk to you about Adam.'

'Adam.' Nina shook herself all over. 'God. Fucking horrible, the whole thing. Poor bastard. I'm glad I wasn't there when they found him.'

'I know. I *was* there, remember.'

'Yeah. That must have been rough.'

'It was … bad. Yes.'

'Sorry.'

'Thanks.'

I looked down at my hands, uncertain how to start. Somehow this conversation was even more awkward than my encounter with Rafael.

Nina sighed gustily. 'To move things along, I might as well say that I know you were bearding for him.'

Oh. 'You do?'

'I had my suspicions from the off. Or nearly. Then I bumped into a bloke who claimed to know one of Adam's exes … well, the details don't matter. You guys put on a very convincing display of lustiness. But lustiness isn't really your style, is it, Lily?' She narrowed her eyes at me over the rim of her mug. 'And then there was Talia. That's when I smelled a hundred-per-cent rat. No way on earth those two were screwing.'

'Did Talia fess up?'

'Nope. Even now, she's sticking to her story. Love's young wet dream.'

'I'm sorry I couldn't tell you.'

'You made a deal and you honoured it. I can respect that.' Nina shrugged. 'Sure, you were actively enabling the PR bullshit machine that sweeps gay people under the carpet and into the closet. And you simulated sexual favours in exchange for work, which gives you more than a passing acquaintance with the casting couch, to my mind. But, hey … no judgement.'

'You couldn't judge me any harder than I'm judging myself.'

'Uh-huh. So how are things going with the thinking-housewife's crumpet? You know, I've always thought rowing is a very homoerotic activity. Squeezed into a tiny boat with all those muscly thighs and sweaty buttocks …'

'Dan's not gay.'

'But in convenient need of some distracting arm-candy.'

'OK, fine. Yes. There's a contract.'

'He suits you better than Adam. Mr and Ms Vanilla.'

'I'm not vanilla.'

Nina gave me a long look. 'No. That's the thing about you. You're not.'

Nina was the third person I told about the pills. Unlike the Momager and Rafael, however, she didn't wait to hear me out but jumped in at every possible moment, asking questions, swearing, exclaiming. And she was entirely convinced of the righteousness of my convictions.

She also had her own theories. 'It's Zalandra whodunit. Has to be. She's the obvious suspect if you've ruled out lover-boy.'

I'd told Nina about the flowers. I could understand if Zalandra wanted to kill me. Killing Adam, though, made no sense. 'She never made any threats against Adam. She was *in love* with him. She hates me, and probably Talia too, I don't know. But Adam – for reasons I'll never understand – had given her a job. Invited her to his party. Even told me how talented she was! That freak show was *exactly* where she wanted to be. She was living every stalker's dream.'

Much as I liked the idea of Zalandra being banged up for murder, I couldn't make it fit.

'OK. So how about the sourpuss sister? Talia seems to think the sun shines out of her arse but Talia thinks that about everyone. From what I remember, the girl spent most of that party looking like she was chewing wasps.'

'That hardly makes her a murder suspect. Adam and Sarah were on better terms than they'd been for years, and even if there wasn't much love lost between them, I can't see her killing the cash cow.' I was impatient: Nina wasn't taking this as seriously as I'd hoped. 'Let's get back to Rafael. What do you think about his blackmail theory? What could Adam possibly have on these people?'

This focused Nina's attention. We looked up the candidates on her phone. Despite everything, it felt good to be cosied up together on the ratty old couch, shooting shit just like the old days. There were moments I almost forgot what was at stake.

After our trawl through IMDb, Nina shook her head. 'The names don't ring any alarm bells. That doesn't mean anything, of course. All sorts of sickos are hiding in plain sight. But what niggles me ... these are powerful men. If some pain-in-the-ass actor was trying to mess with them, threatening to tell the wife about the mistress or whatever, surely they could squish him like a bug? Adam had plenty of dirty laundry of his own; it couldn't be hard to turn the tables on him. Or they could just hire some retired mobster to threaten to break his legs.'

I nodded. 'That's why I'm starting to think either Rafael got this wrong or he made it up to throw me off the scent or whatever.'

'I'll ask around. Do some digging. But if I were you, I'd look for someone a bit lower down the food chain – someone who might give their two cents on casting decisions without having the final say. Somebody with influence but not necessarily much power.'

'Thanks. That's a good idea.' All the same, despondency settled over me.

'You know,' Nina said abruptly, 'I really didn't feed stuff to the gossip blogs about you.'

'Nina, it's fine –'

'You ever consider that Adam did it?'

'*Adam?* Why?'

'The guy was a flaming arsehole. We all know that. I mean, he was such an arsehole someone felt compelled to literally kill him. I can see him getting coked up and firing off some fake tip-offs, just for funsies.'

It wasn't completely implausible, now I came to think of it. 'Maybe you're right. He liked to play games.'

'Nasty games.' Her face darkened. 'He was that kind of player. Like all those industry thugs who'd grab my tits in one hand then slam a door in my face with the other.'

I wasn't sure of the physical logistics of this, but I took her point. 'Adam wasn't always like that. There were good times, too. When he let himself be vulnerable, it felt almost real between us. And maybe it was. I think we were more honest with each other than with anyone else. Because that's how fiction works, right? Films and plays and books … they're make-believe. They're the lie that shows us what's true.' Tears were pricking at my eyes. Nina squeezed my hand and we were quiet for a while.

'What about him and Talia?' I asked at last. 'She acted like everything was unicorns and rainbows between them but, knowing Adam, I'm not sure I believe her.'

Nina pulled at her lip. 'It's hard to say. I mean, I only hung out with them a handful of times. Adam zoned out, basically. Just let her rabbit on. But he seemed fairly … I don't know … chill? Talia is really cut up about the death. She blames herself for not being there. She found her mum after an overdose – did you know that?'

'No!' I was shocked. 'How awful.'

'From what I understand, it wasn't a real suicide attempt. More like a bit of drama during divorce proceedings. Her mother took some sleeping pills and some whiskey and passed out. But, like I said, it was Talia who found her. She thought she was dead. She was only about twelve or so.'

'God. Don't tell her about the pills. Or any of this.'

'I'm not a total idiot. And I can be discreet when I need to be.' Nina fluffed up her fringe. For the first time in the conversation, she looked a little uncomfortable. 'However, there's something I probably should tell you.'

Nina was seeing Dido's Nick, and had been pretty much ever since Adam's party, when they'd roared off into the night in his Porsche 911S.

'He and Dido had their big row, then he came stomping into the room, the main one, where I was dancing like a maniac. (It was Prince. You know what I'm like with Prince.) So he caught my eye, I cupped his balls and ... ka-*boom*.'

They were going to move in together as soon as the divorce papers came through.

Unpleasant surprises had been coming thick and fast lately, but my jaw still dropped. 'But Nick – he's – you're –' *He's awful*, I wanted to say, though I was hardly in a position to judge.

The way Nina's brows arched I could tell she knew what I was thinking. 'The trouble with Nick is that he never should have married someone like your cousin. The Great Dame. Living in that kind of shadow's enough to curdle anyone's spirit. Then there's me, a has-been moppet with a rackety past … He thinks he's saving me from myself and maybe he is. Oh – and you can cross him off as a suspect, too.'

I was caught off guard. 'Suspect?'

'C'mon, we both know he had a motive. Rafael wasn't the only spurned lover on the scene. But I told Nick that Adam batted for the other side pretty much five minutes after Dido dumped him. So if he tore all the way down to Norfolk with murder on his mind, he soon thought better of it.'

'Uh, good to know.' I *had* wondered about the extent of Nick's research for his drug-dealer novel. But the fact was, I found it hard to take anything about the project seriously, including the author.

'God.' Nina stretched and yawned. 'I've got to get going in an hour to compère a sodding poetry slam. The sooner I start life as a mail-order muse the better.'

'You can't give up! You're a far better actor than Nick's a writer.'

'And what do I have to show for it? Living hand to mouth. Tagging along at the edge of other people's shinier lives … Nick's loaded, by the way. It's only Dido who insists on high-brows and hair-shirts.'

'But Nick wants *kids*. It's one of the reasons he and Dido split up.'

'Mm. You know those God-awful "where are they now" column-fillers? "Nina Gill is married with two children and a walk-in wardrobe" is starting to sound a lot better than "Nina Gill was last seen performing improv to three hobos under a railway bridge".' She shrugged. 'The way I see it, there's no way I could do a worse job of parenting than my dear old mum. Could even be fun.'

I got home feeling extraordinarily depressed. I'd been right to mistrust my instincts because it was starting to look as if I misjudged everyone. I'd underestimated Adam's ruthlessness and spite. I'd failed to understand my best friend and the kind of person she truly wanted to be. Even Talia and Nick ... I was starting to think I'd got them wrong too. The idea that someone like me was capable of getting to the truth of anything was laughable.

Then Nina phoned the next day. 'We've got a lead.'

CHAPTER NINE

'Maia Anderson.'

'Who?'

'Twenty-something daughter of Patty Carlton, née Anderson.'

'Right. The producer's wife.' The Carltons had a two-year-old daughter together; Max had two teenage boys from his first marriage, but I'd somehow missed that Patty had another child too.

'Patty had her when she was eighteen. I don't think the dad was around much, if ever.'

I was walking down the King's Road, on my way to meet Dan for lunch. I glanced around and lowered my voice. 'So what's the dirt?'

'A friend of a friend did some modelling with her about six or seven years ago. Maia would have been about twenty.'

'And?'

'Well, my mate's mate said she and Maia hung out a bit. Apparently the girl was a hot mess. A "druggy skank", to quote my source. Blamed her mum for all her issues, too.'

'Don't we all … OK. So where is she now?'

'Get this: she's cleaned up her act and is engaged to the son of a Republican senator.'

I stopped dead in the street. 'So Adam somehow knew about this girl's sordid past and used it to pressure her mother into pressuring her stepdad into giving him Luke Zane.'

'Well, it's a theory,' said Nina, more cautiously than I expected. 'I'm betting someone's done a content clean-up of Maia's online profile – there's not much out there.'

'OK. This is still good stuff. I'll get onto it.'

First I had to get through lunch with Dan. He was becoming more relaxed with me, but I still found our dates surprisingly effortful. With Adam, it was never difficult to think of something to say or laugh about. I also spent a lot of my time with Adam feeling humiliated, angry and exhausted, I reminded myself. With Dan, everything was perfectly pleasant, as well as polite.

With Adam, we'd kissed for real, until I got chapped lips and stubble rash. As the cameras flashed, we'd slide our hands over each other, greedily. The whole time we'd be brimming with secret laughter, catching the glint in the other's eye. We were each other's playthings, our performance pulling a tremendous joke on the world. Even now, after everything, I missed that.

At home, I looked up Max and Patty Carlton again. They looked like every other power-couple in Hollywood: him, fleshy and balding; her a taut-faced blonde. I'd already flagged them, but only because I was fairly sure we'd been introduced at some LA party or other, which meant that Adam had an acquaintance with them that predated Luke Zane. Max had entries on IMDb and Wikipedia, which is where I'd got my info on his family life, but there'd been no mention of a stepdaughter. Patty didn't have a professional profile, and very little came up in the search engines apart from the fact she had an MFA from the University

225

of California and was on the boards of several charities. Nina said she'd only found out about her eldest daughter from an image search.

I looked up the same images, which were mostly of Patty accompanying her husband on the red carpet or posing at fundraisers with assorted ladies-who-lunch. I had to scroll down quite far before I found the photo Nina mentioned – Patty Carlton and her daughter Maia Anderson, attending a celebrity book launch.

Maia was a younger version of her mother, her cheeks plump with youth rather than tight with filler. That's not why she looked familiar, however. I'd definitely seen Maia in the flesh. She'd been at the gala in New York last winter: the blonde who'd looked so dismayed to run in to Adam at the bar. The girl he'd said was an ex-prostitute. *These days, by the look of things, she's a Park Avenue princess. Five or six years ago she was a hooker.*

Patty and Max Carlton had only been married for three years, but even if Maia wasn't raised in the lap of LA luxury, she most likely grew up in very comfortable surroundings. This wasn't some *Pretty Woman*-style transformation. Still, she'd grown up without a dad and had presumably gone through the usual troubled-teen clichés … If she'd had a period of estrangement from her family, it wasn't hard to see how things could spiral. Plenty of wannabe models and actors supplement their income as sugar babies or webcam girls. From there, it can be a mere hop, skip and a jump to a wad of dollars on the nightstand. Every struggling actor gets propositioned by skeevy men offering to help out with the bills; I'd also been approached, once in a nightclub and once at a casting, by a young woman in designer clothes asking if I wanted

226

to make easy money on the side. 'You like to party?' she'd asked. 'You know how to show a guy a good time?' You saw women like this at a certain kind of party in penthouses and aboard yachts. Maybe that's where Adam had first encountered Maia.

But Maia was a privileged blonde from a good home, so it wasn't long before she straightened herself out. Maybe it took a stint in a pricy rehab facility or joining AA. Maybe all she needed was a decent therapist. Either way, she'd cleaned up her act and her online profile, put her brief spell of druggy skankiness behind her and emerged into the light – the stepdaughter of a Hollywood producer, the fiancée of a senator's son.

And then along came Adam.

I tried to imagine the conversation. Perhaps he'd taken a leaf out of Zalandra's book and doorstepped Patty Carlton at her favourite brunch spot or outside the gym. They'd met before – it wouldn't, at first, seem untoward. And even when he made his move, he'd be subtle about it. 'I ran in to your daughter the other day,' he might say. Patty would be surprised. 'Oh, so you know Maia?' 'I hadn't seen her for years,' I imagined his reply. 'What great news about her engagement, especially after all she's been through! The last time I saw Maia was in *very* different circumstances.' And he'd give Patty a look. And she'd know that he knew.

How would he phrase the next bit, I wondered. Some banter about Luke Zane. A self-deprecating reference to the audition progress. Then, 'I do hope you'll put in a good word for me with Max.' Or 'I'd really love to know that you'll be fighting my corner.' And – the killer – 'I'm sure Maia would be grateful too.' Something like that. Adam had been trained in how to make the corniest line sound meaningful. He knew how to exude menace with the sunniest of smiles.

I closed my eyes. Maybe Patty went straight to her husband, told him everything, but still begged him to give Adam the job for Maia's sake. Or else she kept everything hushed up, and when she was asked her opinion on the final casting, smiled sweetly and said, *No question, babe, it's gotta be Harker. Why, just look at that smoulder! Box-office gold!* Sometimes that's all it takes: a little nudge one way or the other, the right word in the right ear.

Either way, the end result was the same. A bottle of poison pills and a corpse in a swimming pool.

Why was Adam killed?

Because he couldn't be trusted to keep his mouth shut?

Because he'd crossed the wrong people and needed to be punished?

Or maybe he was never *meant* to die.

Somebody listened to the whispers of his drug problem and decided to make it public in the most spectacular way possible, before he had the chance to clean up his act. Let Adam's career crash and burn at the ICU! After all, it was sheer bad luck that Adam took the pills alone. His devoted girlfriend, Talia, should have been with him. The fact that nobody at the party was there to witness his overdose and get help was a fluke. What's more, it's extraordinarily difficult to gauge the toxicity of illegal drugs – those fentanyl pills could well have been far more deadly than their procurer intended.

The more I went over this in my head the more plausible it

seemed. For the first time since Adam's death I felt optimistic and energised, as if uncovering the truth might actually set me free. *Little Lucie Turns Detective* … What was I afraid of? Finding justice for Adam would make for an amazing movie. He'd like that much better than some miserable biopic about his death.

Nina confirmed there hadn't been any sort of official guest list for the weekend in Norfolk – 'Adam just fired off loads of random invites. It drove Talia mad.' This didn't surprise me. While it might have been Talia's venue, every other aspect of the night was pure Adam. Thoughtless and extravagant in equal measure.

Security at the party had been minimal: a spotty teenager asking for a password. Still, the fact there was only one entrance to the property, with a camera covering the gates, meant the killer must have been there in plain sight, as one of the guests or waitstaff. The police had taken witness statements from everyone at the scene of the death, and had presumably used the CCTV footage to follow up on the movements of other guests, but it wasn't as if I had access to any of this info. I was looking for a needle in a drug-addled haystack.

The more I considered the scale of the task before me, the harder it was to see how sheer optimism would carry me through.

'I've got an idea,' said Nina at last, 'but you're not going to like it …'

'I can't afford to be picky.'

'OK. The fat goth stalker freak.'

'Zalandra?'

'The very one. She was taking photos throughout the party.

Pissed a few people off, but she still kept taking them. Who knows who or what she might have a record of?'

'Wow, OK.' I bit my lip. Nina was right: I didn't like this idea one bit. Zalandra's threats had felt real, her hate vibrant. The flowers were the creepy icing on her psycho cake. 'She thinks I'm Satan though. Why would she want to help me?'

'You're not doing this for yourself. It would be in service of her Dearly Beloved. Don't go into more details than you absolutely have to. But it's worth a shot.'

'I have no idea how to get in touch with her. I don't even know her real name.'

'Some detective you are. Didn't you say Adam put her in charge of his glory hole – sorry, fan-site?'

So, with a sickly feeling in the pit of my stomach, I looked up the official website of Adam Harker. Zalandra had done him proud. The home page was bordered in black with an *In Memoriam* banner and a gallery of all his roles. It started with a fuzzy photo of Adam aged about twelve, in some school performance at the Fame Factory, and ended with that iconic shot of him in army fatigues in *Tyre*.

These pages stand as a permanent memorial to Adam Harker and the loss felt by his family, fans, friends and colleagues.
Adam was taken from us too soon. But to have moved and uplifted so many people is a rare talent, and his legacy will live on.

The website made me sad in a way I wasn't prepared for. I thought all the comments would annoy me – all that incontinent burbling by people who didn't know Adam and wouldn't have liked him if they did. But even if it was misdirected, the love and grief poured out on the pages seemed sincere. Some of the tributes were thoughtful but the messy ones were touching too. People talked about their own experiences of bereavement, how Adam's films had got them through tough times or how kind he'd been when they'd queued up to see him at a première or bumped into him on the street. It didn't even matter that a lot of these people were probably the same people who'd trolled me. I spent a long time, much longer than I expected, scrolling through all the comments, and when I finished my eyes were wet.

Zalandra had no personal presence on the website, but there was a link to contact the site administrator. I took a deep breath.

> *Zalandra,*
>
> *I couldn't think of any other way of contacting you so this is, in every way, a shot in the dark. To be honest, I was very reluctant to try and get in touch with you at all. I know you have strong feelings about my relationship with Adam. But I hope you can at least hear me out …*

I did as Nina suggested and kept the reason for my request vague. I said I had questions about who supplied Adam with the drugs, and I wasn't satisfied the police were doing enough to follow things up.

I signed off by typing, *I know you're a crazy bitch and you want to make my life all kinds of hell but I'm doing this for Adam. Even if he didn't deserve it. That's what love is, not whatever pathetic, perverted delusion you're high on.* Though I deleted it almost immediately, I felt better for having written it down.

———

231

Nick came to collect Nina after our latest confab. 'Don't worry, I'm not expecting your congratulations' was the first thing he said to me when I answered the door. He looked and sounded as disagreeable as usual.

'I'm sure the two of you make a lovely couple.'

'Like you and that homo?'

'I did try and tell you Dido wasn't sleeping with Adam.'

'Whatever.' He glowered at me. 'I'm resigned to being the villain of the piece. No doubt the Thanes are busy blackening my name with some choice Shakespearean epithets.'

'I wouldn't know. Shakespeare isn't really my thing.' In point of fact, news of Dido's marital breakdown had been received quietly among the Thane diaspora. Even the Momager had contented herself with observing that, now she was back on the market, Dido might want to start tidying herself up a bit and maybe invest in some more feminine shoes.

'Don't act coy, Lily. It doesn't suit you. Now that Nina and I have outed ourselves, Dido will be free to play the Wronged Wife to universal acclaim. It'll be the performance of a lifetime.'

'I know she was genuinely sorry about the way she ended things.'

Nick snorted. 'Salt tears in a salt marsh. Another well-crafted stage effect.'

Nina emerged from the bathroom at this point. She grinned knowingly at me. 'Is Daddy telling you that he'll always love you very much, even though he can't be with Mummy any more?'

Nick ignored this. 'What people don't realise,' he said, 'is that Dido can be extraordinarily vindictive. Petty, too.' For the first time, he looked genuinely wounded. 'She even got custody of the dog.'

———

I answered the call from the unknown number without really thinking about it; I was on my way to do a magazine interview with Dan and I thought it might be someone from his team. Even when I heard her voice, I didn't immediately recognise it. She sounded faded, far away.

'Is that … Lily Thane?'

'Yep. What can I do –' Then it clicked. 'Zalandra?'

'Hello.'

I waited for more. It didn't come. 'Thank you *so* much for calling me back,' I said, channelling the Momager at her most fulsome. 'I really appreciate it.'

In point of fact I hated it. I hated *her*. Every word choked me. It was disgusting, contemptible, that I had to grovel to this deviant for a favour.

'I nearly didn't.' Her breath sighed down the line. 'I'm doing this for Adam. Not you.'

I clenched and unclenched my fist. 'Understood.'

'So … I'll email you the photos, like you asked.'

'Thank you.'

'But I want something in return.'

Oh FFS. 'Flowers?'

There was a dark chuckle. 'No. Not this time. I want … I want you to meet with me. Just the two of us.'

My insides turned over. But at the same time, it struck me that maybe this was a risk I had to take. At some point I needed to confront Zalandra, face to face. Ask her about the flowers, ask her about that party, ask her about when she'd left and where

233

she'd gone. I needed to look her in the eyes and ask, *Just how far would you go to keep Adam from me or anyone else?*

'OK. Sure. We can meet.'

'I can't do it at the moment.' Her voice was now so frail I could hardly hear her. 'I'm … unwell.'

'I'm sorry to hear that.'

'I'm in a hospital.'

'That sounds serious.'

'I get this way sometimes. Feeling … low. Things get too much.'

So she was banged up on some psych ward. That figured. 'I'm sorry.'

'But when I'm feeling better, you'll meet with me?'

I clenched my fist again. 'We can set something up.'

'It's important that you do. You need to understand that.' Her voice was still very faded, yet I could hear the pulse of menace behind it, loud and clear. 'Because I'll come and find you if you don't.'

Zalandra emailed me the photos the next morning. There were hundreds, all in artsy monochrome. Maybe it shouldn't have surprised me, given the overall look of Adam's fan-site, but she had a good eye. The photographs revealed she had a natural instinct for what makes a striking composition, as well as knowing how to focus on the moments of emotion or connection that suggest a story.

Telling details were everywhere – Dido looking haunted in a frame of empty bookshelves. Nick watching as Nina danced, her boobs spilling over, his tongue lolling out. Sarah eyeing a gaggle of Party Blondes with envy and contempt. Rafael stubbing out a cigarette on that weird iron chair. A glimpse of me through a window: a blood-stained wraith, standing in darkness. Another picture of me, a close-up this time, with my eyes widened and lips slightly parted, lit up by the spangles of a disco-ball … Zalandra must have been part of the throng the whole time I'd been at the party, yet I'd never spotted her until our encounter outside the bathroom. The realisation made me shiver.

There were less photographs of Adam than I would have expected. By now, his image was almost as familiar to me as my own. Cinematic stills and movie posters were one thing, but even in these snaps, taken when he was off guard or part of a crowd, he still looked like the protagonist. *(Hero. Villain. Lover.)* I don't think this was because the pictures were framed by Zalandra's eye. It was just one of Adam's gifts.

Most of the people in the photos were strangers, though they looked familiar because they had the kinds of faces and bodies everyone aspires to and so have a likeness that's found everywhere, to sell everything. Many were clearly drunk or high or both. I was on the hunt for someone who looked sober, I decided. This was a cold crime, as Rafael had said.

But the photo that made me sit up and catch my breath wasn't of a stranger. A petite Asian woman had been snapped coming out of a doorway, with Adam behind her. His face was blurred and he was looking down at the floor. She, however, had her head thrust forward, her mouth narrowed to a line, and was grasping her bag so hard the knuckles were white. What was Grace Tang doing at Adam's party?

CHAPTER TEN

Some people are super-matey with their publicists. But the best PRs don't let that happen – Grace herself once told me that a PR who gets too close to a client can lose perspective. Grace was one of the best PRs. She was the director of her own agency, Silver Wing, and although the agency was a relatively new one, it was swiftly developing a reputation for turning up-and-comers into established stars. And she'd objected to me as a choice of beard for Adam. That showed good sense.

Grace had three things in common with Zalandra: she always wore black, had a knack of making herself invisible and could be scary as fuck when required. There was no doubt she was ruthlessly efficient at getting gossip sites to delete photos and shooting down stories in the tabloid press. In Adam's more petulant moments, he used to complain that she was in league with Victor – endlessly trying to cramp his style, spoil his fun. Like they were two old fogey parents and he was the loveably wayward kid. I couldn't see why the hell he would invite her to his house party. Nobody else from his team had been there. So why was Grace?

The more I thought about it the more odd it seemed. It was so unlike Grace, too, to reveal any thought or feeling other than those required for professional advancement. Sure, she'd let me sense her disapproval, but even that was as cool and restrained as the rest of her. 'The Inscrutable Oriental,' Adam had once called her, to her face. And she'd smiled blandly in response. Maybe Zalandra's photograph was misleading, a quirk of timing that captured a flash of hostility that hadn't actually been there. But from what I could make out from the photo, Grace and Adam had been alone in a room together, which was in itself intriguing, since it was hardly the time or place for a business meeting. And their rendezvous couldn't have had a sexual element. Either way, it looked as if it had ended acrimoniously.

Searching for Grace Tang on the internet proved useless. The woman was almost as invisible online as she was when accompanying her clients IRL. 'My job is all about getting the narrative right. PRs are storytellers above everything else,' she said in a rare interview, as part of an article on the 'movers and shakers' of celebrity PR. I stared at that quote for a long time, picking at my nails with frustration.

Then I tried a change of tack. This had all begun because I was looking for someone with a connection to Maia Anderson, the Happy Hooker, and Patty Carlton, the producer's wife. I needed to get back to the fundamentals. So I pulled up my original image search and scrolled through all the photos again. It didn't take me long to find what I was looking for. It was a two-year-old photo taken at an arts fundraiser and published by some online community journal. Patty was name-checked as a board member of the charity in question, but the woman Patty was sharing a joke with wasn't. All the same, it was unmistakeably Grace. I hadn't noticed her the first time simply because I hadn't been looking for her.

OK, yeah, it was a tenuous connection. The woman who Adam had possibly blackmailed possibly knew his publicist. And publicists, of course, get around. Still, it felt as if things were beginning to come together.

Do you remember seeing this woman at the party? I messaged Nina, with Zalandra's photo of Grace attached.

Don't think so, she replied.

She looks angry, right?
Kinda.

...

OMG is she the killer?!?!?!?!
Ha ha who knows. But I'd like to know what she was so pissed off about.

There was something else I'd just remembered. The night of the New York première when I'd had the flu. Grace opening up her hand to offer me the little white pills.

Keeping my expectations low, I rang Grace's office and asked her PA for an appointment. I'd spoken to the PA countless times before, but she gave no hint of recognition, let alone warmth, when she asked me what my phone call was regarding. I replied that someone had tipped me off that there was a story coming out about me and Adam and it wasn't flattering. I said I was in need of advice, and I was hoping Grace might agree to see me for old times' sake. 'I'll need to call you back,' said the PA, which I took to mean I'd never hear from her again.

But lo and behold, I had a voicemail later that evening saying that, yes, Grace could fit me in once she was back from her business trip. Would Thursday at four suit?

'You're looking well, Lily,' was the first thing Grace said to me. 'Congratulations on *The Other Women*. It's created quite the water-cooler moment.'

'Thank you.' Then, because I couldn't quite resist it, 'Unlike *Hollow Moon*.'

The pilot had just aired to high viewing figures but scathing reviews. The actor who'd replaced me as Lys was seven years younger: I could tell the dewy glow of her skin wasn't thanks to Photoshop. She'd survive a flop. Even so, every time I glimpsed her promotional image, a part of me hoped she wouldn't.

(So familiar, this feeling. The scent of vanilla, the taste of bile.)

Grace smiled thinly. 'I'm glad things are working out for you. Now, what can I help you with?'

I looked around the office, which was as severely stylish as its occupant, in search of inspiration. Grace had accompanied Adam and me to countless industry events, and we'd spent hours of travel time together, but of the people I'd talked to about Adam's death, Grace was the most unknown quantity. Even top-notch PRs have occasions when their work is more like a lady's maid's – they hold your bag at parties and umbrellas during rainy walk-abouts. They clear coffee cups, organise vitamin shots. Schedule toilet breaks. Grace knew a lot about me but, I realised, I knew next to nothing about her.

I smoothed down my hair. 'So … it's about … Adam …?'

'You said someone had a story on him,' she prompted. 'Are they threatening to go to the press?'

'Not exactly. The thing is, uh … well … that "someone" is potentially me.'

Grace frowned. 'If this is about dredging up some unfortunate anecdote about your time with Adam, or the more unsavoury aspects of Adam's lifestyle, then I really don't advise going public. It will make you look as if you're cashing in on his death – or, worse, that you're being pointlessly vengeful. Anything that might cause embarrassment or pain to his family –'

'This isn't about Adam's life. Or lifestyle. It's about his death.' I was back on the script. 'I don't think the police know the full story, and before I go to them with some things I've found, I'd like to clear up a few questions. With you.'

'With *me*?' She leaned back in her chair. 'What have I got to do with anything?'

'Well, you were there the night that he died.'

'Briefly. Along with a cast of thousands, as I recall.'

'There were less than a hundred people there. Do you usually attend your clients' house-parties?'

'On occasion. If there's a publicity angle to be pursued. Or when I'm invited in a social capacity.'

'But Adam didn't invite you.' I said this as if I knew it for a fact, even though I couldn't be sure. At any rate, Grace didn't dispute the statement. She didn't react at all, just sat there, waiting. 'So why did you drive all the way down to Norfolk on a Saturday night to crash a client's piss-up?'

'What a peculiar way of framing it. I wanted to talk to Adam, that's all. Something urgent came up relating to Luke Zane and I needed it dealt with sooner rather than later. The whole business took under fifteen minutes.'

'Couldn't you have just called him?'

'Some conversations are better had face to face.' She glanced at her phone. 'And I'll admit I'm struggling to see the point of this one.'

'Maia Anderson.'

'What?' Her face flickered. Though her expression smoothed over almost instantly, I felt a fizz of excitement. Maybe *Little Lucie Turns Detective* wasn't so far-fetched after all.

'Maia Anderson. *She's* the point of this conversation. Adam and I bumped into her once, at a New York gala. Adam knew about her past, and I think he was using it to blackmail her mother. And that's how he manipulated the Luke Zane producer into –'

'Let me stop you right there.' Grace was using the same tone on me as she must deploy on rogue tabloid editors. 'I don't know exactly what you think you know, or how you came to these outlandish conclusions, but the advice I gave you earlier still stands. Anything you think is going to cause embarrassment or pain to others is bound to backfire spectacularly onto you.' She leaned forward. 'This is not just my professional opinion. *It is my cast-iron guarantee.*'

'I'm not out to *embarrass* anyone. All I care about is getting to the truth of what happened the night Adam died.'

Grace continued to look unimpressed.

'Look, Adam told me he wasn't worried about the Luke Zane audition process. He said he had leverage and that sometimes you have to play dirty.' Grace wasn't to know I'd got this information second-hand. 'I ignored him at the time. I thought it was just Adam being Adam. It was only after his death that I made the connection between Maia Anderson, Patty and Max Carlton, and Luke Zane.' I paused. 'And then the other day, I made the connection between Patty and you.'

This time, Grace's whole body stiffened. She was genuinely shocked. 'How the hell do you know about me and Patty? We broke up six years ago.'

It was my turn for a double take. Instead, I cleared my throat and attempted to appear both all-knowing and insouciant. 'But when Patty was in trouble, she still came to you for help.'

There was a long pause. In a movie, this would be the point where Grace got up to fix herself a drink while she debated whether or not to come clean. In real life, she just fiddled with a pen for a bit.

'Patty and I weren't ever serious,' she said at last. 'Patty was bi-curious and I was … well, open to being a short-term experiment. After things came to an inevitable conclusion, our paths crossed maybe twice in the last six years. But she knew I was Adam's PR. So, yes, she came to me for advice.'

'Because Adam was blackmailing her?' I needed to hear Grace say the words.

'Right. And let's get something clear: what annoys me almost more than anything else is the sheer idiocy of the enterprise. Yes, some producer's other halves get over-involved in the casting process and, yes, Max values Patty's opinion. But the idea that she had some kind of *vote* … I honestly don't know what Adam was thinking. The kindest explanation is that he was desperate. Or off his head.

'Anyway. As it turned out, Patty didn't need to do anything because Adam was always the front-runner for Zane. There was no need to play any tricks, dirty or otherwise. But the whole business was obviously very upsetting. Of course, Patty was mostly distressed on Maia's behalf.'

'I can imagine. How well do you know Maia?'

'We've never met – she was estranged from her mother during the time Patty and I were seeing each other. From what I understand, she made a stupid mistake during a very unhappy and confused time. When I heard that she and Patty had reconciled, and that Maia had turned things around, I was naturally very pleased for them.' Grace said all this as dispassionately as if she was reading out a statement at a press conference.

'Maia's admitted to "acting out" in the past, but her fiancé and his family don't know the extent of it. Neither does Max. Patty worked herself up into a state about whether Adam could be trusted to keep his mouth shut and who else might come crawling out of the woodwork. Of course, I advised her and Maia to come clean to their loved ones. Get ahead of the story – that's what I say to all my clients. Avoid prevarication. Apologise and contextualise; move on.' She shrugged. 'Now that Adam's dead, of course, they may decide the immediate threat has passed.'

'So …' I held my breath. 'What did you say to Adam?'

Grace smiled faintly. 'I told him that he was a despicable piece of shit. And that if he ever pulled a dumb-ass stunt like that again, I'd ensure his name would stink worse than Jeffrey Epstein's at a girl-scout slumber party.'

'Yikes.'

'Oh well. It's not the first time I've had to read some pissant actor the riot act and it won't be the last.' She'd become almost relaxed, swivelling idly from side to side on her chair. 'That's the problem with B-listers. You'd think the biggest stars would be the most demanding, but A-list talent understand their job and know what they're there for. C-listers are new and excited and eager

243

to do whatever you need. B-listers, though … They're about to launch, but they also know they aren't nobodies, so they push boundaries with you. And Adam's boundaries were always going to be more of a problem than most.'

Then she centred the chair and straightened up again. 'Now. You said that you started looking into all this because you had questions about Adam's death. That you don't think the police know the full story. How does Adam's blackmail attempt fit into this?'

This was tricky. I didn't want to let on the extent of what I knew about the pills. 'The police seem to have given up on finding who supplied Adam with the drugs. For all his faults, I do actually believe Adam wanted to get clean. So I'm interested in people who might have a motive for … enabling … him to relapse.'

I was braced for Grace to react with fury to the implied accusation. She merely looked contemptuous. 'You actors – always with the melodrama. Nobody ever needed to "enable" Adam to do the wrong thing. God knows I had more than enough dirt on him to end his career several times over if I'd wanted to.'

'Weren't you tempted?'

'Why ever would I do that?' she asked, surprised. 'Naturally, I was angry on Patty and Maia's behalf. Adam's actions were reprehensible. But he was shaping up to be one of my most important clients. He'd have been the perfect Zane. Then there's the amount of blood, sweat and tears I'd already invested into rehabilitating his reputation …' She pulled at her lip. 'How out of control did the party get? I left before nine, and at that point things were fairly tame.'

At nine, I was still in the studio, the bag of drugs beside me on the bed. If Grace was telling the truth about her timings, then it was highly unlikely she could have swapped the pills.

'There were drugs, but nothing extreme. That's why I was shocked at how it ended – for Adam.'

'He seems to have inspired a surprising amount of loyalty in his plus-ones. You know, I'm sure, about the drama school that Talia Templeton is helping his family set up in his name?'

I blinked. 'What?'

'I'm doing some work on it for her and the Harkers. They plan to turn the Norfolk property into a residential summer drama school, with scholarships for underprivileged kids. You really hadn't heard? I gather your cousin Dido is going to be one of the patrons.'

'How splendid.' I couldn't be arsed to feign sincerity at this point. 'Adam was, after all, a great champion of disadvantaged youth.'

Grace let out a most uncharacteristic snort. It emboldened me.

'Look, I'm sorry – I know this is impertinent – but didn't you find it, uh, difficult, working so hard to disguise who Adam was, given …?'

'Given my own sexual orientation?' Her voice was very dry. 'I wasn't involved in Adam's decision to play straight. That was set up well before I came on the scene. But for what it's worth, I think he made the right call. He wasn't the right kind of gay to come out.'

'What does that mean?'

'It means that Hollywood will tolerate exactly two types of gay male stars. One's the camp, bitchy sidekick with a heart of caramel. The other is the clean-cut homo who plays it straight on both sides of the screen. He's the one with a nice husband, a white picket fence and a couple of surrogate-hatched kids. That was never going to be Adam.'

Never? Adam, who believed that everyone has a destined life partner. Adam, who fantasised about raising babies in the orange groves. I thought of him on that star-spangled midnight, conjuring his dreams. Then I blinked the image away.

'We both know Adam was the kind of man your mother doesn't want you to meet,' Grace concluded. 'Volatile, promiscuous, coke-snorting trouble.'

'That could describe a lot of famous leading men.'

'Indeed. And they're all straight.' Her brows lifted. 'I find it interesting that *you* are questioning *me* about the ethics of bearding.'

I felt my cheeks go hot.

'You're probably aware I never thought you were a good fit for Adam.'

'Because I'm not properly famous?'

'If it wasn't for your family name, and that Christmas film, you'd most likely be modelling sweaters in the Boden catalogue. At best. That was my first impression of you. But the more I saw of you ... you and Adam ... and now all this ... Well. I suppose I'm coming round to the idea that you have what it takes, after all.'

'Thank you.'

Her face was impassive. 'Don't assume that it's a compliment.'

CHAPTER ELEVEN

For once, luck was on my side. After I left Grace's offices, I went for a wander and ended up on Bond Street. Who should I spot there but Talia herself, in a fancy coffee shop with Sarah Harker and her mother.

I drew back into a doorway to survey them better. Unsurprisingly, Mrs Harker looked sadder and sloppier than when I'd met her, but Sarah looked good. *Really* good. She'd had her face lasered so that the acne scars were all smoothed away, and her skin looked as uncanny-valley as Talia's. Her rather lank dark hair had been restyled into a sleek bob. The clothes were designer and so were her teeth. So were the shopping bags on her and her mother's arms.

Talia, I could see, was paying for the coffees. She turned back to smile at the other two with a look I knew very well – happy, nervous, eager to please. I knew exactly what she'd be saying, too: *My treat.*

As soon as the coast was clear, I phoned Nina to ask if she knew about the proposed Adam Harker Academy of Dramatic Tricks. She was out with Nick and distracted. 'Ask Talia yourself,' she said. 'It's about time you two started talking again.'

'I will. I just want to get some background first.'

'I don't know much about it, to be honest. It's a Harker family initiative; then Sarah asked Talia to get involved. Talia – or her dad, technically – is donating the house.'

'Blimey.'

'Talia's as generous as she's gullible. We know that.' Nina cackled. 'I mean, I've been leeching off her for years.'

Is that what was happening here? Adam said he'd given his family various handouts, and maybe there'd been a bit of cash from his estate, but it couldn't have been all that much. He'd said himself that he'd snorted most of his earnings up his nose. Luke Zane was meant to be his big payday.

So maybe Talia was Sarah's.

Talia wasn't the only person I needed to reconnect with. Zalandra had emailed me, saying she was now back at home and ready to arrange our promised meeting. I hadn't replied. And I'd had two missed calls from Dan during my interview with Grace, as well as three from the Momager.

To get the worst over with first, I started with my mother.

'You know I don't like to meddle, but I think you're being *very* cavalier with poor Dan,' was how she began the conversation. 'He got in touch with me this afternoon because he's concerned he hasn't heard from you today and you haven't replied to his last message. Quite apart from your contractual obligations, I would think you'd be more sensitive to Dan's emotional well-being. He's still in a very vulnerable place. Good communication is key to any successful relationship. And, frankly, *I* would appreciate some communication too.

Where have you been? What are you *doing*? Have you even started on that life-in-a-day piece for *Stylist*?'

'I've been following something up … research …'

'Research for a role?'

'Right. Lead detective.'

'Don't play games with me.' Her voice sharpened. 'You'd better not be pursuing more ridiculous conspiracy theories about your wastrel fake ex. If I've told you once, I've told you a hundred times: any muck you rake up will inevitably end up all over you.'

That's what Grace had said too.

'No muck-raking, just mending fences. I'm hoping to meet up with Talia, in fact. Apparently she's helping to set up a drama school in Adam's name.'

The Momager's breath hissed. 'That *viper* … I'm only surprised she's waited this long to capitalise on the junkie's death. She's an even more shameless self-promoter than that trampy mother of hers.'

'Talia's just the money guy. It's Adam's sister who's running the show. Oh, and Dido's going to be a patron. Maybe I'll be invited to be one too.'

I didn't mean this seriously but my mother was part-mollified.

'Well,' she said righteously, 'after everything you did for Adam, it's the very least you deserve.'

So I heard about the summer school, I messaged Talia. *I think it's an amazing idea.* Then – eye roll – *Adam would have loved it.*

I was still surprised when she called me back.

'It's me …' she said ten minutes later, her little-girl voice all

249

of a tremble. 'Talia?' Like I'd forgotten who she was. 'I know you think I've been avoiding you. But please don't be mad.' On she swept, in that breathless, hiccupy way of hers that made me want to give her a slap and blow her nose for her at the same moment. 'I'm sorry, I'm sorry. I just couldn't think what to say. Adam – the funeral – his family, his fans – the press – I got overwhelmed. And you were practically the only person – well, the only person I cared about – who knew the truth about Adam and me. I didn't know what to do with that. I suppose it seemed easier to pretend you weren't there. That you weren't a part of any of it.'

'A part of the lies?'

'No! I see them more as … make-believe. It's nicer that way, don't you think?'

I pulled various faces at the mirror and counted to ten. 'Well, I'm just glad something good will come out of Adam's death. Turning that house into a summer drama school, helping young actors … it's an exciting project.'

'Really? You really think so? You promise? That's such a relief, you have no idea. Mummy and Pops won't take it seriously at all. They think I'm just, you know, playing around, like with the beachwear and the face creams and stuff. But I'm determined to help the Harkers memorialise Adam. It's a *real cause*. The whole family have been so inspiring in their grief, so dignified – his sister especially.'

'That's … nice.'

'I think it was kind of hard for Sarah, growing up in Adam's shadow? But the more I get to know her, the more I see the ways in which they're alike. The same sense of humour, for instance. It's almost spooky. Spooky, but sweet.'

'Mm. I'm glad you're supporting each other.'

'People are being *so kind*. I've even got Adam's publicist to do the PR for us. She's drafted a press release for next week, for when the Harkers make the announcement, and we're filming a promotional video this Saturday down at the house.' Talia paused. 'Oh! Here's an idea! Why don't you come and join me after we're done? Sarah can't stay on so it will be just the two of us. There are some gorgeous walks, you know, if the weather's good. Autumn by the coast is so dramatic. Say yes! Or else we can just curl up by the fire and talk and talk and talk ...'

'Just to be clear: this is the house where Adam died?'

'His spirit's definitely there. But in a good way. It's very peaceful. Walking through the door, it feels ... OK, this will sound strange, but it almost feels like a blessing?'

It didn't just sound strange. It sounded creepy as hell.

'We'll have the afternoon to ourselves,' Talia continued, 'but maybe I should invite Nina too, for later? That could be fun. And if you get there early you can say hi to your cousin.'

This made me sit up. 'Dido?'

'Right! I still find her a teensy bit scary, but I'm starting to realise she's a softie at heart. And her theatrical connections are *gold*.'

'And she'll be in Norfolk because ...?'

'We're going to film Dido walking through the grounds, showing the place where the actual theatre is going to be built. She'll explain why giving young actors support at a really early stage is so important – every time she talks about it I get goosebumps, I swear.'

'You know that Nina is together with Dido's ex?'

'I *know*. Awkward! But we can make sure they don't cross paths. Dido's leaving as soon as the filming's done, with the journalist who's doing the interview. He's a friend of hers. And as for Nina and Nick … I can see why Dido would be upset … but it's not like there was an overlap.'

I snorted. 'Indeed not. There was a distinct break. Of a whole five minutes.'

Talia giggled. 'You know how much I adore Nina – I love her to *bits* – but her impulses are all over the place. She even tried it on with Adam that same night.'

'*What?*'

'Sarah saw them and messaged me. She was all over him, Sarah said. Practically jumped Adam outside the bathroom. Of course Adam wasn't having any of it – though not for the reasons Nina probably imagined.' Talia giggled again. Then she lowered her voice, even though there wasn't anyone to hear us. 'I feel bad for her, actually. Sarah said Adam was very rude. As in, *super mean.*'

I didn't like any of this. I knew all too well what Nina was like when she was coked up and horny. I could imagine, too, the viciousness of Adam's rejection. It was starting to look as if Nina hadn't guessed Adam's secret after all. Or else this had been her half-baked way of putting her suspicions to the test.

'Sarah thought I'd be mad, but how could I be? It's Nina. Nina! We all know what she's like. She always does crazy shit when she's drunk and then *totally* regrets it in the morning. It's hilarious. She probably doesn't even remember.'

'You're probably right.' I was thinking, hard. 'Listen. It would be great to catch up with you. There's some things I think we need to talk about. About Adam, and … and the night he died.'

'Yes. You need closure,' Talia said earnestly. 'I do too. I mean, that's part of the reason I'm getting so excited about this summer school. As Sarah says, it's about creating something positive out of a tragedy, but it's also about drawing a line. Honestly, I think it would do you good, coming down there. It might be what you need to lay Adam's spirit to rest.'

'OK,' I said, before I could think better of it. 'Count me in.'

It was now twenty-four hours since Zalandra's message requesting a meeting had gone unanswered. In the interim, I'd had six missed calls from an unknown number and five emails with no text but WHEN AND WHERE???? in the subject line. The sixth was more ominous: I WILL ALWAYS FIND YOU. So I fired off an apologetic message, saying that I was extremely busy with work but would be in touch as soon as possible. Toodles!

I knew I couldn't fob off Zalandra for much longer, and that it was probably dangerous even to try, but there was only room for so much crazy in my life. Talia was spamming me with links to self-help guides (*Grieving Mindfully: Unmask the Healer Within*). Nina had sent me a deluge of gifs and memes on the theme of girl detectives. Scooby Doo also featured. I was starting to wonder if she'd ever taken my investigations seriously or if she was just playing along.

Besides, I needed to focus on the job at hand. Man in hand, that is. Before Dan and I went out to dinner, I had to spend a good half-hour reassuring him that, yes, I was fully committed to the continuing success of our arrangement. I found I was apprehensive about telling him that I'd be going to Norfolk, since it meant cancelling an appearance at one of his colleagues' birthday drinks.

As it turned out, however, Dan was incredibly solicitous. Which of course made me feel like an ungrateful arse.

'It must be huge deal for you, revisiting the place where Adam died.' He laid his hand on mine and looked deeply into my eyes. I smiled bravely back, sensing our fellow diners drinking it all in – Grace couldn't have arranged a more touching tableau if she'd tried. 'I don't like the idea of you going there at all, really, though if you say it will bring closure then of course I have to respect that. But you can't schlep all that way on the train. Absolutely not. It wouldn't be appropriate, let alone comfortable. The place is, what, a two-hour drive from London? Two and a half? That's nothing. I've got an old school friend who lives in that part of the world. The two of us can have a pub lunch en route, I'll drop you off at the house, then go catch up with my mate, and we can reconnect later.'

It wasn't a bad idea. Nina had tried to persuade me to drive down with her in Nick's Porsche, but she'd no doubt insist on discussing assorted murder plots and Hollywood sex-rings the whole journey, with the kind of lip-smacking relish I was increasingly exhausted by. I was unsettled, too, by the fact she hadn't told me about coming on to Adam. She was probably embarrassed. Or, as Talia said, she didn't even remember. But I felt I needed a bit of a distance before meeting up with the two of them and Dido. Sarah, too, might still be lurking when I arrived. Before facing any of them, I wanted to keep my head clear.

'Are you sure about this?' I asked.

Dan smiled. He had a good smile: it made his eyes crinkle and lit up his whole face, so that the bluntness softened. 'Absolutely. What are friends for?'

More flowers arrived the morning of my trip to Norfolk. The blooms were intact, this time. They were wrapped in a pink satin ribbon stained with what looked like blood. Some of the roses had blood on them too. The note read *I'll Always Be Here for You*.

I took a photo, then put the box carefully away on top of the wardrobe. Whether the blood was animal or human, there might well be all sorts of incriminating evidence to be gathered from the contents. Then I'd turn up to my meeting with Zalandra with a recording device and make sure she let rip with the crazy, before taking everything to the police. Screw her. She was a sad-sack psycho who was most likely going to spend the rest of her life in an asylum.

As for me ... I knew what the scene outside my flat on Saturday morning must look like. An attractive couple, all smiles, getting ready to set off in a fancy car for a country weekend. Bags packed with cashmere knits and designer wellies. Eyes bright with the anticipation of muddy walks and dirty sex, most likely in front of a crackling log fire. #CountryStyle #BackToNature #Getaway

Who would guess that my hunky fake boyfriend was actually just giving me a lift down to the house where my gay fake ex-boyfriend was murdered?

#Haunted #TrueCrime #Killer

But there were still moments when it almost felt like a holiday. As we loaded our overnight bags into the back of Dan's convertible, he fussed about whether I'd remembered to pack walking boots and if my waterproofs were suitable. 'The catering is on me,' he said, holding up a bag bulging with gourmet junk food. 'You can't have a road trip without good snacks. Almost as crucial as good music.'

Dan was an unabashed petrol-head, and once behind the wheel, he was more relaxed than I'd seen him for ... well, ever. We were soon bantering about our rival playlists and reminiscing about the car-ride games we'd played as children. Dan talked about his daughter, Lulu, which wasn't something he often did because it made him emotional, and the road trips he planned on taking her on once she was older – 'Route 66, obviously; that's the classic. But then there's the Great Ocean Road, Australia. Has to be done. And we could start closer to home, in Ireland, with the Wild Atlantic Way ...' We talked about our favourite travel destinations and the people we'd met there, and the best ways to let off steam after dealing with difficult colleagues. I realised it was a long while since I'd had a conversation that was entirely free of intrigue or regret.

My phone rang several times during the first hour of the journey. An unknown number. Zalandra, no doubt.

'Shouldn't you get that?' Dan asked.

'No, I know what it's about. Some nonsense I have to deal with once I'm back.' I switched the phone to silent, pushing thoughts of the bloodied pink ribbon away. 'I don't want to think about it now.'

He looked pleased.

As we zoomed onto a particularly green and pleasant stretch of road, Dan put down the roof of the convertible. Cold bright air whipped through my hair; I closed my eyes and tilted my face towards the open sky. Foo Fighters blasted from the stereo. Maybe, just maybe, everything was going to be all right.

The pub Dan had selected for our lunch was an English tourist board's wet dream: a higgledy-piggledy warren of inglenook fireplaces and age-blackened beams, set in a leafy hamlet complete with duck pond. The landlady had apple cheeks. The menu was heavy on craft beer and game pies. On requesting a quiet spot, we were ushered away from the bar and into a private snuggery with its own wood-burning stove and snoozing cat. Here, the landlady asked for a selfie with Dan. 'We're all such fans,' she said, blushing furiously. 'Aww. The feeling's mutual,' he said, giving her shoulders a matey squeeze.

He meant it, too. 'What a gem,' he said, once we were alone. 'This is the life. Lovely stuff. Funny how it's only once I'm out of the city that I remember how much I hate the place.' He stretched in his chair. 'I owe you one.'

'For recruiting you as my chauffeur?'

'Ah, but I'm only in it for the snacks.'

We smiled.

Rain started to spot the window as our food arrived. 'Is something wrong?' Dan asked, seeing me play about with a forkful of mushrooms. They were gritty with parsley and slimy with cream.

'No, it's good. A bit heavy, that's all.'

'You eat like a bird. You need feeding up. Here – try this.' He brought a steaming forkful of venison pie to my mouth. 'Open wide.'

It felt rude not to, so I obediently swallowed. 'Mmmm.'

His thumb lightly rubbed the side of my mouth, and I drew back.

'You had a clingy pastry crumb.'

'Oh. Thanks.'

It was beginning to feel stuffy in the small room, with the stove pulsing out heat and the thick tapestry curtain drawn against the doorway. The mouthful of venison lay in an indigestible lump in my stomach. I excused myself to go to the bathroom, where I splashed water on my flushed cheeks. On returning, I found Dan standing by the window, looking out towards the pond. 'Here,' he said, beckoning me over. 'Look at this.'

A little old lady and a little old man were feeding the ducks in the drizzle.

'Sweet,' I said, though, to be honest, I thought the scene a bit dismal.

Dan rested a hand on my shoulder. 'Isn't it? You know, that's all I ever wanted for Jenny and me. We'd find a nice little place in the countryside, grow old together. Feed the birds in the rain.'

It was a pity Dan's expressions of marital regret always sounded so mawkish.

Feeling disloyal at the thought, I patted his hand. 'You'll still have all that, but with someone who deserves you.'

He turned to look at me. Seriously and deeply, like he had in the restaurant when I'd first talked of revisiting the scene of Adam's death. 'You really mean that?'

'Of course I mean it.' I tried to think of what Talia might say in a situation like this. 'You're an extraordinary person, as well as a great catch. You're bound to find someone who's extraordinary too.'

'I can't tell you how happy I am to hear you say that.'

Then he leant in and kissed me.

In the first moment of shock I just stood there, motionless, with his tongue in my mouth. It was still flavoured with gravy. Dan took my lack of reaction for compliance, for his tongue began to move, vigorously – thrashing about, in fact, as his hand held the back of my head, clamping my face to his, and his other hand began to roam around my body while he emitted small noises of satisfaction and pleasure. They were very similar to the noises he'd made while eating the venison pie. I came to my senses and pushed him off, with more force than both of us expected, so that he fell against the table.

'Shit. I'm sorry,' I said breathlessly. 'Are you OK?'

'No, *I'm* sorry,' he said, though he looked annoyed as well as startled. 'I didn't mean to take you by surprise.' He rubbed his hip and attempted a gallant smile. 'I suppose my baser instincts got the better of me.'

I tried to smile back. 'Crossed wires, that's all. I'm sorry if things got … muddled. But as you know, I'm not looking to date – date for real – at the moment. I'm still not over Adam.'

Dan shook his head. 'You can't let an ex overshadow the rest of your life. I appreciate that you feel some kind of survivor's guilt, but it's obvious you've been ready to move on for a while. My instincts might be base, but they're not wrong. And I *know* we have a connection.'

'Look, there's no doubt the, uh, play-acting aspect of our arrangement can be confusing.' The room was too small, too stuffy. My lungs felt cramped. My chest was tightening. 'But the lines were set out very clearly at the start. We need to keep our focus. We need to think of the bigger picture here.'

'Screw the lines. Screw the rules. The heart wants what it wants.'

He was advancing towards me.

'But what if the heart wants something … wrong?' To my shame, tears stung my eyes.

'Lily! You're crying.' Now Dan looked stricken. 'God, this is so awful. And all my fault. You're making me feel terrible. You're so pretty when you cry, but it's still the worst sight in the world. I can't bear the thought that I've upset you. It's unbearable. I'm so, so sorry. Come here. Please.' Somehow he was now hugging me, murmuring his sorrys into my hair. This, too, was wrong. But again my body was lagging behind my brain. 'There,' Dan was saying, 'is that better? Does it feel good? It does, doesn't it? Everything's going to be fine, I promise. It's been a confusing time for both of us, but I know how to make it up to you. You'll see.' And he moved from stroking my hair to stroking my cheek.

'*Don't touch me.*' I twisted free, hands protectively raised. 'Don't you *dare*.'

We were both breathing hard. He was visibly trembling. There was a horrible pause. Then, 'Were you like this with Adam?' Dan asked, and I realised he was, in fact, shaking with rage. 'Hot and cold? I bet you were. I bet you played him like a puppet on a string.'

'This isn't –'

'Maybe Adam liked that. Maybe he was a masochist. He was an addict, after all. You were part of his problem, I bet. His addiction. Yes. I know the damage girls like you do. It's not just that you're a prick-tease. It's that you're an emotional terrorist.'

'Jesus fucking Christ,' I said, staring at him. 'No wonder your wife left you.'

It was probably just as well this was the moment our waitress returned to clear our plates. We both stayed frozen in place. A small part of my brain found time to wonder exactly what the girl had heard and how much of this might end up in the press. The clatter of cutlery shook us from our stupor. Tight lipped and white faced, Dan flung a wad of notes in the waitress's direction, grabbed his coat and blazed out of the room. I followed him because, after all, I had nowhere else to go.

In the car-park, the elderly couple who'd been feeding the ducks were now sharing a packet of crisps on a bench. Without looking at me, Dan yanked my bag out of the car, flung it on the tarmac and took his place behind the wheel. The engine roared. He stuck his head out of the window to get the last word in. 'Frigid little bitch.'

CHAPTER TWELVE

So there I was again. Stranded in the arse-end of nowhere after a blazing row with my (ex) fake boyfriend. This time it was raining, too.

The first thing I did was find a sheltering hedgerow to throw up in. The idea of that greasy wad of venison being inside me made me feel faint. I leant against a tree for a bit and tried to gather myself. At this point, my main thought was *My mother is going to kill me.*

Eventually I took out my phone. There were twenty new messages in my inbox. The subject line of the latest one was *BETRAYER*. I started laughing weakly to myself. Sure, the Momager would be out for my blood – but she'd have to fight Zalandra for it.

Our lunch had been a late one; it was getting on for three. I figured I was still about an hour's drive from the house. Who could I call? I tried Talia but she didn't pick up. Neither did Dido. Filming must have overrun. Nina would be in the car but she wasn't due to arrive much before six. There was nothing for it but to slink back into the pub and ask about a taxi.

The place was a lot busier than before lunch. When I walked into the bar the assembled drinkers fell comically silent. I doubted this was in tribute to my scene-stealing turn in *The Other Women*.

Our waitress must have spread the word that an emotional terrorist was on the loose.

I explained to the goggle-eyed bar staff, with all the briskness I could muster, that unfortunately my friend had had to return to London due to a family emergency, and I needed to find a cab. Teeth were sucked and heads shaken. The local taxi number was tried to no avail, but after further consultation, Joey's-mate's-nephew was called and an arrangement reached. There was a moment when I thought Joey was about to ask for a selfie as his reward, but I channelled the Momager's best blood-freezing stare and he thought better of it.

At least there was a cashpoint just outside the pub. I took out my fare and found a quiet-ish corner to sit and wait for my lift. On the table in front of me were the leftovers of a weekend news supplement. I flicked through it idly. Anything to distract me from wondering which of the tabloids the waitress was busy emailing with her Hot Tip!!!, and whether the elderly duck-botherers would be in on it too.

Even though the confrontation with Dan was long over, the disgust lingered, like the taste of vomit in my mouth. I kept having to wipe my clammy palms on my jeans. Worst of all, I still had to face the house. Dido. Sarah. Talia. The swimming pool. How much, I wondered, would Joey's-mate's-nephew charge to take me speeding home to London?

When the man himself arrived, there was a moment when I thought he was the same spotty youth who'd manned the gates at Adam's house party. He wasn't, but I was finding the parallels to that night increasingly disorienting. The car was even similar to Tig's – an ancient rust bucket smelling of weed.

My new chauffeur held the door to the backseat open for me. I could feel his eyes on my arse as I clambered in. 'You're the actress who was in that kids' film, aren't you?' he asked as he settled into the driver's seat. 'The Christmas one, with the goblins.'

'Mm.'

'*And* you dated the dead actor. The one who drowned at the orgy.'

'It wasn't –' I stopped myself. What was the point?

'Terrible business.'

'Yes.'

'It's still the most exciting thing that's happened round here for fifty years, mind.' We lurched onto the main road. 'So are you here for the film festival?'

'Festival?'

'I heard the actor's girlfriend is going to set up a film festival down here. Get all the big celebs in. Hey! Maybe this time next year I'll be giving Casilda Fernandez a lift back from the pub.' He laughed. 'And you know what I'll tell her? I'll say I had that – what's your name again?'

'Lily. Lily … Thane.'

'Right! I'll tell her I had that Lily Thane in the back of my cab once.' He laughed even more uproariously. 'So … what're your plans for the weekend, then, Lily? Fishing? Boating? Bird-watching?'

'I'm just seeing some friends.'

'Ah. Well, if you and your friends are looking to "party", I might be able to help out.' He turned round and winked broadly. 'With supplies and such, if you catch my drift.'

Jesus. 'Thanks. I'll pass.'

I'd absentmindedly taken some of the newspaper along with me, and now I shook it out and held it up in front of my face as a conversational deterrent. By a strange coincidence, the pages I'd opened included a profile of Casilda Fernandez. Her curves seemed even more luscious, her glow even more golden, than in her *Wylderness* days. The full cast list for her next feature had just been announced. I read the précis of the movie, and my breath caught.

I was so preoccupied when we pulled up outside the entrance gates that it took me a moment or two to realise we'd reached our destination.

'So this is the actual house where the bloke actually died?' my driver asked, craning his neck in vain hope of seeing past the trees to the scene of death-and-orgies. He was clearly disappointed when I said dropping me off by the side of the road was fine.

At least the intercom was working better this time.

'Oh. It's you,' said Sarah Harker, her voice thick with dislike.

'*Lilyyyyyy!*' squealed Talia, drowning her out. 'Yay! Come up, come up, come up!'

The gates creaked open. I squared my shoulders.

The last time I'd been there it had been a sunny June morning and the place had still looked fairly austere. It was mid-November now, and though the rain had cleared, austere had intensified to bleak. The high concrete walls, soaked by the recent downpour, were a splotched and darker grey. A fret from the salt marsh sent trails of mist through the dripping black pines.

I walked up the drive, once more hearing the lonely tap of my feet on the tarmac. This time, however, the grounds looked freshly trimmed and tended. No weeds in the drive, no tufty hillocks in the lawn. All the building's lights were blazing. The bright glass under the dusk-grey sky made the blocks of the house seem oddly insubstantial, as if another switch could be flicked and they too would start to glow from within, like paper lanterns rather than cubes of granite.

Talia herself came running out of the house to greet me. 'Lily! This means so much to me, I can't tell you. Are you excited? Say that you're excited!'

I gently extricated myself from her embrace. My cheeks were smeared with goo from her lip gloss, and her perfume was making my eyes water. 'Thank you so much for inviting me down here. You've got a lot going on.'

'Ha, yes – naturally everything's overrun. It's been fun but *utter* chaos. Your cousin's being an absolute *saint*! Anyway, come in, come in. We're just about finishing.'

When she saw me hanging back, she took both my hands in hers. 'I know how you feel. I really do. But the energy of this place ... it's healing.' Her eyes shone. 'Breathe deeply, and let the light in.'

I struggled to keep a straight face. But when I walked through the door, the house did feel different. For one thing, it was immaculate. Not one speck of dust on the shelves, not one smudge on the window panes. For another, there was now some actual furniture – of the low-slung white and pouffey variety. And there were flowers everywhere: cascading profusions of pale blooms and dark ivy. They, and the scented candles scattered about the place, put me in mind of a church, or possibly a temple. Talia, now I came to look at her properly, was dressed a bit like a high priestess in a long gauzy dress of white and silver.

'That's quite some gown.'

She giggled self-consciously and gave a twirl. 'It's a bit much, isn't it? Sarah convinced me, though.'

I followed her into the kitchen. We'd passed a pile of cables and other technical equipment in the hall, and I could hear people moving about and talking overhead. I wondered if Sarah was among them.

'Are you appearing in the promo then?'

'That's all Dido, but me and Sarah are doing a print interview too. I wanted the photos and so on to be done outside, but obviously that's tricky at this time of year, what with the weather and the light and so on. We had a hard enough time getting footage of Dido by the theatre site. So the photo shoot was mostly done in the house.'

'Mm. It all sounds great. But, you know, once everyone's cleared off, and before Nina gets here, I'd really like to talk to you.'

'Absolutely! That's what this weekend is all about, isn't it? I mean, we've always been friends – *good* friends, I like to think – but the things we now share, things that only the two –'

'Adam. Exactly. I'd like to talk about him, and …' I hesitated. I couldn't put this off any longer. 'I'd like to talk about how he died, if that's OK.'

I expected Talia to be all of a flutter. Instead, she inhaled slowly and closed her eyes. 'Yes,' she said, once the moment was over. 'You're right. We should talk about that.'

'Talk about what?' Sarah demanded. She was framed in the doorway, wearing a crisp black trouser suit, with her hair

267

slicked back. For a disconcerting moment, it was almost like looking at Adam.

'One of my endless work dramas,' I said smoothly. 'You look great, Sarah. It's a wonderful project you're setting up here. Adam would be ... amazed.'

'Uh-huh. Thanks.' She looked both impatient and bored. That, too, was a look I knew well from her brother. It seemed incredible that the last time we'd met had been at his funeral. Sarah had been half-crazed then, spitting her grief and bitterness into my face. And here she was, dressed in black again, but with the edges all polished. #InstaReady. 'Tally? Daniel's asking for us again.'

Talia looked torn. 'Go,' I said, gently shooing her. 'I'll be fine. We can catch up later.'

'Are you sure? *Sure?* OK, well, I shouldn't be long. There's heaps of food in the fridge – help yourself to anything and everything. And look,' she exclaimed, beaming, 'here's your cousin to keep you company! You girls have fun and I'll be back before you know it.'

'Lovely Lily,' said Dido smoothly. 'What a treat.' After a perfunctory air kiss, she went to the fridge and helped herself to a bottle of water. She was wearing a man's velvet smoking jacket over bare skin, with leggings and muddy biker boots. It was as ridiculous an outfit as Talia's but, being Dido, she carried it off much better.

'Well,' she said, leaning against a counter-top. 'I don't expect either of us imagined ever being here again.' She took a swig of water. 'I take it you're also "doing it for the kids"?'

I shook my head. 'I'm just here to support Talia. The Adam Harker Fame Academy's all yours.'

'How so?'

'You're starring in the film. And I hear you're going to be patron.'

'We'll see. The film's just a promo to use in presentations – to lure sponsors, win over potential NIMBYs. That sort of thing. Three minutes of me preaching about the importance of theatre in the lives of the Youth. Lots of waving my arms over a muddy patch of grass and saying, "Imagine the marvellous theatre that will rise from the marshes of untimely death."'

Her flippant tone surprised me. 'It's a long way to come for a charity gig.'

'Oh, I shouldn't sneer. It'll be an impressive project if it comes off. Bringing art to the regions, opportunities to the underprivileged ...' Dido lowered her voice a little. 'To be *completely* honest, I thought Grace Tang would be here. Or at least more directly involved in the process. I'm hoping she'll rep me, so this would have been a good opportunity to connect.'

Interesting. 'So Grace isn't around?'

'No. She sent someone from her office instead. Still, it's a good sign that the Harkers are using her firm. Adam's sister is surprisingly capable.'

It struck me that in explaining her reasons for getting involved, Dido hadn't mentioned the obvious one. 'I wonder what Adam would think of it all.'

'His name's just a hook to hang a good cause on.' Her eyes narrowed. 'It's rather touching you're so supportive of Talia's part in all this. From what I heard, your excitable little friend got together with Adam almost as soon as your plane left the runway. That must have stung.'

'It did, at the time. Speaking of rebounds,' I said awkwardly, 'I only recently found out about Nick and Nina. It was quite a shock … You know that, er, Nina's arriving later?'

'Which is why I'm getting a lift home pronto – if I didn't know better, I might think I was being set up for one of those ghastly reality shows where women are always throwing drinks in each other's faces.' Dido looked around, nose wrinkling. 'That would be in keeping with the McMansion makeover, anyway. Look – do you want to get some air? I could do with stretching my legs before the drive.'

This was the opportunity I'd been hoping for, even if I took it up without much enthusiasm. Outside, it was chilly and damp, but my cousin's one of those people who never feels the cold. She lit up a cigarette and dragged on it greedily. 'De-*licious*,' she said, shaking out rivulets of dark hair. 'You want one?'

'I've quit.' Dan hated smoking. It had been an unofficial add-on to our contract that I'd give up the fags. (In more ways than one, *ho ho*.) Now, of course, I was free to return to whatever filthy habit I chose.

'Good for you.' It was almost as if Dido knew what I was thinking. 'How's it going with your new beau? Danny, is it? I gather he's some kind of TV personality.'

A lurid jumble of tabloid headlines flashed before my eyes. 'Little Lucie's an Emotional Terrorist!' 'Lily Thane's a Frigid Bitch!' But any attempt at a PR whitewash would have to wait. Right now, I had other damage to control.

'I don't think it's likely to go anywhere,' was all I said.

270

'That's a shame.'

Dido stalked about and smoked in silence for a while. I wondered where our conversation was leading, but wanted Dido to be the one to begin. Presently, she led the way down the hill to where the garden ended and the salt marsh began.

It was close to five, and the sun was setting. The rain clouds had partly cleared, so the sky was a lurid pink streaked with charcoal; the rippling mud of the creeks carried the faintest pink cast. I breathed in, smelling salt and rot. There was a low chatter of geese somewhere ahead, the birds slowly rising like a plume of smoke on the horizon.

'Feels like we're right on the edge of the world, doesn't it?' Dido murmured.

'It was the end of it, for Adam.' I immediately winced. This was the sort of grandiose statement only someone like Dido could get away with.

But she turned and looked at me, grave as an effigy. 'That was a terrible night,' she said. 'In every way. Like a fever dream. I know I shouldn't bring my miserable little marital breakdown into it, but I think that's another reason I agreed to do the filming in person. I suppose I thought it would exorcise a few demons … Isn't that why you're here too?'

'Partly. I also wanted to talk to you.'

'We do live in the same city, you know.'

'Right.' I rammed my cold hands into my pockets. 'The whole trip's been very … spontaneous.'

Dido nodded, but she wasn't really listening. 'This is where I ended my marriage. Pretty much at this exact spot.'

Salt tears in a salt marsh, as Nick had described it. I hadn't realised he was being so literal. *A well-crafted stage effect.* It was true the marsh made a grandly desolate backdrop for Dido, with her muddy black garb and swirling hair. I looked back up the hill: in the rapidly increasing gloom, the house blazed even brighter, but also seemed further away.

'You must have been in quite a state,' I said. 'Especially as you'd just found out that Kash Malik wasn't going to turn you into a movie star, after all.'

Her head whipped round. 'What's this? What are you talking about?'

'Kash's new feature: the "feminist Woody Allen movie". Adam set you up with Kash because Kash is an auteur on the up, and you can't have an auteur without a muse – Adam convinced you that you'd be the perfect fit. And things with Kash must have gone well, *really* well, I guess, because you started telling people you'd got the part. But Kash didn't cast you in the end, did he? At the very last moment, he decided against a little-known Shakespearean stage actor. He went for an A-lister instead. Casilda Fernandez. It was in the paper today.'

There were two spots of red burning high on Dido's cheeks. 'I should have known better. I got carried away – I *never* get carried away. But Adam …'

'Adam led you on.'

'I would never have considered auditioning if it wasn't for him,' she said throatily. 'Adam told me that Kash was already a huge admirer and that it was time for me to be "discovered" on screen. I could trust Kash, Adam said. He'd bring me to a global audience.'

So theatreland's youngest and brightest *grand dame* was in fact hankering for a silver-screen smash – red carpets and razzle-dazzle. I'd have thought I'd feel good about this. I didn't.

'It was an ego-trip for Adam,' I told her. 'That's what he liked to do: seduce and bedazzle. He'd make grand promises, then sneer at you for believing them.'

Her mouth twisted. 'I've known disappointment, obviously. It's integral to the artist's life. But when I took that call from my agent ... God. Adam had assured me I was a dead cert, that he'd heard it direct from Kash. I'd started to tell people – or rather, I'd dropped unmistakeable hints to friends. Frenemies too.' She lowered her voice to a whisper, even though there was no one to hear us. Part of her probably didn't want me to hear this confession of weakness either. 'It wasn't the rejection that floored me – it was that I'd let myself be so exposed.'

I nodded. 'I understand, I do. And I'm sorry. But what I *don't* understand is why you still came down here to Adam's party, knowing how he'd strung you along. Why would you do that?' At the party, I'd congratulated Dido on her forthcoming 'Hollywood début' and had been surprised by the stiffness of her response. I'd thought her reticence was just a pose. In truth, she must have been seething.

I thought, again, of Nick's description of the end of their marriage. *What people don't realise is that Dido can be extraordinarily vindictive.*

When had she got that devastating call from her agent? Two, three days before? Or earlier – early enough to plan her punishment?

In any case, Dido didn't answer my question. She just stood there, gazing into the gathering darkness, a graven image once more.

Looking at that noble profile – the proud sweep of that impossible Thane nose – I felt a spasm of rage. I reached out and gave her a shove. There wasn't much to it, but because she was startled, she almost fell.

'What the hell, Lily?'

'Look at me,' I said. All the fears and frustrations of the day – week – month – year – had suddenly converged. My throat was so tight I could hardly get the words out. '*Look at me*. I know you didn't dump Nick in public, in the middle of the party, like you said at the funeral. You ended things right here, alone by the bog. You just admitted it. So why lie about it? Why lie to me?'

'I didn't – that is, I don't remember – we were at a funeral, Lily – I wasn't thinking straight. And why does it matter, anyway?'

'Because it was your explanation for the message you sent me the night of Adam's death. "I need to talk to you. I've done something dreadful."'

'Oh, please. It was a stupid text. I was drunk and emotional, hiding out in a bedroom so I didn't have to face the crowd … It meant nothing. You should have ignored it.'

'How could I? It frightened me. I was so frightened, in fact, that as soon as I got it I ran over to this house and found my ex-boyfriend dead in a swimming pool. So what was the dreadful thing, Dido? *What did you do?*' I was so close to her our faces were almost touching.

'Lily – stop it – you're starting to frighten me –'

I took another step towards her, backing her towards the marsh. Muddy salt water was already creeping over the base of her boots. The pink of the sky had faded to a dull red smoulder at the horizon. The geese had gone, but all around us small rustlings and ripplings in the undergrowth made the darkness seethe.

'All right,' she said, holding up her hands and shifting unsteadily in the ooze. 'All right. I'm sorry. You're right. There's something I need to admit to you, and I should have done it a while ago.' She licked her lips. 'Here's the truth. There was a time … during your and Adam's relationship … when I may have sent a few bits and pieces to a gossip site.'

All the breath left my body. '*You're* Tinseltattles's source? How … *why*?'

'Well, Adam wasn't the type to hold back, was he? He used to share all sorts of ridiculous anecdotes about your time on the road. I just passed on the best of them, that's all.'

'And what about the other crap?' I clenched my fists. 'Like the allegations I was on drugs, that I was blackmailing Adam, that I was an actual *prostitute*? Was that you too?' I gave her another shove – a hard one this time, hard enough to send her sprawling into the marsh. She gasped. 'Why? Why would you do that – to me, or anyone?'

She lay there spreadeagled among the reeds and the rot, her face flecked with mud. But she was still Dido Thane. She raised her head and curled her lip and she could have been Schiller's Mary Stuart, facing down Elizabeth. 'Because that's the world you've chosen – a fake world built out of shoddy tricks. We both know why you were with Adam. He was just another shortcut. You were using the profile he gave you as a stand-in for *real* talent, *real* ambition, *real* grit. Things other people bleed for. Why should you be taken seriously? You don't deserve it. You haven't earned it. You never will.'

I suppose she had a point.

Dido squelched up to her feet. Disdainfully, she removed a slick of weed from her hair, smoothed down her sodden jacket. 'And after the Kash Malik debacle, I didn't think Adam should get away with anything either. I planned to do a Tinseltattles hit on him too. I knew enough about his habits to know his behaviour at the party would be incriminating. That's why I came, if you want the truth. I intended to find some dirt and publish it.'

'Except Adam ended up dead.'

'Yes. But before that, he apologised. Handsomely. I'd expected him to brazen it out or sneer at me, even. It wasn't like that at all. He ended it by saying he was embarrassed, but not as embarrassed as Kash Malik was going to be once he realised his mistake. Cassie has none of my intelligence, he said, let alone craft, and he should know because he'd dated her.' She shook her head. 'So I was ashamed of my intentions. Just as I was ashamed of how I'd treated my marriage and of the mischief I'd caused you … I suppose it was a night of assorted reckonings.'

I almost laughed, in spite of myself. 'It must have helped that the apology was so handsome.'

A plaintive voice called to us from the hill. I'd almost forgotten about Talia. Her white dress was just visible in the gloom. She was calling and waving. We ignored her.

'Adam knew what it's like to have a calling,' Dido said, gazing out towards the invisible sea. 'He took the craft seriously, if nothing else. He understood the irony that every performance I've ever given can only survive as a memory or an anecdote. Even the great Sir Terence Thane – what's his legacy, really? Nostalgia and newspaper clippings. His name on some poky theatre bar. So

Adam said I owed it to myself to find another, better Kash: a filmmaker who can turn an actor into a living, breathing work of art … *forever.*'

'Adam was right to encourage you.'

'I'm glad you think that, Lily.'

'Of course.' I smiled my most Californian smile: the one spun from sunbeams and sugar. 'A cheap phony like you is made for Hollywood.'

CHAPTER THIRTEEN

I let Dido go ahead of me up the hill, striding past Talia as if she wasn't there. Nostrils flaring, hair a-billow. Her indignation was so stately I almost admired it.

Following behind more slowly, I found Talia looking flustered. 'Dido looks *really angry*. Is it because the shoot went on late? How can I make it up to her, do you think? Did she talk to you about the project? Is she still going to be patron? Was there an accident – why is she covered in mud?'

'I'm sure it's fine. You know actors: they like to make a grand exit.'

'I thought it was their entrances they cared about.'

'Us Thanes make the most of both.'

This was the point at which Adam would have made a dirty joke. For a heartbeat, I thought I saw him reflected in the window, rolling his eyes at me. Then I saw it was Sarah.

Inside the house, a handful of people were milling about in a purposeful manner: zipping up bags, rolling up cables, having a last check through their clipboards or scroll through their phones. Sarah, to my relief, went upstairs to take a phone call. Dido had already disappeared, presumably into the sanctuary of her friend's car. I went through the larger living room and sat down on one of the low-slung sofas, suddenly overwhelmed by tiredness. 'Is it too early for a drink?'

Talia beamed. 'Never! *Brilliant* idea. What would you like? Champagne? Vodka? Cocktails? I've got *everything*.'

'Let's leave it a few more minutes.' I patted the space next to me. She came and sat down on the sofa, obedient as a child. 'Before Nina gets here, there's something I'd like to talk to you about.'

Talia nodded vigorously. 'About Adam and his death. Shouldn't Sarah be here for this too? She's just calling her mum – I'm not sure how long she'll be.'

'I thought Sarah was, er, leaving now?'

'Well, actually, she said she'd like to stay on. I hope you don't mind? *Do* you mind? Be honest. I know I said we'd have some quality time together, just the two of us, but at the same time, I don't feel I can, like, *abandon* Sarah. Not when she's worked so hard for this shoot and the PR launch and everything, and done so much to include me. Even though she knows me and Adam weren't, you know, a conventional couple, she totally understands the bond we had and really respects it. And she's been feeling so lost, so adrift, since her brother died.'

Huh. Funny how Sarah hadn't been quite so respectful of my own 'unconventional' role in Adam's life. Presumably my inability to fund designer shopping sprees had something to do with it.

I gritted my teeth. 'Poor Sarah. That must be so hard. I definitely don't want to trouble her with any of this. I don't want to trouble *you*, either.' I glanced around to check that we couldn't be overheard. 'I just wanted to ask … well, I don't know how regularly the police are updating you and the family, but a fair amount of time has passed, and I wondered if they were any closer to finding out who supplied Adam with the drugs?'

'Oh. There hasn't been any sort of breakthrough, I'm afraid. I know that his usual dealer has an alibi – he was in Ibiza all summer. Then there's my friend Jorge – well, actually, I don't know Jorge *that* well. I met him and Stassia this one time in San Tropez, but they seemed lovely … Anyway, I gather Jorge got in a bit of hot water because of the cocaine? But his lawyer apparently sorted it out, so it was all right in the end.'

'It bothers me, that's all. The idea of those dodgy perks. For an addict, Adam was surprisingly careful about what he took and where he got it.'

Talia pouted. 'You know I don't like the A word. I mean, Adam had his issues, definitely, but he was also fully committed to living a healthier life. He was seeing a drugs counsellor.'

'I saw his goodie bag at the party. It was full of the usual treats.'

'Yes. I know, and –'

She was interrupted by the last of the PR team coming to say goodbye, which led to a flurry of air kisses and thank yous. When Talia got back from waving them off, she was holding several sheets of scented notepaper.

'I think I know why you're so fixated on Adam's death,' she announced.

'You do?'

'You haven't said a proper farewell. I haven't either. That funeral … it was mostly a blur. I mean, it was *surreal*, wasn't it? I spent the whole time thinking I was going to be sick.

'Anyway, so I had this idea – OK, I saw it on Instagram, but Sarah loved it. It's basically a ceremony of letting go. What you do is write a message to the person who's passed, and then you fold it up into a beautiful little origami boat, and you take it to the sea or a river or a lake – it has to be *living* water, that's crucial – and, finally, you set it on fire as it sails off. Like the Vikings!' She held up a paper boat with a flourish. 'This is the one Sarah made earlier. Isn't it pretty?'

'You want to burn that in the bog?'

Her face fell. 'When you put it that way, it just sounds silly.'

'No – no, I didn't mean that,' I said lamely. 'Sorry. It's a lovely idea.'

'So you'll do it then? Yay!' She actually clapped her hands. 'You won't regret it. I think it will be very *liberating*, watching the little flames ride the moon-lit sea, taking our farewells to Adam with them ...'

'Fine. Just as long as it doesn't end up on Instagram.'

Talia passed me a piece of paper and a pen. Then she crouched down by the coffee table to write her own message, chewing the end of her glittery pen between scribbles, her brow furrowed with concentration. It was the first time I'd seen her write on anything that wasn't a keypad. Soon the paper was densely packed with her loopy, curling script and adorned with hearts and exclamation marks. Meanwhile, I stared blankly at my blank page.

Talia looked up and smiled encouragingly. 'Just try and imagine if Adam was standing here now. What would you like to say to him?'

I miss you.

What are you wearing?

Partypartypartypartycomecomecomecome

cum

??

do you miss me

sorry

sorry

Please?

God. I needed to get a grip. I gave myself a shake and wrote, *Adam, I'm sorry we didn't look after each other better. I'm sorry about a lot of things.* I was impatient with myself for indulging Talia in the charade – it was a relief when the buzzer went. Nina could at least be counted on to inject a dose of salt into the saccharine.

Here was a grand entrance: Nina, her old fake-fur jacket slung over a new (vintage) Vivienne Westwood Boucher-print corset, a bottle of Maker's Mark tucked under one arm. She'd had her teeth whitened; because they were still crooked, her smile looked freshly fanged.

'The bitch is *back*!' She sashayed into the living room, plonked the booze on the floor and marched over to the stereo. In an instant, Prince was blaring out 'Soft and Wet'. There was still little in the way of furnishings, let alone people, to absorb the noise, and the bass line seemed to make both the glass and granite hum.

Talia swept our farewell messages under a cushion and went to turn down the volume. 'Actually, I was going for

282

more of a chilled-out sort of vibe? To keep things, you know, contemplative?'

Nina flung herself down on the sofa and blew out her cheeks. 'Sheesh. I didn't spend three hours on the M11 wrecking Nick's brake pads just to gaze at my navel.' She took a more considered look around the room. The fake fire was flickering briskly away and there was a sheepskin rug fluffed up in front of it, but there were still no curtains or blinds, so the entire north side of the room was a square of glazed darkness. Our reflections shimmered in it like figures underwater. 'I like what you've done with the place, Tals. But what's with the bridalwear?'

'Don't you like it? It was for the photo shoot.' Talia smoothed down the gown.

This was the moment Sarah made her entrance.

Nina stared. 'And here's the groom. Congratulations, you guys.'

Sarah flushed to the roots of her hair. She looked furious but she kept her composure. 'Hi. You must be Nina. I've heard a lot about you.'

'We've already met, actually. The last time we were partying here.'

When Sarah saw Nina putting the moves on Adam, a few short hours before his death.

'Right! Which is why it's so wonderful that Talia and Sarah are reinventing this place,' I babbled. 'As, you know, Adam's legacy. It's going to be incredible. Though it must have been especially hard for you, Sarah. Returning to the house, I mean.'

'Yeah,' she said stiffly. 'You could say that.'

Talia was looking anxious. 'It's so great that you're here, Nina. Lily and Sarah and I were thinking of ways to say goodbye to Adam. As our own little ritual.'

'Aha, *now* the robes and the candles make sense. It's an exorcism.'

Sarah's eyes narrowed. 'What do you mean by that?'

'Nothing, nothing … A private joke.' Nina turned to me. 'What did you do with Danny-boy, by the way? Did you shut him in a closet for the night?'

'Oh, that's right – your new boyfriend drove you down here.' Talia gratefully seized on the change of subject. 'I'd love to meet him if there's time before you go. Danny Bowers always seems so warm, so genuine. That's how he comes across on his show, anyway.'

Nina grinned. 'Yes, Lily does love a good *show*.'

I glared at her. 'Show's over. We broke up.'

'No!' Talia gasped. 'Why?'

'We had an argument on the way here.' The humiliation, and ugliness, of the encounter was still raw. 'I don't want to talk about it.'

'Well,' said Talia, rallying, 'how about a drink then? There's Nina's whiskey, so we could do Manhattans. Or old fashioneds are fun. I *do* love a maraschino. They're so pretty, aren't they? Like a sticky pink kiss in a glass! And there's always champagne –'

'Let's start with the fizz,' said Sarah brusquely.

'Have you got anything soft?' Nina asked.

I was incredulous. 'Since when are you teetotal?'

'Since I'm trying to get knocked up. They say cutting out the fun stuff helps.'

284

'What's the big rush? Trying to lock in Nick and his trust fund before he changes his mind?' Yes, this was bitchy, but I was smarting from the showmance reference.

'No need for locks,' Nina said, giving her corset-bound boobs a jiggle. 'I've got plenty of ways of ensuring Nick's devotion, believe me. He owes me and he knows it.'

'Owes you for what?'

'I'm sure Nick's *crazy* about you,' said Talia.

'Lucky guy,' Sarah dead-panned.

Talia and Sarah went off to fix the drinks.

'What the fuck is the Ugly Sister doing here?' Nina demanded as soon as they'd gone. 'And I'm talking about her personality, by the way. It's almost as bad as her brother's.'

'Talia invited her. She feels sorry for her. And tone it down, will you? This evening's going to be awkward enough without you stirring the shit.'

'*Me?* You're the pissy one. What did Danny do – dock your lunch allowance? Or threaten you with a lifetime of floral skirts and velvet scrunchies?'

'Oh, shut up.' Nina gets like this sometimes. Bullish, abrasive, inclined to either lash out or self-sabotage. Adam was the same. They'd both get this dark and feverish glitter about the eyes, and I knew it was time to watch out.

'All I'm doing is trying to lighten the mood. This isn't supposed to be a wake. And to be honest, it kind of gets on my tits the way that you and Talia mope about like Adam was your knight in white satin armour.'

'You know why I can't move on from Adam's death.'

'Yeah, and your obsession's getting unhealthy. Good on you

285

for following the leads, but it's not like you've found a smoking gun. Or a smoking anything.'

'I thought you were supporting me.'

'I *am*, Nancy Drew. I believe you, for one thing. Somebody definitely wanted the wanker dead. Or at least bundled off to rehab in a blaze of bad publicity. What I find harder to get my head round is why you care so much. About getting justice, I mean. What are you trying to make up for, Lily? What do you think it's going to change?'

'God, Nina. Maybe I'm just concerned that a killer's on the loose.'

'Fine! Then go to the police with what you've got or else let it go. Because holding hands with Talia while crying into your quails' eggs isn't going to help anything.'

'What's not to help?' Talia had come tottering back, bearing a silver tray with three champagne flutes and a Diet Coke. Sarah followed with assorted canapés. Quails' eggs were, indeed, among them.

I gave Nina a warning shake of the head over the rim of my glass. She ignored it. 'Lily and I were talking about Adam's legacy. Has it not occurred to you that a drama school in his name is pretty much the last thing on earth Adam would have wanted?'

'I … I don't understand you.'

Nina laughed. 'Insecure jerks like Adam – and, to be fair, most other actors – don't want to nurture the talent of the bright young things coming up behind them. They want to crush them beneath their heel.'

Talia looked as if she'd been slapped. 'Nina! I appreciate you're trying to make a joke or whatever but I actually think that's really harsh. Unkind, even. Especially in front of Sarah.'

Sarah pulled at her lip. 'No, it's OK.'

'You mustn't put a brave face on it –'

'I'm not. It's true, I can't see Adam being interested in helping other kids follow in his footsteps. He was way too selfish. All the opportunities he messed up, all those second and third chances, all the people he hurt … He always assumed he'd get away with it because it was his *right*.' She shrugged. 'Doesn't mean we can't try and make something worthwhile out of his memory.'

Sarah had voiced similar resentments at Adam's funeral. And I knew she had a point. But it still pissed me off. 'Adam was generous to you,' I said. 'Wasn't he?'

'Here and there, now and again. It was a power game to him.'

I frowned. 'He didn't owe you anything.'

'No? "Adam has the beauty; Sarah's got the brains." That's what my dad likes – liked – to say. Which was a sick joke, right, because Adam wasn't stupid, was he? So where did that leave me?' She looked at us fiercely. 'Adam got me to sign an NDA before he let me come to his party. Like I was some pathetic groupie. Or a *servant*. Do any of you know how that felt?'

We were all silent.

She abruptly got to her feet. 'I'm going out for some air.'

'Wait, Sarah, please –'

Talia pattered after her. When she came back a few minutes later, her face was as stern as I'd ever seen it. 'Sarah's going to lie down. She's very hurt. Very unhappy. As am I.'

Nina, however, was unconcerned. 'C'mon, Talia. It's clear Sarah's got a ton of issues with her brother that have nothing to do with us.' She dug into the wasabi shrimp. 'Because, really, how well did the three of us know him? Two beards and a bitch.'

I finished my drink and put the glass down on the table with a bang. 'It's not for you to say how we choose to remember Adam.'

'Sure. Because I'm just the sidekick. The disposable gal-pal. But for a walk-on part, I've got some killer lines. Wanna hear them?'

I shook my head. Obviously, Nina ignored me.

'Adam used you as an emotional punchbag and Talia as his personal ATM,' she said, jabbing her finger for emphasis. 'He bullied his sister, physically assaulted his boyfriend, put his stalker on his payroll and blackmailed his way to top billing. Yeah, he was hot, yeah, he was talented, and yeah, he had his "troubles". But let's not pretend the end of Adam Harker was some great fucking tragedy. In fact, I'll go so far as to say he had it coming.'

'You're right: those lines *are* killers.' Talia's over-plumped lips had abruptly thinned. 'And nobody could mistake you for a walk-on part.' Tossing back her hair and breathing hard, she grabbed her iPad from a shelf and set it up on the coffee table.

'If you're about to show us a montage of Adam's greatest hits, then I'm officially outta here,' said Nina.

'Not *his* hits, no. It's a TikTok video my friend Jenna uploaded to her private account the night of the party. I watched all of them because I had to stay home in London and had major FOMO. Look.' She swung the screen round to show us.

Jenna was one of the Party Blondes, bumping and grinding with one of the Party Dudes. Barbie 'n' Ken, giving it their best to 'Big Pimpin''. In the background, the swimming pool glimmered. People were sitting and smoking on the side, legs dangling in the water. Another couple were snogging, half-undressed, in the shallows. Nick and Nina. Nina wriggled out of the embrace and clambered out, dripping. She disappeared through the door at the far end of the pool garden. Only a moment or so later she returned, waving something triumphantly over her head. Nick was out of the pool now too, and she leapt towards him and wrapped her legs around his waist. Clutched in one hand was a bag, clearly emblazoned with the Union Jack.

Jenna and her boy toy twerked and gurned. Jay-Z rapped. The swimming pool glimmered and the video cut.

'That's Adam's bag,' I told Nina, and my voice had a crack in it. 'That's his drug stash.'

Her chin was up and her shoulders squared. 'So?'

'So … why did you take it? Why'd you give it to Nick?'

'I knew where Adam was bunking and that he'd have kept the good stuff back for himself. I figured he owed me a little fun. So I stole his blow.'

Her insouciant shrug infuriated me. 'Because he'd rejected you?'

'What? Jeez. Of course Adam didn't *reject* me. Why the hell would I come on to a gay dude?'

'Maybe you hadn't realised he was a gay dude.'

'What the fuck are you saying, Lily? You know I didn't mess with his fucking pills. Why would I? Nick snorted a line off my tits, then I dropped the bag back to the studio, and the two of us roared off into the night – high as kites and happy as Larry.'

'OK, maybe *you* didn't touch the pills. What about Nick?'

'*Somebody* must have touched them, I think,' Talia piped up. She'd been silent during the video clip and the exchange afterwards, picking at the skin around her nails. One of them was now bleeding and she wiped it distractedly on the sofa. 'Lily says Adam would never have bought dodgy pills and I think she's right. He was too careful.' Her voice trembled. 'What if … what if someone gave him bad drugs, though? As in – you know – *swapped them out?*'

It was a struggle to look Nina in the eye but I did it. 'You said Nick owes you. And … and that Adam had it coming.'

Nina turned bone white. 'Nick "owes me" for getting him free of his toxic ex. Not for helping him to poison yours.'

'Why didn't you tell me you'd messed with Adam's stash?'

'The same reason you didn't tell the police you'd taken one of his pills,' she hissed through clenched teeth. 'It doesn't make me look good. Doesn't make me a killer, though, any more than you, Lily-pet.'

We stared at each other. I could hear my pulse loud in my ears. My breaths came fast and shallow. Talia was crying softly in the background.

'Look,' I said eventually, 'let's take a moment and try and calm down. Things have got out of hand, and if that's my fault, I'm sorry. We need to step back and –'

'Fuck you.' Nina lurched to her feet and grabbed the unopened bottle of whiskey. 'And fuck this fucking ambush.' She'd started to cry. Not like Talia's snuffles – she was snotty and gulping, her make-up running down her face like a freak-show clown's. She scrubbed at her cheeks with shaking hands.

'Nina, please –'

In moments, she was at the door, fumbling for her car keys. I ran after her. 'Nina, wait, don't leave. Please stay –'

She spat in my face.

'You're dead to me,' she said.

CHAPTER FOURTEEN

I went back to the living room, unsteady on my feet.

There were tear-tracks running down Talia's make-up too, but she was trying to compose herself, pressing her palms together and doing some sort of deep-breathing exercise. I wiped my face on one of the paper napkins and gulped down some more champagne. Maybe tonight was, after all, a good night to get obliterated.

'What shall we do?' Talia said at last, in a very small voice.

I closed my eyes. 'I don't know.' The booze had hit me quickly; everything around me seemed insubstantial and far away. Dance music continued to pulse in the background. 'Can you turn that off?'

The silence when it finished was unsettling.

'Should we get Sarah?' Talia asked. 'She hasn't seen the film yet. I think she should, though, shouldn't she? And what was Nina on about when she was talking about blackmail and stalkers? Is there some, like, *major conspiracy*?'

'Let's not think about this any more. Not till the morning.'

But I couldn't let go of it just yet. My eye rested on the little origami boat, lying crumpled on the floor. Something tugged at my tired mind. 'Talia … the marsh. The creeks. Do people sail on them?'

She nodded. 'There's the local fishermen, of course. And tourists go bird-watching and boating in the nature reserve. But the creeks can be dangerous if you aren't, like, a native.'

So it was possible to get to the house by water. Not just through the gates by the road.

The marsh had always seemed impenetrable to me but what would I know, as a landlocked Londoner? I rubbed my head groggily. Everything seemed an insurmountable effort. I was sick of the whole business and tired to the bone.

'Why do you need to know?' Talia asked. 'Oh! Oh! Are you thinking that Adam's drug dealer came by boat? Because that would totally exonerate Nina! There's a boathouse in the pinewood, you know. Shall we go and check it out? I can get a torch.'

The idea of blundering around a pine wood in the dark did absolutely not appeal. 'Better wait until morning.'

'Yes,' she said, nodding, 'you're probably right. That's more sensible. What if we –?'

I screamed.

Talia screamed too, in reaction. 'What? *What?* Lily!'

'There!' I pointed at the window. My hand shook. 'Did you see it? A figure – I swear – somebody – outside in the night.'

We both ran to the glass and peered out to the sloping lawn and the marsh below. Beyond the spill of light from the house, the landscape was black and densely blotted.

'Could it have been an animal?' Talia suggested, hand still fluttering over her heart. 'A cat or something? Or, like, a tree branch in the wind?'

'Maybe.' Now that my own heart had stopped pounding, I was

beginning to think it more likely I'd imagined something. 'Or it might have been Sarah, I suppose. She said she wanted some air.'

'Sarah went to lie down in the studio. The poor thing got up at the crack of dawn and hasn't been sleeping properly for weeks.'

'The *studio*?'

'Well, she said she wanted to be in the last bed Adam slept in before he died. To, you know, feel close to him.'

I had a powerful urge to lie down too. 'Why'd she want to feel close to someone she basically loathed?'

'Oh no, Sarah *loved* Adam. *And* resented him. She's very conflicted – I think that's why she's working so hard to make something good out of his death.' Talia chewed her lip. 'You know what? I think it might be a good idea to check on her.'

I stayed at the window, staring out at the dark. I'd been so sure I'd seen someone. But my mind could have been playing tricks on me. My thoughts were too scattered to be sure of anything.

That's why it took a minute or so for me to realise that Talia had left the room.

I was gripped by the same sense of foreboding I'd felt that sunlit June morning, walking along the dewy verges to where Adam lay dead. Why had I let Talia go to find Sarah alone? Talia said that Sarah had loved Adam, but all I'd seen was bitterness. And rage. All those years of seething resentment …

I set off, a little unsteady on my feet, to the other end of the house and the sliding doors to the patio. I definitely shouldn't have had that second glass of champagne, not on an empty stomach. Outside, pinpricks of damp misted the air. The revamp hadn't got as far as the garden: the solar lights set in the walls were wan and flickering, and spindly dead shrubs spiked the beds.

I faltered on the threshold. 'Talia?'

Was another shadow on the move, there behind the tree? My eyesight had gone blurry again.

'TALIA!'

Finally, her voice floated back. 'Over here!'

Relief flooded through me. 'Are you OK?'

'Of course! Come and see!'

She was calling from the swimming-pool enclosure. I didn't want to face the pool again. But I didn't want to be alone in the house either.

It felt good to be in the fresh air. The heat from the fire and the sickly sweetness of all those scented candles had been more oppressive than I'd realised. Maybe that was why my head felt so foggy.

Or was it from the fall onto the rock? I checked my hands for grazes before remembering that was a different night – the other night at this house. God. I needed to pull myself together. I pinched the soft skin at my waist, hard enough to make myself gasp, then pushed through the door to the second garden.

There it was, gently steaming and glittering before me. But this was another swimming pool again – a swimming pool from an entirely different time and place, perhaps even a different world. The water was a rich inky blue, the colour of midnight. Tiny silver bowls bearing tea lights floated on the surface. And there were flowers, too, scattered across the darkness: silvery-white water-lilies, even more star-like than the candles that flickered in the breeze.

I looked closer. I realised the water must have been dyed. The flowers were made of silk and the tea lights were battery-operated.

'What do you think?' said Talia's voice from behind me.

'It's … magical. Did you set this up for the photo shoot?'

'No. I did it for *us*. You and me and Sarah. Adam's three favourite girls.' She took me by the arm. 'I'm so glad you like it.'

I rubbed my eyes. 'I think … too much champagne … I think I need to go back inside. Did you check on Sarah? Is she OK?'

'Sarah's fine. Sleeping like a baby. Sit down here for a minute – rest.' Gently, she helped me to a sitting position at the side of the pool.

'What are you doing?'

She'd pulled off my boots and was taking off my socks.

'Talia – ! Stop it.' I swatted her away but, giggling, she reached for my feet again. Then she slipped out of her silver sandals, hitched up her dress and sat down next to me, trailing her feet in the indigo depths.

'I like to come and sit here, sometimes, thinking of Adam. Remembering. The water's gorgeous …' She rested her head on my shoulder. 'You should try it.'

'I'm not swimming in your weird-ass shrine.' Lumberingly, I got to my feet. My bare feet. How had that happened? I made it to the bench and sat down heavily.

Talia pitter-pattered after me. 'You should think about it,' she said earnestly. 'As you're here. It will bring you closer to Adam. I know how much you miss him. I do too. But you came first, of course. I've always known that. The connection you two had … You're way prettier than me, and *much* more talented, and effortlessly cool … yet even *you* couldn't keep him, in the end.'

'Adam was never mine to "keep",' I said effortfully. 'He was a gay man. We were in a professional relationship. The end date was literally written into our contract.'

'As was mine,' said Talia, nodding. 'Set to finish as soon as Luke Zane wrapped. I'm not *stupid*, Lily. *Obviously* Adam was always going to move on from me. He'd find a co-star or a proper pin-up and he wouldn't need me, or my money, any more. I was only ever a stop-gap. I know that. I also know that the only reason Adam was nicer to me than he was to you was because he basically thought I was a child. That's all right. I didn't mind.

'What I didn't expect was how ... real he made me feel. Solid and shining. Someone who other people actually *saw*.' She smiled dreamily. 'Because they see me now, don't they? They chase after me, in fact. *Everyone* wants to talk to me. About Adam and our time together ... It's lucky Sarah depends on me so much – for guidance, as well as other things. It means I'll be free to concentrate on all the important and exciting ways I'm going to keep Adam's memory alive.'

I closed my eyes. As if blocking out the view would block out the words that were coming.

'You were his best girl. But I was his last girl. I'll always have that.'

Dark water was pouring through me. 'Oh Talia...' I whispered. 'What did you do?'

She took my hand in hers. 'The same as you. I did the same as you and Adam and Dido – I turned myself into a different person. A wig, new eyebrows, this funny prosthetic nose ... I had no idea how easy it was. Honestly, I was *transformed*. Inside and out! The boatman I hired assumed I was a stripper. As a surprise for the party, you know. I was able to buy a bunch of drugs off him too. Then the two of us snuck off on his little motor boat, puttering through the creeks at the dead of night. And all that lurking in the pine wood! I really did feel as if I was in the movies …

'Anyway. The boatman took me back to the village half an hour later or so, I paid up, then went to change and get into my car. Do you want to know something funny? What I *really* worried about was that people would somehow realise the croissants were stale. I'd picked them up in the evening, you see, before the drive down, so they were *sawdust* by the time I got to the house. *Obviously* they couldn't have been freshly baked that morning.

'But I was quite confident my boatman was never going to come forward. Not when the police said they were searching for whoever supplied Adam with the drugs. (Turns out the local fishermen do a roaring trade!) The man couldn't know the stash I bought from him is sitting at the bottom of the salt marsh. I had to be very selective, very specialist, about where I got the fentanyl from, after all.

'The truth is, Lily, I never expected you to be at the party that night. When Sarah messaged me to say you'd turned up, I felt betrayed, actually. It was a real blow. I don't mind admitting that now. I really believed Adam when he said you and he were over. I suppose it was inevitable you'd start asking questions – that you wouldn't be able to let things go. I'd feel the same, probably, if it were me. But it's just such a terrible, awful shame. I can't tell you how sorry I am.

'Because there's always been something a little … bleak, I guess, about you? Not many people pick up on this, but then they don't know you like I do. And the awful thing is it's made things easier. I could never have planned you breaking up with your boyfriend, for example. Or whatever went on between you and Dido down by the marsh. Though I suppose that horrible fight with Nina was inevitable once you saw the film. I was lucky there, too. Poor Nina always gets herself into trouble one way or another, doesn't she?'

'Nina ...' I slurred.

'She'll be fine.' Talia squeezed my hand. 'I'll look after her, and Sarah too. We'll all rally round. It helps, of course, that you said goodbye.'

'Good– good– goodbye?'

She closed her eyes, inhaling deeply. '"Adam, I'm sorry we didn't look after each other better. I'm sorry about a lot of things."' She opened her eyes again and smiled. 'That's the note we'll find, you see. Closure is a comfort of sorts.'

She had me by the arm now and was pulling me off the bench, towards the pool. I tried to resist but my body had gone limp. 'Wh– wh– wh–?'

'A little something in your champagne, that's all. Similar to the sleeping pill I gave Sarah – I hadn't expected her to stay on, but there's a lot to be said for the power of spontaneity. We all have to be flexible; we all have to acknowledge when it's time to let go. So please don't struggle. It's not worth it, not in your last moments. Close your eyes and it will be even more like falling asleep.'

I was so sleepy, and my brain so coddled in cold fuzz, it was almost hard to feel fear. Close up, the dyed water of the pool was so dark as to look black, its depths infinite. I flailed about, floppily, and tried to scream Sarah's name as Talia gripped me beneath the arms, but the breath in my lungs was as thin and feeble as the rest of me. I was dimly aware that Talia was being careful of me, taking her time – of course, I thought, she doesn't want there to be any signs of a struggle.

It had begun to rain. Pockmarking the water, pattering on the paving stones, slanting silver in the lights. My bare feet slipped and skidded about, futilely searching for a grip. All those hours in the gym and spin classes had paid off for Talia – she was small but pitilessly strong. I collapsed on the paving with a groan. Her hands were on my side now, briskly rolling me over to the pool's rim. She leaned over my face, and her eyes were bright with tears.

'Go to him,' she said softly. 'Go to Adam. You can have him for always now.'

I heard my own scream like the echo of something very far away. Still, the shock of the water revived me a little. I thrashed about, tipping over the little silver bowls, getting my arms entangled with the fake lilies. *How apt*, a distant part of my brain observed. I grabbed at the side of the pool even though I knew it was useless, that I was useless, that Talia was right, and giving up without a struggle was the simplest thing to do. But cold rain pecked at my face, and the warm, inky water smelled of chemicals, burning my throat and lungs. And so I gurgled and moaned, uselessly, and splashed, uselessly, even as the numbness slunk through my brain and my sodden clothes took on the weight of armour. And all the while, Talia gazed sadly down, hands clasped between her breasts, one tiny tear trembling on her cheek.

Until she crumpled to the ground, with a grunt.

A dark figure stepped out from behind her.

I thrashed and gurgled some more.

'Boo,' Zalandra said.

CHAPTER FIFTEEN

Talia had slipped a benzodiazepine into my drink – one of the standard anti-anxiety drugs that date-rapists use, the kind that leaves the body after a few hours without a trace. It was detected in the blood tests I had at the hospital, and a prescription bottle with Talia's name on it was found in the house. Her story, of course, was that I'd taken it of my own free will, after being left distraught by the break-up with my boyfriend and a fight with my best friend. Talia hadn't known how much I'd been drinking when she offered it to me. After combining the medication with alcohol, I'd become disoriented and confused and wandered out of the house while her back was turned. Then I'd fallen – or jumped – into the swimming pool.

Zalandra's role in all this was slightly less clear. In Talia's version of events, Talia was moments from dragging me out from the water when she was disturbed by an intruder. In her confusion, she lashed out in self-defence, only for Zalandra to respond in kind. Zalandra had, in fact, dealt a blow to her head with one of the globed solar lights she'd plucked from a flower-bed.

When Zalandra called the emergency services, she said that she'd struck Talia because she believed Talia was preventing her from giving assistance to me. She was not an intruder, she explained – the doors to the house had been left open, she was acquainted with both Talia and myself, and she had come to Norfolk to follow up an appointment she had made with me. But she withdrew the statement she gave to the police, on the grounds that the prospect of appearing in court would put her under intolerable mental strain. She had, in any case, been too late on the scene to witness Talia's alleged confession or to be sure of how I had come to be in the water. Or so she said.

Either way, it was lucky for me Zalandra had made good on her threats and tracked me down so relentlessly. Apparently she'd got hold of my mother's contact details and fed her some bullshit story about being a casting director, angry I hadn't shown up to an audition. On learning I'd gone to Norfolk, she'd caught the train down that same day, arriving at the house not far behind Nina and with no plan other than to bide her time and wait for an opportunity to confront me. She was rewarded when Nina made her furious exit, slipping through the entrance gates moments after Nina had driven out. Exactly what she'd witnessed, she kept to herself. But with her talent for watching and waiting, I suspected she'd had a ringside view.

If so, Zalandra was probably wise not to admit to it. Almost as soon as she recovered consciousness, Talia was armed to the teeth with the sharkiest lawyers money can buy. Sarah certainly wasn't saying anything – not about the sleeping pill Talia had given her nor the alcohol she'd watched Talia serve me. Presumably she was too busy with her work for the Adam Harker Foundation to help with police inquiries.

I was ultimately persuaded – by the police, my parents, my agent, my own lawyer – that the case against Talia was too weak for charges to be brought, either on my behalf or Adam's.

Meanwhile, the court of public opinion was having a field day. What, exactly, had transpired at the celebrity death-house? Rumours were mongered, titbits leaked. A murderous catfight! A suicide pact! A lesbian sex cult gone wrong! The old Tinseltattle slurs were dug up and recirculated. Conspiracy theories abounded, including one that Adam had never really died, just gone incognito – like Marilyn or Elvis – and was living a quiet life in Norfolk the whole time, until his two exes tracked him down, forcing him to go on the run.

Nina asked me if I'd thought about Adam in what were almost my last moments: drugged and drowning in the same pool, under the same wide East Anglian skies. I told her the truth, which was that I'd thought only of myself. Certainly, there'd been no supernatural energy present. No merman or mer-demon to raise me from the depths or drag me down to hell. I felt only the choking horror of my own foolishness. I suppose Adam must have felt that too.

Nina was the only person who really believed my version of events, despite the Momager's protestations and my lawyer's platitudes. In some ways, this made everything harder because, of course, I had chosen to believe the worst of her – twice. The fact that Nina didn't bear a grudge about this was the biggest proof, if proof were needed, that our friendship was over. She forgave me the first time; the second was more of a letting-go.

Nina was the one who told me that Talia had suffered a full-blown psychotic breakdown. Apparently she was whisked off to a secure mental-health facility somewhere in the American desert. It would be five-star, naturally. Kale smoothies and cotton sheets with a thread count higher than my mortgage. There was probably even a swimming pool. 'I can't see her ever coming out,' said Nina.

So Talia had passed behind the ultimate red rope: *it keeps us separate to keep us safe.*

After the final round of police interviews and legal consultations, I returned to my aunt and uncle's Brecon hideaway. The last time I'd gone had been a self-inflicted punishment as well as an escape; I suppose I thought the deprivations of the place would improve me. This time I knew that nothing could be salvaged. Yet my first days there were peaceful. I didn't mind the cold or the rain or even the *Collected Works of Bertolt Brecht*, which was still waiting for me next to the inhospitable sofa. All I wanted was silence. However afraid I was of my thoughts, I knew I had to be alone with them. Otherwise, I feared the tremors of regret and guilt and fury and terror I felt beneath my skin would intensify into quakes and thunder-claps and grow louder and louder – thrumming through my blood, juddering in my bones and cracking my brain into a thousand dark fissures.

But I was not alone for very long.

Three days after I arrived, I came back from a walk that had been cut short by a sudden downpour. There was an unfamiliar car in the muddy yard and a familiar figure waiting on the doorstep. Zalandra.

'How did you find me?'

She hunched her shoulders. 'I asked around.'

I put my keys in the door. Perhaps a part of me had been expecting her. 'You'd better come in.'

———————

'You saved my life,' I said, sitting down on the bony sofa. Zalandra elected to stand. She hadn't chosen to wait for me in the car or even wear a coat, and she must have been outside for a while, as her hair was slicked down with water and her clothes were sodden. The room soon filled with the fuggy smell of wet wool. She still wasn't as wet as when she'd pulled me out of the swimming pool, of course. 'I'm glad I'm finally able to say thank you. I think I was too out of it at the time.'

She hunched her shoulders again. 'It's what anyone would have done.'

'But you hate me.'

'Even so.'

'Talia didn't hate me, yet she tried to kill me. You know why, don't you?' I watched her carefully. 'You heard the things she said before she pushed me into the water.'

Another shoulder hunch. 'It's not my story.'

Not her story to tell? Or not the story she'd chosen to remember?

'What *is* your story, Zalandra?'

She was silent. It wasn't like the first time she'd approached me, in the coffee shop. Then she'd been hesitant. Fidgety. Painfully shy, painfully resolute. But I sensed a similar calculation going on behind those pale eyes.

I waited, and waited some more. Frustration got the better of me. 'I mean, I don't even know your real name, for God's sake.'

'It's Zalandra. I changed it officially not long after we met in that café. It was a spur-of-the-moment choice … but it's grown on me.'

Bullshit. 'You chose it because of Adam. Because you're a superfan. Of those films – the *Wylderness Chronicles* – and of him.'

She gave one of her small, crafty smiles. 'Oh, I was never a Wylderbeast. I mean, I saw the first movie when it came out. I didn't revisit them, though, until after Adam died. It only seemed right, since I was doing his memorial for the fan-site. They're … OK, I guess. Not my sort of thing.'

I shook my head in an attempt to clear it. 'I don't get it,' I said flatly. 'You named yourself after Adam's love interest in the film that made him a star, you followed him to LA, somehow persuaded him to give you a job, turned up at his party.' Not to mention harassed me, his alleged girlfriend. 'And I'm glad you were so, uh, involved, because otherwise I'd be dead. But let's not rewrite history here.'

She blinked. 'I thought you wanted to hear my story. This is how I tell it.'

'Then I'm listening.'

'OK.' She was doing that blinking and fidgeting thing again. The heavy breathing too. 'OK. Adam was a good actor. I mean, I liked what I saw of him. But I never paid him much attention until he started going out with you. Suddenly your name and your face were everywhere. Or that's what it felt like. It felt as if I couldn't get away from it – from you. I did try. I really did. I knew it wouldn't do me any good. But then I bumped into you, the day in the café. And I suppose something snapped.'

I went hot all over, then cold. 'Wait, so you were really st– you were interested in *me*, not Adam? The whole time?'

'Zalandra spends most of the first film in disguise,' she said, so placidly I knew her mildness had to be deceptive, and I felt another

305

flash of heat and ice. 'She's trying to avoid her destiny. Until Kastor – Adam – arrives, and she realises it must be confronted after all. Which is a huge letdown, don't you think? The so-called powerful heroine who still needs a hero to give her agency? All the same, it resonated.'

I waited.

'Ask me my name again,' she said at last. 'Ask me my old name.'

'What's your old name?'

Her voice was the thread of a whisper. But her gaze was steady and never left my face. 'I used to be a flower, like you. I was *just* like you, Lily, except I was a rose. I used to be a girl named Rose Huntley.'

It took me a moment. A long moment, perhaps the longest in my life, longer even than the moment it took for Zalandra to plunge into that pool and drag me back to air and light. I suppose I'd never looked at her properly before, otherwise I would have paid more attention to the bleached blue of her eyes and how they were fringed with pale lashes. Zalandra's colouring had always seemed off – the black hair dye she used was too harsh for her kind of pallor. Now I saw that her roots needed retouching, revealing a seam of fair hair. It was faintly reddish, a colour that – if allowed to grow, to be nourished – might be described as strawberry blonde.

She stood there impassively, as I stared at her as if for the first time. The baggy black clothes. The unflattering haircut. The layers of fat. Not happy fat, not the lush curvaceousness of a body at ease with itself and the world, but sad swaddles of flesh, acquired joylessly, compulsively, to cover up the person inside. Zalandra was a heroine in disguise.

Because I remembered the person inside. I remembered Rose Huntley: blue eyed, strawberry blonde, dainty as a doily. Six months younger than me and twice as pert. Rose Huntley, who seemed to book two out of every three jobs I went for and would pass me at castings with a sly little smirk.

'I remember you,' I said.

CHAPTER SIXTEEN

'Hardly anyone else does,' replied Zalandra.

Because Rose Huntley had vanished. Off screen and out of memory. Just one of the hundreds of thousands of juvenile leads who age out of their USP into a life of anonymous adulthood. It's only the iconic ones who get asked why.

Puberty's a tricky time for everyone. That's one of the reasons fresh-faced young adults tend to be cast in teen roles. No sudden bursts of acne to worry about. But the main reason, of course, is so that producers can avoid the bother of child performing licences and tutors and chaperones. So when the call went out for girls aged between twelve and sixteen to be cast as non-identical twins – tweenagers – in the pilot of a big new US/UK co-production, practically every girl at the Fame Factory went for it, including me. So did Nina, I think. So did Rose.

Rose wasn't at a theatre school. She didn't even have a stage mother. Her parents were high-flying businesspeople of some kind; at any rate, she was always accompanied to auditions by professional chaperones. Both she and the chaperones kept themselves to themselves. When the two of us read together at the final audition for the twins, giving our best facsimile of sisterhood, we smiled and nodded at each other, cool as you please.

The swish of her strawberry-blonde hair, the flash of her sugar-'n'-spice smile … Her silver-blue eyes, bright with malice.

The scent of vanilla. The taste of bile.

This Time Tomorrow was to be one of those multigenerational, emotionally manipulative dramas along the lines of *Brothers and Sisters* or *This Is Us*. The hook was the long-distance relationship between an uptight Wall Street widower and a bohemian London artist. The banker had a stroppy teenage daughter and a cantankerous mother; the artist had a meddling ex, depressive teenage son and wise-cracking twin girls. Us. Rose was cast as the alpha-twin – that was clear from the start. She had the lion's share of the best lines and last words. Wardrobe ensured her skirts were always a little shorter, tops a little tighter. Hair and Make-Up set her ponytail higher on her head so that it swung with extra sass.

At fourteen, Rose was my only peer, since the rest of the 'juvenile' cast were nineteen plus. Still, we kept our distance the moment the director called cut. The Momager approved of this. She didn't believe in getting friendly with the competition.

The pilot was filmed in one of the big London studios, with Toronto standing in for New York for the US exterior shots. Right from the start, it was an unhappy set. Rewrites and gripes kicked off at the table read and continued through rehearsals and reshoots.

The only person who made a concerted effort to keep things upbeat was the actor playing the Wall Street dad. I'll call him Sam. Sam was college buddies with the showrunner and so could get away with a certain amount of clowning around. There were a few pranks, a lot of comic ad-libbing. When people had a particularly bad day, he'd send boxes of doughnuts to their trailers. He flirted mildly with the Momager. He kept saying how grateful he was,

309

after so many years as a walk-on, to have his first lead role on such a great show with such terrific people. It should have been grating, and to others it no doubt was, but I felt I understood his yearning to feel lucky, to conjure success through the power of magical thinking alone.

One day, Sam found me snivelling outside Wardrobe after a fitting. 'Hey, hey,' he said, 'what's this? Why's my favourite girl been crying?'

'I'm about to be cut,' I said. 'I know I am. Everyone likes Rose better.'

Rumours were spreading. The twins were too samey … the sisterly chemistry wasn't working … one of us needed to go. It didn't matter that I had better timing and delivery than Rose. I had puppy fat and the Thane nose to contend with.

It was the Easter holidays. The idea of going back to school and confessing I'd been dropped, mid-shoot, felt like annihilation. Even after the *Hollow Moon* debacle, after Adam, after everything, I've never felt a rejection that cut so jaggedly or so deep. And it was my fault, too. The Momager kept sighing woeful sighs. 'You need to show people what you've got. Who you are. Where's your *spark*? I hardly recognise you these days, sweetie.' I was a drag, and my own mother knew it.

Sam shook his head. 'Come to my trailer, and let's get you cleaned up. We can't have people seeing you like this.'

I followed him, of course. Nobody noticed, or if they did, they didn't think anything of it. The crew were overstretched and distracted. And I'd been nagging my mother to let me have more independence on set. I didn't need her babying me, I'd said, only that morning.

In the trailer, Sam goofed around a bit to make me laugh and wiped my eyes with a spare T-shirt. He told me what a great little actress he thought I was. 'The trouble, I think, is that Joel's looking to take the part – the younger sister part – in a more grown-up direction.' Joel was the showrunner and head writer, Sam's college pal. 'Strictly between ourselves, he's told me that future storylines are going to be a bit more edgy. He needs someone who's going to be comfortable with exploring that.'

Here was official confirmation that the twins were kaput. I started crying again.

'Hey, hey.' Sam tucked my hair behind my ears and dabbed my eyes with the T-shirt. 'It's not over. Not by a long way. You mustn't let yourself be intimidated. There's still time to show us – Joel – what you're capable of and why you're the best fit for the part.

'Look, Rose is a sweet kid – she's got the sunny-side-up thing down pat. But we're looking for something with more grit here. And I think *you've* got grit, Lily. You're, what, nearly fifteen, and you've been acting since you were six, right? There's a certain worldliness that goes with that. *That's* what you need to draw on. Experience.'

'I'm not very experienced,' I mumbled.

'Aw, I don't believe that. Sure, you make a terrific ingénue. But there're moments – very intriguing moments – when you seem like so much more, Lily. When you seem like someone on the cusp of all these exciting things. Someone who's already blossomed, but just can't see it yet.'

Funny. When I try and picture his face, I can't. I just see a composite of every other forty-something blandly attractive actor

I've shared a screen with. I do remember how old he seemed, up close – the coarseness of his open pores. And that there were still traces of foundation by his hairline.

His face was almost touching mine. His hand was on my bare leg, sliding up under my skirt. 'Show me you know what you want.'

I pushed him off, lightly. Weakly.

He laughed. His breath smelled of sugared doughnuts. 'That's right. Try and do it with a little smile next time. A teasing one. You know exactly what you're doing, remember.'

So we were acting?

'But … I don't … know what we're doing …'

He pulled a comical face. 'It's just acting, sweetheart. Just playing about. C'mon. Improvise with me.'

He moved in again. His mouth was on mine. 'That's better,' he said a moment or so later, all smiles. 'See, you had it in you all along. All you needed to do was to relax. You're a natural.'

I don't remember what I said next. I'd like to think it was something devastating. Or at the very least dignified. I'm certain it was neither. But I stood up and I shook my head and I got out.

I got out.

It seems extraordinary, but I was almost more upset about losing the job. There was no way I would keep it now. If there had ever been the slightest chance I'd be picked over Rose, Sam would ensure that wouldn't happen.

I found Rose by the catering truck, chattering away to one of the PAs, while her dopey chaperone sat with her headphones in at a nearby table. Rose was sipping an iced latte. I didn't drink coffee – another one of those adult tastes I was yet to acquire.

'Hi, Lil.' I hated 'Lil'. Like I was the barmaid in some crummy soap. 'What happened to your face?' Rose wrinkled her cute little nose. 'You've gone all blotchy.'

'Yeah … no … I was talking to Sam …'

'Sam! Isn't he great?'

I hesitated. I know I did. I know there was a moment, a knife-edge as sharp as it was shining. 'Sam –' I said. 'Sam – he – I –' My voice caught.

She rolled her eyes. 'God, Lil. Time to work on your delivery much?'

I suppose that was enough. I suppose I might even have smiled. 'Sam's been *really* helpful. Coaching me, giving me tips.' I lowered my voice. 'For when they decide which twin to keep.'

Rose's face tightened. I'd got her attention now. 'So it's official – one of us is getting dropped?'

'Or both. Joel wants the role to go older. More sophisticated.'

'Shit.'

'Yeah. That's what Sam was helping me with.'

I suppose I've always been better at playing innocent than experienced. Perhaps I even managed to fool myself. I'd told Rose the truth, hadn't I? Just not the whole truth. Not the truth that mattered, that would have kept her safe.

After that encounter with Sam, I wasn't scheduled to be on set again until the end of the week. The night before I was due to return, we got the call. Script rewrites, plot rethink, incredibly difficult decision, blah blah blah.

It was all very bad luck. They thanked me for my hard work and wished me every success in the future.

Despite its bumpy start, the pilot did well enough in audience tests for the show to be picked up for a full series. *This Time Tomorrow* ran for a respectable five seasons in the end. But there were major changes between the pilot and the first official episode. For one thing, both Rose and Sam's parts were recast. Since the pilot was never aired, this stayed a non-story.

Rose wasn't seen at any more auditions. The first whispers were that she'd got stage-fright, the second that she'd got spots. There weren't any whispers about Sam. But that's hardly surprising: he died in a car accident in Houston about a year after the pilot was filmed. An obscure actor dying an obscure death was barely reported, even in the industry press. I only found out because the Momager had kept tabs on him. His charm offensive had left her with a bit of a crush.

She did her best to hold back on the recriminations when we heard Rose had won. The girl was a conniving little madam, that was plain to see. As a consolation prize, the Momager began to take my complaints about my nose more seriously. 'Still, we need to put some work into fixing your figure first, don't you think, darling? A little podge can be rather sweet on the under-tens. But you're a big girl now – and not in all the right ways.'

The first time I saw my pert new nose in the mirror, I cried. It was like looking at my slimmer, prettier twin. It was like looking at Rose.

CHAPTER SEVENTEEN

Meeting Rose's eyes again was the hardest thing I've ever done.

'I thought you'd work it out once I sent you the flowers,' she said. 'His "flower girls" – that's what *he* called us. Or is that something else you've forgotten?'

Roses and lilies. Rotten, torn, bloodied. I hung my head.

'You knew,' she said quietly. 'You knew what that man was. You knew, and you didn't warn me or anyone. No, you as good as *sent me to him*.'

'You have to believe … I didn't realise … I never …' I thought she'd get a fright. I hoped she'd embarrass herself. That was all. I'd walked away from him, hadn't I? I'd got up; I'd got out. 'I – I didn't understand what I was doing.'

I didn't understand. I *couldn't* have.

I had done my best to not understand what I'd done every day and every night for the last eighteen years. I had weighed the memory down and sunk it deep. Into the waters, into the marshes.

'I didn't have your luxuries, Lily.' Her voice was so calm. 'I didn't have my mother on set. I hardly even had her at home. My parents were always away, always working. They said I got my drive, my ambition, from them, and even though they didn't understand it, it made them proud. My self-sufficiency, that is, more than my success. I organised the chaperones and the head shots and the showreels and the licences, and they paid for them. But they weren't there. I was on my own. Before. During. After.'

I flinched at each word.

'It would be different now, probably. People are much more careful. Girls like us are much more aware. Back then, I think one or two people guessed all the same. I think that's why he got dropped after the pilot. But it was too late by then, wasn't it?

'It was too late even when he died. You'd think that it would make me feel better – as if a shitty death was the next best thing to actual justice. But I didn't feel relief when I heard, or not much. I had all the same anger and now it had nowhere to go. I suppose that's why I came to fixate on you. The one who got away.'

The airless room smelled of wet wool and sweat. Rain hissed on the skylight. I could hear my own breaths, shallow and fast. I took a step back.

Zalandra-Rose gave a small laugh. 'You're not frightened of me, are you? If I'd wanted for you to die, I'd have left you to drown.'

I swallowed. 'Weren't you tempted?'

She considered this. 'No. I knew your death wouldn't change anything. All I ever wanted was to talk to you – to take you back to that day, so that you'd see what you'd done. To force you to face me and recognise yourself. Adam understood that.'

Adam. I had forgotten him entirely.

'Adam … knew?'

'The first time we ever talked was outside his agent's office, some time after the two of you broke up. I'm not even sure what I'd hoped to get out of accosting him there. But I knew I'd frightened you and that it had backfired, because you'd disappeared, and even if you came back, you were always going to keep running away from me.'

She smiled a little. She was so poised, so fluent. A different woman to the stammering, stumbling creature who'd accosted me before. She'd been rehearsing this for eighteen years.

'Adam was one of those people who feed off the fascination of others. He couldn't help it, probably. I think he was always on the lookout for infatuation, and that's why he also noticed when it wasn't there. He worked out quite quickly that I was after you, not him. He said he'd always figured you came with a ghost.

'So I told him my – our – story. And he said he'd help.'

'Help?'

'To bring the two of us together. He told me that you weren't the monster. You didn't abuse anyone. I know this. Obviously. Even so … maybe I needed reminding. Anyway. Adam thought there was something in you that needed rescuing. He said what happened to me was unforgivable, but that there was a chance I'd feel … lighter … if I saw that you weren't free of it either.

'I'm not sure if I buy that, to be honest. When I saw you in that café, for the first time after all those years, you looked untouched. Untouchable. Even now, you're doing fine. You've still got that TV show. And, OK, people think something creepy, or sordid, went on between you and Talia and Adam and that swimming pool, but you can get past that. It might even do you some good, giving Little Lucie a bit of edge. People like to forgive pretty blondes, don't they?'

I flinched again. 'Could you … forgive … me? Ever?' And

then I blushed, because the line sounded soapy, histrionic – a cliffhanger ending to *This Time Tomorrow*. Zalandra-Rose raised her eyebrows and, despite everything, I saw she was amused.

'I'd like to forget you,' she said at last. 'I'd like to forget a lot of things. And maybe, someday, I will.

'It's possible Adam was right, and there's a case to be made that you're a victim too. You were young and stupid and thoughtlessly cruel in the way teenage girls are. I understand that, or I can try to.

'Because in all the important ways we were the same, weren't we? Rose and Lily, Lily and Rose. The flower girls. That's why we had a duty of care to each other. An unwritten contract, I guess. That's what I can't forgive. You broke it so lightly … you broke *me* so lightly. And for what?'

After Zalandra had gone, I stayed on the sofa without moving for a long, long time. Minutes rolled into hours and still I couldn't move. I emptied my mind of everything except the tick of my pulse and the patter of the rain and the lengthening shadows, as the bare little room grew dark around me.

When thoughts began to swim, dimly, into view, they were mostly of Adam. Our last meeting. He'd been trying to tell me, I realised. He thought that now he knew my secret he'd be able to put me right. Fix the sadness, the wrongness, he'd always been able to see. And had always relished, in fact. Because his own wrongness kept tripping him up. We were alike in that way. Bringing Zalandra and me together on that riotous night – what was he hoping for? Redemption, but also drama, I had no doubt.

That was the thing about Adam. As vicious as he was generous – our Lord of Misrule.

Let's pretend, I told him once. Let's pretend we can be happy, let's pretend we can be good. But now I think we could have done better than that. We – I – could have tried so much harder to make our lies true.

This is what haunts me. Because if I had calmed down and actually listened to Adam that night, then I would have stayed at the party. Whatever might have transpired between me and Zalandra, our paths would have been set on a different course. Adam might have stayed sober. Or I might have got wasted with him. Either way, he wouldn't have been alone.

He knew the worst of me and yet he hadn't turned his back. Neither, in the end, had Rose.

I was not Adam's killer. I was not Rose's abuser. But I'd left both of them to their fates.

And for what?

All around me, the rain drummed down. As it came down harder on the sky-light, the noise of the water became first insistent, then thunderous, like the clapping of a thousand hands. I closed my eyes. And after a while, all I could hear was the roaring of applause.

ACKNOWLEDGEMENTS

I'm unlikely to ever make a speech at the Oscars, so here's the next best thing.

Thank you to my editor, Sarah Hodgson, for her inspiring insights and innumerable improvements. Thank you to my A-list agent, Sue Armstrong, for her tireless support and to Emma Dunne, my copy-editor, who has truly shown the patience of a saint. A big shout-out, too, to Kirsty Doole and Aimee Oliver-Powell and the rest of the magicians at Corvus.

I've led a very sheltered life so the research required for this story took me down several unexpected rabbit holes. When Google failed me, the following people were unstintingly generous with their help and advice. A hearty thanks to Dr Paula Maria Heister, Louisa Macdonald and Miriah and Brent Garrard. Any mistakes or fictional liberties are mine alone.

Ali – I hope you don't guess the twist.

Isaac and Eden – you're way too young for this, so get your sticky paws off.